Dancing
in the River

a novel

GUERNICA
PRIZE
4

**Canada Council   Conseil des Arts
for the Arts   du Canada**

**ONTARIO ARTS COUNCIL
CONSEIL DES ARTS DE L'ONTARIO**

an Ontario government agency
un organisme du gouvernement de l'Ontario

Canadä

Guernica Editions Inc. acknowledges the support of the Canada Council
for the Arts and the Ontario Arts Council. The Ontario Arts Council
is an agency of the Government of Ontario.

We acknowledge the financial support of the Government of Canada.

Dancing in the River

a novel

George Lee

**GUERNICA
EDITIONS**
TORONTO · CHICAGO · BUFFALO · LANCASTER (U.K.)
2022

Michael Mirolla, general editor
Lindsay Brown, editor
David Moratto, interior and cover design
Guernica Editions Inc.
287 Templemead Drive, Hamilton, (ON), Canada L8W 2W4
2250 Military Road, Tonawanda, N.Y. 14150-6000 U.S.A.
www.guernicaeditions.com

Distributors:
Independent Publishers Group (IPG)
600 North Pulaski Road, Chicago IL 60624
University of Toronto Press Distribution (UTP)
5201 Dufferin Street, Toronto (ON), Canada M3H 5T8
Gazelle Book Services, White Cross Mills
High Town, Lancaster LA1 4XS U.K.

First edition.
Printed in Canada.

Legal Deposit—Third Quarter
Library of Congress Catalog Card Number: 2022930927
Library and Archives Canada Cataloguing in Publication
Title: Dancing in the river : a novel / George Lee.
Names: Lee, George (Author of Dancing in the river), author.
Description: Series statement: Guernica prize
Identifiers: Canadiana (print) 20220150036
| Canadiana (ebook) 20220150133 | ISBN 9781771837569 (softcover)
| ISBN 9781771837576 (EPUB)
Classification: LCC PS8623.E4375 D36 2022 | DDC C813/.6—dc23

I had melancholy thoughts ...
a strangeness in my mind,
A feeling that I was not for that hour,
Nor for that place.
   —**William Wordsworth,** *The Prelude*

Dance, when you're broken open.
Dance, if you've torn the bandage off.
   —**Rumi**

This book is dedicated to:

my grandma, who needs no foot-binding in Heaven,
my parents, who still live in this book,
my wife, Rachel, whose love has healed my deep pain, and
my children, and their children.

Prologue

"WHAT'S THE BEST early training for a writer?" a young writer once asked Ernest Hemingway.

"An unhappy childhood," Hemingway famously replied.

I grew up in a mountain village on the Yangtze River in China. For a long time, I had been pondering whether to pen the story of my early life as a coming-of-age tale like *David Copperfield*.

Before long, though, I discovered that I'm no Charles Dickens.

As I recall, my writing journey began on my third birthday when I was given a fountain pen, which I've kept to this day. After a pair of tiny hands gingerly uncapped the pen, I tried, for the first time in my life, to draw an "I" (我), which, however, looked like a "search" (找). Seeing my error, my father added the last stroke on the top of the latter character to make "me" complete. To my young eyes, the two Chinese words looked identical. (Chinese characters are very complicated, as are Chinese minds.)

Late at night, in our home in Canada, I would imagine that I—now very old—was reading my own novel to my grandchildren lying beside me on the comfy couch, mentally rehearsing this dialogue:

> *"Is this a true story, Grandpa?" A pair of young, curious eyes fixed on mine.*
>
> *"Surely it is," I replied, looking down at him from above my reading glasses.*
>
> *"Is the Yangtze a long river?"*
>
> *"Yes, it's very, very long. That's why it's also called the Long River."*

"Are you the boy in the novel, Grandpa?"
I paused for a moment, unsure how to reply. "Sort
of. But he's like every other boy in China in those days."

From time to time I felt called to write about my early life through the lens of my blended cultural sensibilities. At one point I even attempted to write the book in my mother tongue; however, my tongue refused to agree with my thoughts. I was stunned when words failed to flow out, as if clogged in the underwater channel.

For some reason my audacious goal was stalled for many years. I invented alibis, as many of us do when facing confession of a task too challenging. However, every day I devoted time to mental construction of the plot. By this time, I had learned that a plot is different from a story. For me, a plot is synchronicity, karma, fate.

Looking back, I realized my life stories had unfolded themselves, not from the outside, but from the inside. No coincidences in life. For me, this is a multi-dimensional book.

In it, I am both the author and reader, the experiencer and the experienced, the thinker and watcher, the dreamer and the dream, the father and the son. Most importantly, between the two ends of the spectrum, I am a silent witness as well. To that end, the characters in this book walked into my life both literally and symbolically. Some of them represent the unfathomable depth of reality. My grandmother is such a character; so are some of my childhood friends.

This book carries an allegorical burden: to unearth the truth about the mystery of life and of myself. My journey began at the river, travelling from body to mind, then to soul, from learning to becoming, from the visible to the invisible.

Over the years, in the deep corners of my mind I kept hearing the waves of the river crashing against every cell of my inner being until, one day, I could no longer ignore them when my mind was thrown into a swirl of great tides as the memories flooded back.

To my surprise, I discovered that my memory is like a multi-layered onion. As I peeled it layer after layer, tears welled up at the hurts deeply buried in the corners. But soon after I embarked on this journey, the healing process had also begun.

Most of the events in this book occurred in my early life. My memory knows what I have remembered, and it agrees with me.

As green as I was about the world, I stood, still and alone, on the edge of the river, observing myself with a young, distanced eye, listening to the solemn whisper of the waves, attempting to catch a glimpse of light hidden behind the clotted clouds. The sentences rattled in my brain and banged on the door of my heart. Finally, the pages opened in the wind and carried this tale far and wide.

As I was writing this book, I felt as though a mighty hand was guiding my thoughts and my pen. The mind is like a river flowing through human consciousness into a deep ocean. Upon entering the depth of my soul, I found a stream as it trickled down toward a long river. And when I waded into the river, currents of dreams and emotions flooded wordlessly through my consciousness.

I use English words to bridge the gap.

PART ONE

Reality exists in the human mind, and nowhere else.
—**George Orwell, 1984**

There is a Chinese legend about a nine-headed bird
that hovered above the mountains, watching over the
land. One day, when the First Emperor of China
journeyed through the land on horseback, he was
blocked by a tall mountain. Angered by this unbowed
giant, the emperor lifted his horsewhip and sliced the
body of the mountain in two. In the wink of an eye, a
great river snaked through the halved mountains and
the bird, the legendary phoenix, vanished.

But, like the bird, the story still hovers on the edge
of the memory of the land.

IN THE BEGINNING, humanity is inherently good; the same is true of human nature. It is the nurturing that triggers alienation. So say the old Chinese teachings.

Long before my life began, fate tossed me to this old, mysterious land where nine-headed birds danced and sang.

For her entire life, Grandma was unable to pen her own name. I didn't "drink the ink," she used to say, since her mother was too poor to send her to school.

In my earliest memories, Grandma, a small woman with a slight hunchback, is a shining gemstone. Her frailty could not hide her inner strength. When she spoke, the ancient earth under her tiny feet resonated with the sounds of assent.

"Look at your feet, Grandma, as tiny as the baby's," I said, teasing her.

"But you see the beauty?" She grinned.

"Beauty? No."

"You see virtue?"

"What is virtue, Grandma?"

"Filial respect. Foot-binding is a rite of passage."

I nodded, but unable to understand what it meant to her, or to me.

"Was it painful, Grandma?"

"Yes, of course."

"Why did you not refuse it?" I shook my head, disbelieving.

"I did. I protested, I screamed, but met with deaf ears." She went on. "Every day, my mother—your great-grandma—squeezed my little feet. Relentlessly. Layers, layers, layers of cloth. Once, for three long days, I refused to eat, I refused to drink. But your great-grandmother never gave in."

"What happened then?"

"For your great-grandmother, upholding tradition was more important than her daughter's pain." Grandma seemed to be searching in her memory. "She told me: If you don't eat bitterness, endure hardship, how can you rise above others? And I believed her."

The daily torture that eventually deformed the tender bones of such a young girl must have hurt Grandma beyond imagining. My little mind couldn't comprehend why anyone would take pleasure in the torture of human beings and I was appalled by her story.

Whether Grandma grew numb to the painful daily ritual or whether she decided that no amount of crying or screaming would change her fate, I do not know. But eventually she endured the torture with teeth-grinding whimpers.

"In those days, no man want marry a big-footed girl, you know," Grandma said with a smirk.

Fate toyed with Grandma's life as well.

In those days, as was tradition, girls were "sold" to wealthy families and grew up to be daughters-in-law in exchange for money or property. The girls would first help with housework for the new families, then wed their sons upon reaching early teenhood. In Grandma's time, such arranged marriages were quite common for girls from poor families.

Grandma was only ten when she was sent to a family in Phoenix Town, along with a pair of blood-jade bracelets as her dowry. These old red bracelets were passed down from her mother's mother.

The town is named after its mountain; the mountain is named after the legendary bird; the bird has nine heads. How old is the town, Phoenix Mount, or the Yangtze? No one knows. Phoenix towers over the town; the town descends abruptly toward the river; the river flows through the heart of the land like a giant dragon.

That same year, the Japanese, or the "devils from the East Oceans," as Grandma used to call them, invaded China. The Japanese fought all the way from the oceans to the river, then went upstream along the Yángtze to Phoenix Town.

Rumours of the Japanese soldiers raping pretty girls travelled like the wind. The air was filled with petrifying tales of the invaders burning, plundering, killing.

Phoenix Town was terrified.

"I smeared my face with soot, to disguise as a rough boy," Grandma said.

One day, she fled with the villagers to the mountain where they survived for days without food. They chewed tree leaves, gnawed on peeled bark. When the trees in their hideout were denuded, they dug into the moist dirt, gulping down the dirt-encrusted worms.

"Hunger sharpens your teeth, you know," Grandma used to tell me. "When you're starving to death, your teeth are like a saw."

Forever after, Grandma was haunted by nightmares, fierce stomach aches, abhorrence of the Japanese "devils". Forever after, she would go to sleep fully-clothed. Even in hot summer days. Many times in the dead of the night I could hear her screaming through her dreams: "Run quick, quick, run ..."

During the day, when the torture from chronic bowel problems became unbearable, she would rush to the kitchen, grab a butcher's knife, and take out her pain on a wooden stool beside her bed, slamming the blade down again and again until her pain and rage subsided. "Kill you, death! Kill you, death!" she screamed. Silently the stool withstood Grandma's furious revenge for years, its face marred, its edges jagged.

Sometimes, I stood by, pounding her back to ease the pain.

My fate began with a bowl of water, Grandma told me.

One day, when an army platoon was journeying through Phoenix Town, a young soldier from the People's Liberation Army (aka the PLA) stopped by Grandma's house.

"Can you kindly fetch me a bowl of water from the river?" the young man in green uniform said. "My name's Peace Song. Call me Peace."

Grandma looked at him, nodded, then summoned her young daughter to run down to the river.

The bowl of water did not quench the young man's thirst, however. As soon as he set eyes on the pretty young lady who had served him, he poured the water into his mouth, then said, "The water's sweet, but your smile even sweeter."

At that moment, my fate was sealed in the bowl of water. I belonged to the bowl. I was in the water.

"Can I carry water from the river to fill your tubs?" the young man asked.

"Today?" the shy lady said.

"No." He gazed at the blushing young maid, who was fiddling with her braid, and said: "Forever!"

2

MY BIRTHDAY COINCIDES with National Day.

Whether by chance or by fate, I was born with a noticeable birthmark on my right thigh.

"Must be a mark of fate," Mother said, giggling as she rubbed it gently.

Since my time in the cradle, my lullaby has been the sound of the waves lapping the levees in the quiet of the night. Even after I left my childhood behind, for a long time, I couldn't fall into sleep without recalling that familiar sound.

I overstayed in Mother's womb.

One day, as Grandma's tiny feet lurched across the hand-laid cobblestones along Main Street, she stopped at a brick house with grey tile roof topped by a chimney. She hurried back, sat on my mother's bed and revealed the secret brought from the fortune-teller's house: "Boy child. Mr. Yi said boy."

"He said so?" Mother's small eyes opened wide.

Grandma nodded, repeating, "SON," then went out of the back door, carefully navigating stone stairs leading to the riverbed.

Mother's lips cracked weakly into a smile. Footsteps approaching. Father pushed open the door and saw Mother's broad smile.

"Son!" Father said, cheering. "I had the same hunch."

As night fell, the boats and ships on the river passed by in reverent silence. The quiet evening was soon broken by my mother's whimpering groans.

Grandma kept busy in the kitchen in the rear of the house. My four-year-old sister was already despatched to fetch the village's sole midwife, who arrived on our doorstep ten minutes later, carrying a wooden case wrapped in a red scarf. She organized her professional tools and sat beside my groaning mother, listening intently to her pulse. First on the right wrist, then the left. Father and Grandmother stood anxiously beside the bed. "Almost ready. Bring hot water, clean towels," the midwife said.

She shooed my father and my sister, hiding behind him, from the room, closing the door tightly.

Mother's moans grew deeper and longer as each minute passed. Father paced outside the bedroom. He took out a pack of Globe brand cigarettes and began to smoke one after another. My sister soon dozed off at the dining table. Father carried her to bed.

For a short while, silence fell in Mother's room. Grandma hurried in, bringing a small tub of hot water. She wrung out a hot, white towel, then applied it to my mother's forehead.

Excruciating pain shook a cry from my mother's mouth. In the kitchen, Grandma cracked open two eggs into the steaming pan filled with long noodles, then summoned the midwife. Despite practiced reluctance, the midwife hurriedly sat at the dining table to eat.

"Don't you worry, Old Song, her water's not broken yet," the midwife said to my father, while wolfing down the long noodles from a large china bowl.

Despite the cold, Father unbuttoned his faded army uniform, glancing from time to time at the watch on his left wrist. He inhaled deeply from his cigarette, then exhaled a long breath.

When I began to understand things, Father told me his wristwatch had been a present from his army captain, who later became our regional governor.

Father's uncle reluctantly adopted him when his father died, on the condition that Father call him Papa. This, my father would never accept. He would chop wood and fetch water but he could not bend his young mind to calling his uncle his father.

"How dare you disobey me while I raise you like my own son?" his uncle screamed while whipping him.

Father tiptoed out of his uncle's house into the black cover of night when the PLA passed through the village. Once among the soldiers, my father asked who was in charge. In no time, he found himself thrust before a tall man wearing a four-pocket green uniform.

"I want to join the PLA," Father yelled, finally letting out the thoughts long held in his young head.

The officer, pulling him closer, looked at this audacious boy with disbelief, then shook his head. "Join the army? Not even as tall as rifle," the officer said, pointing at the weapon slung on the right shoulder of the soldier standing beside him.

Father, however, didn't want to give up his plan of escape so easily. "I *am* 18, truly 18," he protested. He then dropped to his knees, clung to the officer's leg tightly with both arms, crying: "I will not let you go if you don't take me."

The officer burst into loud laughter. Tossing aside his burning cigarette, he stooped down to pull my father up by the arms that were encircling his legs. Yet my father would not let go, screaming, "Where you go, I follow."

Touched by the boy's crazy stubbornness, the officer decided to enlist my father as an orderly. He ordered his men to cut a uniform's long sleeves to fit my skinny father.

Father wanted to fight on the battlefield. But the Nationalist Army had retreated all the way to the island of Taiwan. So, instead, he learned to read and write in classes aimed at erasing illiteracy among soldiers.

I learned most of these details from Father's lips.

➤ By now, darkness had enveloped the mountains, and the deserted streets fell into silence. The crescent moon hung in the sky like a cradle, surrounded by glittering stars. Mother gnawed on a towel to muffle her cries. Toward midnight, Grandma summoned her son-in-law. "Bring more hot water."

Carrying a jug of hot water, Father attempted to open the door but Grandma blocked him. She took the basin and promptly shoved the door closed with her rear end. He stood outside, strained his ears against the door and lit another cigarette.

Mother's tiny room was warm, the windows heavily draped. A kerosene lamp flickered and shadows jumped on the white-brushed walls, dancing amid the sporadic groans.

Finally, an inevitable force pushed me down through a dark tunnel until I fell into a widened opening. I slipped out of Mother's womb, uttered my first human cry, the umbilical cord twisted around my neck. A pair of scissors severed the cord.

"A *son*!" the midwife declared.

Just then, the wall clock chimed and chimed. Twelve times in total.

Amid the cries and cooing, Father banged the door open and stopped to see the fresh little me lying on Mother's bosom, greedily sucking her breast.

"Have name yet?" The midwife looked up at my father's perspiring face.

"Long time had it," Father proclaimed in a tone of apparent authority. "The sun gives light to the moon, the moon gives light to the night, the night is brightened by the dreams of man. Welcome to the human world, Little Bright!"

(In Chinese, the word "bright" symbolizes a union of sun and moon.)

And so, I was called Little Bright.

3

As a toddler, I would tug at Grandma's apron, begging her to tell me about my early years.

With the moonlight flooding into her bedroom, Grandma would fetch a basin of hot water and soak her tiny, aching feet. I would sit on the edge of her bed, my eyes wide in the flickering lamplight, my ears soothed by the rhythm of the wavelets lapping at the levees of the river.

One October morning, word of my arrival had travelled along the wings of the morning birds. "A stone has finally dropped to the ground," people murmured.

Uncle Wang was the first to come. "Fortune has descended on your door." He grinned, handing a red envelope to Grandma. Pretending to be displeased for a few seconds, she finally tucked it into her pocket with feigned reluctance. Uncle Wang was our town's mayor. He'd been in the PLA too. His wife was estimated to deliver in December. "If it's girl," he joked with Father, "she'll be your daughter-in-law."

"Good, good!" My father handed him a Double Happiness cigarette with both hands.

Grandma emerged from the kitchen, holding something wrapped in a crumpled newspaper that Father had read the night before. She whispered into Uncle Wang's ear, then tucked the parcel into his hands. Uncle Wang's face brightened. Without waiting to sip his steamy mug of tea leaf, he edged to the door.

➤ Now, with her door shut and the window drapery drawn against the daylight, Mother would have to lie in bed for thirty moons. Grandma would not allow her daughter to break with tradition. Her feet could not touch the ground nor could her hands feel cold water. Coldness was associated with illness as much as discomfort.

Mother had been waiting for this moment for a long time. Now she put me onto her breast, wrapped her arms around me, holding me gently against her bosom as if protecting her son from the kidnappers rumoured to be roaming the land.

The night before, Grandma had stewed a bowl of soup for hours in an old earthen pot that stood on a wood-fired stove. When Grandma carried the stew to bed, Mother was still tasting the droplets of her salty tears from the night before.

"Eat all," Grandma ordered. I was sound asleep against Mama's bosom.

Mother spooned the concoction into her mouth.

"What's in here?" Mother asked, hiccupping. "Tastes horrible!"

"Placenta," Grandma mumbled.

"What?" Mother threw up, vomiting pieces of the stew onto the bed and all over the floor.

"You see!" Grandma shrieked, upset at her daughter's reaction.

Mother's jaw dropped. She wiped her mouth and looked up at her mother, incredulous, her face a mixture of disgust and horror.

"You are saying what?" She still couldn't trust her own ears.

At length Grandma brushed away her own indignation with a wave of her hand. "When you were born, my mother offered me the same. It's the tradition."

Before Grandma could say more, Mother took a deep breath and had to fight down the gushing in her throat. Retching horribly, Mother almost vomited her entrails in front of her perplexed mother.

The fetid stench seemed to float in the room for weeks; however, my mother and her infant gradually grew accustomed and forgot to notice.

After the placenta incident, my poor mother insisted on a meagre regimen of rice and vegetable soup, but the diet only provoked further nausea. Consequently, Mother's breast milk ran dry. With winter knocking at our door, Grandma was worried about her grandson's well-being, so she began to feed me spoonfuls of rice, which she would chew into a mush, then say, "Yummy!" before spooning the pasty substance into my mouth.

This continued until my third birthday.

On that day, Grandma cooked a bowl of long steamy noodles, and added a peeled, hard-boiled, red-dyed egg. (Called longevity noodles.) She chewed the concoction first in her mouth before trying to feed me a spoonful.

"No, no, Grandma," I pushed away the spoon, refusing to be spoon-fed.

Clamping my mouth tightly, I turned my head away, stubbornly thwarting her efforts. Whether I was disgusted by Grandma's chewing or was simply eager to bite the food by myself, I do not know. Or remember.

Our people say a boy's fate can be revealed by how he behaves on his third birthday. This, my father believed. So, on my third birthday, my family huddled to divine my destiny. First, Grandma retrieved an old silver coin tightly wrapped in silk and placed it carefully on the table. Then, my father put down before me a copy of Chairman Mao's Book of Quotations (also known as the *Red Treasure Book*).

And finally a new fountain pen was laid before me by my mother.

When my time came, I snatched the pen. With my left hand. A repeat test confirmed the same fate. The pen became my witness. Joy exploded around me. A worrisome cloud, however, passed over my mother's face: her son was a lefty. After Mother quietly spoke of this mishap, silence fell in the room.

"How can a left hand wrestle with the right?" my mother asked worriedly.

Here, life is to be lived by following crowds, other people's beliefs; being different is akin to being a political contrarian, which is akin to being suicidal. Apparently, my parents understood this simple logic.

This unwritten rule would be deeply inculcated in my brain.

Undaunted by the frightening omen, Mother set out to rectify my impediment. I was the odd child in the family. But her teaching fell by the wayside, unheeded. It was not because I turned a deaf ear to her but because I couldn't help being that way. How can you change something that is born to you? I could, of course, have asked my parents that question. Nevertheless, my father's faith in the rightness of the norm remained unshaken.

Also on that day, a ponytailed girl hopped into the picture, followed by her father, Uncle Wang. The red, silky ribbons in her hair were like two butterflies dancing on her head as she jumped. Her name was Red.

I gave her my hand and she stole my childhood heart.

4

NOT FAR FROM the end of Main Street was a footpath leading to
a yellow-sanded beach at the edge of the river. We called it Turtle
Beach, because turtles liked to crawl from the river onto the sand
to enjoy the sun. The half-sided mountain stood erect on the opposite side of the river. In the distance, birds flitted around the
branches of the trees surrounding the mouth of a huge crevice on
the side of the mountain facing the river. A bird sanctuary.

In summer, the beach became our rendezvous, far away from
the adult world. There, we built sandcastles and joyfully buried
ourselves in the warm sand. With our fingers, we sketched words
on the soft surface. It seemed that our adult life would be much
easier if we could erase the old with a wave of fingers and rewrite
our new life while lying lazily under the sun.

When I walked barefoot in the sunlight, I discovered a mystery:
I have a shadow. When I moved, it moved with me. When I stopped,
it played dead. If I headed north, it followed; if I headed south, it
trailed behind.

But I did not believe the shadow was me.

So, I ran. But I found it strange that it followed me, silent as a
ghost. My little mind therefore concluded that, whenever the sun
shines, there is a shadow and when the sun goes off to sleep behind
the mountains, the shadow grows into the darkness and merges
with the night.

After some time, I had to admit *I am the shadow.* The shadow
belongs to me; the shadow is me. We are one and the same, even
though the shadow in me cannot be seen with the naked eye. Eyes

reside on our face; the mind resides in our heart. Grandma called it the eye of the heart.

One afternoon, I asked Red to meet me at the beach. She didn't come alone—she brought some other boys and girls. We all played tag for a while. After the fun ran dry, boredom set in. Red toyed with a new idea. "Let's play house." I loved it, and nodded assent. So did the boys, including Bubble and Ear. (I've long forgotten Ear's real name. People used his nickname because he was born with only one ear.) The girls also agreed enthusiastically. We paired off by playing rock-paper-scissors.

To my dismay, Ear was paired with Red to play hubby and wife. This I couldn't stand. But he shrugged and said nothing until Red said to me, "You can play daddy if you want."

Ear raised his forefinger, pointing at Red. "No! You are MY wife!"

"No way!" I shouted, throwing my own finger at him. "Shame on you. Red's agreed to play my wife, not yours."

Even though Ear was a head taller than I was, I wasn't going to be intimidated—even at the risk of losing my girl.

"Don't you even try, little twerp," he retorted angrily. "You're a lefty—disqualified—or you could play my left-handed son."

"Your mother!" I spat. (Spitting at someone's mother was among our community's worst—and most popular—curses.) Furious, I pushed him hard before anyone could intervene and he landed on his backside in the sand.

Picking himself up, he charged at me like a bull in the arena. It would have been a fierce battle if Red hadn't come between us, yelling at the top of her lungs: "No fighting! No more fighting!"

Meanwhile, Red untied her two red ribbons, handing one to Ear and one to me. This gesture immediately pacified Ear, but not me. This was a devastating blow. Jealousy was burning in my little pounding heart. Red belonged to me, and no one could snatch her away. I was angrier at Red for giving my rival a lovely symbol of her favour than I was at the ugly earless jerk.

After that, I didn't speak to Red and avoided her for days.

One day she approached me at home, asking me to join her at the beach. "The two of us alone," she said.

I nodded with feigned reluctance.

On the beach, the gentle waves splashed the sand, foam dancing in their wake. She ran barefoot in the water; I kicked off my sandals and chased her. When I caught her, both of us were soaking wet, but we didn't care. We lay in the sand to wait for the sun to go to its rest behind the mountains. We counted the passing boats going upstream, downstream. A great wave of joy washed over me. The world would have been a more beautiful place if my childhood had lasted forever like this, with Red lying beside me. I was dancing in the stream of my thoughts.

Finally, we sat up, my throat dry. Timidly, I breathed out the long-withheld words: "Will you be my wife when you grow up, Red?" I wanted to put my arms around her but didn't dare, afraid her rejection would stab my heart like a piece of broken glass.

Red lowered her head, blushing, a lovely smile spreading her lips. She extended her hand and I held it in mine, my heart leaping into my throat. I was thrilled. Any beautiful words I might come up with now could never describe my emotions at that moment. My joy illuminated the cloudy sky above us.

I don't remember how long it was before Ear and I reconciled, but it was because of Red that I apologized to him. Children so easily forget their bitterness because the spirit of reconciliation dwells in the hearts of the innocent. Once again, Ear and I were friends.

However, our time on the beach was not always fun and games. One evening as we waded in the water and ran along the crescent beach, Yellow, my blonde-haired dog who sometimes accompanied me to the beach, started barking at something in the distance. Following his gaze, we caught sight of two swollen bodies that had washed ashore: a man and a woman tied together at the waist with a sodden, knotted rope, their bodies moving with the dying waves.

A swarm of flies buzzed, mosquitoes hung above the corpses, and the air reeked of pig dung. In an instant, our laughter froze, our horror hanging in midair.

We ran off like the devil himself was at our heels, the dust whirling up behind us.

For a long time, that scene was burned onto the film of my memory, and I wished the image could be erased with a wave of a finger as easily as my sand drawings.

But fate doesn't give you that choice.

Later, we learned the man and woman were secret lovers from Li Family village, a town thirty miles upriver that was known to birth beautiful women. When the woman found out she was to wed the headman of her village, who was twice her age, she and her lover vowed to tie the knot in the river.

Sometime after the spine-chilling discovery, village folks began to say the beach was haunted by two young ghosts strolling hand in hand along the shore. Since then, whenever Yellow prowled that area, he'd bark several times toward the beach, then scurry away.

5

WINTER HAD COME overnight.

The Spring Festival—an annual indulgence—was at hand, and the cold, clear air rang with the happy festivities.

A few days prior, one of my upper baby teeth grew wiggly and started to bleed. But I soon forgot about the discomfort when Mother promised me a pair of the new leather boots that I'd long coveted. She also informed me that my big uncle, who was a director in the city's propaganda department, would join us on Chinese New Year's Eve (Big Feast Eve)—the night before Lunar New Year's Day.

On his previous visit, I had begged my uncle to tell me about his time spent fighting the Americans in the Korean War. Instead, he gave me an empty Marlboro pack, which I added as a rarity to my collection of cigarette packs.

"My job was to make friends with the American captives and convert them so they would turn their backs against their own country," he said.

"How did you do that?" I asked, curious.

"We washed their brains."

"What? What brain?"

"Wash their brains."

"But how?"

"With words. Words work miracles and they carry more power than guns and cannons."

"Like washing your face?"

"Yes, day after day. You'll understand when you grow up."

But I was still confused. I was only interested in how he had gunned down the Americans like I'd seen in the movies.

One night, when I was lying on my bed thumbing through my favourite picture book, *The Monkey King*, I overheard Father murmuring about selling our house pig to the slaughterhouse.

Soon I drifted into the realm of dreams. (Grandma explained when we sleep, we enter the hometown of dreams.) In the dream, I was wearing my shiny new leather boots. When I ran, the shoelaces suddenly turned into a long, thick rope curling around me like a snake, its long tail tightening around my neck. I was suffocating and struggling for air. When I woke up, I was still panting.

Usually, when I opened my eyes in the morning, Yellow would be there to greet me, wagging his tail. But today, Yellow was nowhere to be found. The same was true for our fat pig.

My father searched for that pig everywhere before finally locating it. "The stupid beast," he said when he returned, rubbing cold hands against his face, "was hiding in the heart of the haystacks at the village threshing ground."

I realized then it was the place where I used to play hide-and-seek.

The next morning, my father and mother tied up the pig to one of the posts in the wooden pigsty in the backyard. The pig squealed like a baby, then bent down on his front feet as though in prostration toward his master, which reminded me of when we used to *kowtow* (knock our foreheads on the ground) in front of the headstones of our ancestors' tombs.

I could not believe my own eyes: there were tears rolling down from the pig's two small eyes.

"Old Heavens!" Grandma shouted, referring to her supreme deity also known as Lord Above. "This beast crying like baby."

I looked away. Mother was motionless. My father stared, speechless. I ran away from them, tears rolling down from my own eyes.

Poor pig, destined to the butcher's blade. He'd always been

conscious of the fate awaiting him. How he found out about his doomsday remains a mystery to me.

Later, I followed my father on the cobblestone streets along Main Street before turning into a slaughterhouse not too far from People's Square. On the cobblestones were the prints of the pig's dirty feet, in the shape of a heart.

On many occasions, I watched as a butcher thrust a long sharp blade into the throat of a bellowing creature until the last drop of its steamy blood oozed into a wooden basin lying on the blood-stained floor.

These creatures (and their predecessors) were all carried by four strong butchers into a huge wooden container filled with simmering water to remove their hair before they were skinned and dismembered. Their livers, kidneys, ears, tails, feet, and every other part would then be displayed on a long bloodstained wooden counter. Their hearts, while still palpitating (or so I thought), were wrapped in yellowed, crumpled newspaper before being passed to the villagers.

The red-brick house was packed with animated little crowds, some discussing our pig's mysterious tears. Saying nothing, I ran outside. I leaned against a red-brick wall; the sounds of shrieking erupted from the slaughterhouse and continued echoing into the distance. I covered my ears tightly with both hands. In my mind's eye, the night opened its mouth, baring its teeth like a wolf.

Late that night, Mama came to my room. She untied her apron, took out a folded five-yuan note from her pocket, then sat on the edge of my bed.

"I'm going to buy you a pair of leather shoes tomorrow," she said.

A pause. Mama took time to smooth out the crumpled bill on her knee with her hands, which trembled.

"Don't want leather shoes," I exclaimed, my tone calm but strained. That was not what I wanted to say, but I couldn't say anything else.

A heavy silence fell between us. She stared at the money and said nothing. Finally, she hung her head and quietly left the room, her feet heavy and slow.

I felt sorry for Mama.

She worked hard day and night. The kitchen was her kingdom but also the battlefield for her three children. My younger sister, who was four years my junior, always cried for more food. One day, I kicked her when she cried for more. But her screaming grew louder, which rattled the glass windows and shattered Mama's heart as well. One day, I took three fresh eggs from my pocket and gave two to her. She immediately cracked the eggshell on the ground and gulped the white and yolk down in a few seconds and then looked at the second egg. "I'll save it for Mama," she said. During the evening meal, Mother held her egg, asking me, "Where did you get this?" I hung my head, not daring to tell her the truth. "Brother stole eggs from our neighbour's house," my sister blurted.

"What? How dare you!"

Mama smashed the egg onto the floor and slapped my face hard. I held my cheek, crying. Mama burst into tears. She held me against her bosom and cried with me. "I'm sorry, son, I'm sorry. It's all my fault."

We huddled together and cried.

Later that night Grandma told me a story I never forgot.

Once, a young boy stole an egg. The boy's mother did not discipline her son; instead, she was proud of her son's shrewdness. As time went by, the boy fell into a habit of stealing. By and by, the boy grew into a young man who committed big crimes. In the end, the authorities decided to execute him. On the day of his execution, the prosecutor asked him if he had a last wish. "Yes," the young man said, "I want to cast a last look at my mother."

When his mother arrived, he said: "Mama, can you grant me one last wish?"

"What is it, son?" the devastated woman said, sobbing.

"I want to suckle at your breast one last time."

Without hesitation, the mother bared her breast, opened her arms to her son and held him like a newborn baby. Seconds later the mother shrieked in horror and pain: her son had bitten off her nipple!

"It's *you*, Mother, who deprived me of my life today," the man bellowed, wiping the blood from his angry mouth. "I hate you!" Then he walked alone to his execution without turning his head.

After that night, I learned to say at the dinner table, "I am full, Mama." Then I would swallow my saliva.

Mother knew I was faking but swallowed her tears, hiding her anxiety under the shadow of her eyebrows. Eventually, even her laughter became part of our torment because we knew that she faked it to please us. From time to time, our stomachs growled and we were tempted to dip our heads into the steaming pot to lick the bottom. Slumber became my best food; I cooked satisfaction in my head, and it made my mouth water in my dreams as I recalled licking the chopsticks, savouring them. The whiteness of rice flew around me like fleeting clouds. But when I woke up hunger was still walking at my side like my shadow. When I looked out, the moon turned into a mooncake.

Mother loved her children. On meagre days, she would often go to the mountains to dig for wild plants to supplement the rationed rice, but she was never free from worrying about us. Worries, guilt, and sorrow filled her eyes and marred her strained but kind face, so she hid her eyes in the dark veils of night.

"When you worry too much, your hair stops growing," Mother said.

The night cried out: life is food; life is clothing; motherly love is measured by the size of the rice bowls and the colour of fabric. For her, life was moving too slowly, as though each second had grown longer, like a slow-motion scene in a movie. Worries freeze time and slow life down. They made the wall clock stop ticking.

Every day, when Mother pulled open the lid of the steaming iron wok in the kitchen, she would repeat her wishes: to live in a house with stairs, lightbulbs, telephones. To her that was heaven. In time, her wish became her dream.

Of course, it may take years, even decades, to achieve our heavenly dreams. Our ancestors endured much hardship for a long, long time. Tens of hundreds of years. Tradition is not yet sick of waiting. Even if we are stabbed in the heart by a knife, our eyes will never blink. Such is the stolid character that resided in Mother's blood.

I could picture this dream but could do nothing about it. When you are a child, you cannot exchange your situation for a better one, just like you cannot move Mount Phoenix, but I did pick up the habit of escaping by creating imaginary dialogue in my mind.

That night, I was not sure how long I had been lying in bed. Soon, I was shaking with fear. Out of the blue, the roof caved in and a huge rock came down from the sky and hit me on the chest. I was lying in a pool of blood. Then a flock of albatrosses in the sky flew from behind the mountains and circled above the village. They moved westward in two groups, flying in an inverse V shape. One of the birds called out to me and told me he was Yellow, my dog friend.

"How did you change into a bird?" I asked.

He related his captors slaughtered him and placed his body on the feast table, but his soul flew away.

I giggled; the rock that had hit me shrunk into a baby tooth.

When I woke up, the blanket was stained with blood; I must have spat out the lost tooth in my dream. Now, when I spoke, a whisk of breeze gushed from the crevice beside my remaining front teeth.

Feeling both thirsty and hungry, I went to the kitchen. On the table, a gloomy kerosene lamp flickered, and a huge bowl lay in the centre. I dropped my head into the bowl and sucked up a mouthful of the congealed liquid inside, which smelled like rotten fish. Before I could gulp it down, I threw up; it was pig's blood. My revulsion continued emptying from my stomach and I threw up again, in the same kitchen where, despite my current puking, I had once experienced many happy moments.

Outside the house snowflakes danced in the wind, oblivious, as if nothing had happened. When they hit the ground, they lay silent as death, blanketing the whole village in white. A rooster started to crow in the distance; in no time, its peers joined in.

Yellow never came back. After days of searching, I fell into despair. People suspected Yellow had been in the dishes served on Big Feast Eve, but I refused to believe. For a long time, I continued to hope that, someday, Yellow would show up at my bedside, wagging his tail. But that only happened in my dreams. Humans have dominion over the fate of lesser creatures, but what about the fate of a little human being like me, I wondered.

Whether I submit myself to my fate or struggle to break free, these pages must reveal it all.

6

AN OLD EYE cannot see new things, people say.

Loudspeakers were new things in town when they were planted on every available spot, on wooden poles at every major intersection, on the trees around People's Square. The poles towered over the dirty streets, the ragged passersby and the trees choking in dust.

In no time, the voice of the loudspeakers climbed high above the walls, penetrating every house in town. The voice was everywhere in the air—it became one with the air. When you breathed, the voice already spoke in your head. No MUTE buttons to push.

On a sunny July morning in 1967, the loudspeaker lady first announced the weather forecast, then the compulsory parade. As Grandma listened, she shook her head in disbelief. She could foretell the weather more precisely than the loudspeaker lady.

Her way was unique: she looked up at the sky and weighed the clouds with her eyes.

"Look," she said, pointing her finger at the clouds hovering over the mountain. "Clouds in the belly of the sky are threats of storm."

So she urged me to carry an umbrella under my arm. "To shade yourself against the baking sun or to shield your body against a thunderous storm," she explained. "Clouds are unpredictable and deceptive, just like crowds."

Much of her homespun wisdom still rings true today.

I can see with my own eyes, Grandma, I heard myself thinking. A wind blew past my ears; so did her words.

Ear scurried down the lane to see me. He was wearing a white shirt, black trousers, a pair of Liberation brand shoes, made of green canvas cloth; I wore the same. White over black signified the colour of unity with folks in the parade. I asked him to invite Red but Ear shook his head. "Just the two of us this time, man to man." I nodded in agreement.

This guy has begun to understand things better than I do, I thought. Every summer Ear grew taller and his trousers became shorter. Meanwhile, the hair on my head grew longer, the voice in my throat had lowered but my body seemed to stop growing—up. All because of that fateful summer night, I grumbled.

At the heart of the town lay People's Square.

The restless crowd waited for the sacred moment when representatives from Lin Valley would hand out copies of Chairman Mao's *Red Treasure Book*. A propaganda team was summoned from our county's capital to mark the occasion. Such a historic moment deserved to be celebrated with sing-songs and dances in the streets.

"When you read the *Red Treasure Book,* it clarifies your thoughts, brightens your eyes, strengthens your bodies," Uncle Wang declared, holding a cone-shaped, tin amplifier to his mouth and standing on a makeshift platform of dinner tables.

The *Red Treasure Book* and its words were our treasures, a possession that would bring us joy and happiness. To us, the words of Chairman Mao were as holy as the Holy Bible is to Christians. I did not hear about the Bible until much later.

The crowd swelled. Eager people shoved Ear and me to and fro, eventually, nudging us out of the centre. At the edge, I could see only heads and shoulders. At my wit's end, I pushed my way through to the willow trees at the edge of the square. I climbed up a tall tree and perched on a branch.

Now, I could see the square like a bird. I had never been happier.

Trumpets blew, drums thundered, cymbals clashed and then the parade snaked out behind a gigantic portrait of Chairman Mao lifted high. Wearing a green uniform and a Red Guard armband, Chairman Mao raised his hand to salute the crowd; all eyes trained, no doubt, on the huge mole beneath his bottom lip. That was a symbol from Heaven and a lucky sign for China, people explained.

Meanwhile, an equally gigantic portrait of Vice-Chairman Lin Biao followed close behind the supreme leader, in which he held aloft the *Red Treasure Book*. Our Vice Chairman was born in Lin Valley and joined the Revolution later. How lucky we were to be so closely associated with the second greatest leader in the land. You could utter a long sentence about that connection, but no words were sufficient to describe that feeling of pride inside each of us.

Having lost Ear, I tried to locate him but distinguishing whose head sat on whose shoulder in a sea of people dressed in black and white was out of the question.

It was time to climb down from my perch. Just as my shoes touched the grass, a large boy rushed at me, snatching the Chairman Mao badge pinned to my shirt. Before I could speak, the thief had disappeared into the throng. The bastard had stolen my most precious possession. Luckily, I'd amassed a coveted collection of artifacts, so I would be able to get it back from my peers by trading it for a less desirable badge.

No tears, but the incident affected my mood. So instead of following the crowd out of the square, I sat on the grass, my back against a tree. So far, I had enjoyed the crowd, which served as a buffer between my fear of being left out and of loneliness. At the same time, I was afraid of the crowds, which are unpredictable. I saw proof of it that day.

While I thought, hunger climbed up my throat and I remembered the two eggs that Mama had hard-boiled for me. Peeling off the cracked shells, I stuffed the eggs inside my mouth.

➤ People's Square was not unfamiliar to me.

A regular film night there turned out to be my weekly thrill, helping crush my childhood boredom. Back then all the films were black-and-white. Volunteers erected a large white transparent canvas as a makeshift screen. Amazingly, one could watch the movie from the back as well as from the front. When the front of the canvas became crowded—it was a popular event—I often sat at the back of the screen.

But when you watch a movie from the back, everything reflected on the screen is a mirror image of what's projected in front. In any scenes when people walk to the left on the front side of the screen, for example, they walk to the right when viewed from the back. Since I was left-handed anyway, left was right for me. I didn't mind the backward view of that imaginary world.

Too young to understand the movie, it nevertheless revealed a side of the world far beyond my small town.

One night, at the end of *A Tale of the Red Lantern*, the crowd thinned out and dispersed into the dark. My eyes focused on the man at the projector's table as he packed up his equipment.

"Uncle, where did all the actors go after their performance?" I asked.

Perplexed for a moment, the man looked down at me and replied: "They get off the screen when everyone has left."

I blinked, but believed him, despite the chuckle he worked to contain while shaking his head.

And so, at the end of the following week's screening of *Guerrilla on the Railway Tracks,* I was determined to touch the pistol held by my hero, Commander Li, who gunned down numerous Japanese invaders. I waited and waited. Afraid to blink. But Commander Li did not show up.

I don't know when I fell asleep, but Grandma came and found me with the help of a flashlight. The big screen had been dismantled. Only two remaining poles stood silent and naked in the moonlit square. Disappointment hit my head like a brick.

"Five years old now; you don't understand a thing in this world," Grandma said, sighing.

For my little mind, the world was like a big stage on which all people were players. The real world was too sophisticated for me to grasp.

(Years later, I learned that Shakespeare had said the same thing about 400 years earlier.)

In time, I understood the world on the big screen had been created by the projector. And many years later, I learned that human minds are like the projector, the white screen a mirror image of our thoughts; our minds create the reality.

One day, a fateful event in People's Square changed our lives forever.

As evening fell, the sun had climbed over the mountains and moved slowly down the ravine. It wasn't long before clouds began to gather and float high above the four winds. Before evening had settled on People's Square, townsfolk had come down from all parts of the village to set up their stools and benches in rows before the stage, where the propaganda team would perform the *White-Haired Girl*, a popular piece of communist propaganda in the form of a play, as well as a movie.

The townsfolk were bubbly and excited in the heat of that summer night.

I had watched the movie version here many times and it was a personal favourite. I could recite almost every line of the dialogue.

Here's how it goes: New Year's Eve. Yellowed Prosperity, the wealthy landowner, rushes to Yang's shed to collect a debt. (Yang's name is a pun, a play on words meaning "a sheep labours in vain.") Poor sheep has no money to pay; Prosperity seizes Yang's daughter Joy as his concubine. Later, Joy flees to the mountain. Like my grandma. Joy births a baby, whom she stones to death in horror. Fruit of evil! Sorrow whitens her hair overnight. Not because of her baby, but because of her lost virginity. Then comes the Revolution. All landowners executed.

People have spoken: all landowners deserve death!

My reverie was broken by the sound of footfall on the stage.

A running dog (the nickname for anyone associated with land-owners) toyed with an abacus. His fingers flew through the beads, calculating interest.

"No money?" shouted the Villain. "Sell me Joy!"

Yang knelt before the Villain, begging for mercy.

As our history shows, villains never show mercy for the poor. Instead, the Villain grabbed Yang's thumb, forcing it into a red-ink box, to create a thumbprint on the sale paper.

An old man jumped onto the stage, charging at the Villain and crushing his head with a red brick.

This scene was new, not part of the familiar script in the movie. I was baffled.

Roars erupted from the human sea as the townspeople stood, throwing their fists like grenades.

"Avenge the white-haired girl!"

"Down with all landlords!"

"Down with all running dogs!"

"Long live Chairman Mao!"

Yellowed Prosperity, the actor, lay in a pool of black, glossy and very real blood.

The bellowing mingled with a sudden rumble of thunder. Lightning struck, bathing the town's rooftops and people's faces in eerie yellow. Big raindrops pelted the dispersing crowd. The sky spat out thunder, lightning and rain.

Frightened by the commotion, I struggled for safe footing and I fell, hard, to the ground. My left arm broke on impact.

‿⁊⁊ℯ

MY FORMAL EDUCATION began with a bowl of bitterness.

On the first day of school, I sat in the first row beside a pony-tailed girl whose name meant "daughter of the moon," so we called her Moon.

At that time, blushing and stumbling in proximity to a girl my age was an inconvenient mystery. But having one as my tablemate? I would be disgraced and drowned in the gossip of my peers.

Moon was not pleased either. She used a pencil to draw a bold vertical line down the middle of the table.

"This is the 38th Parallel, which you *cannot* cross." She stared at me.

I immediately knew what that meant: 3/8 also means March 8, which is International Women's Day. The 38th Parallel is also the military demarcation line between North Korea and South Korea. The girl had started a gender war but I would not bow to her rules.

On purpose, I let my left elbow challenge her by inching out and encroaching on her territory. War had been declared between North Korea and South Korea. But who was north and who was south? North Korea, we were told, was China's ally and the South was the enemy, like the Americans. Angry eyes wide, Moon shot scathing looks at the offending elbow. I did not withdraw. In the end, she looked away with a long sigh.

At least I hadn't lost face in the first round.

Red sat in the second row and Ear sat behind Red.

The school bell rang. Principal Jia—whose eyes jittered under a black slash of eyebrows— entered. He was followed by a grey-haired man holding a basin covered with a white towel, whom he introduced as Master Fu, the new school inspector appointed by the authority.

Master Fu was the much-acclaimed hero of the *White-Haired Girl* play who'd fatally bricked the villain's head. That bloodstained red brick had changed the course of the revolution in our town. Today, it was Master Fu's responsibility to lead Phoenix Elementary down a new revolutionary road, the principal declared.

"Close your eyes, class," Principal Jia ordered. We obeyed. "Now, imagine you're the master of a house filled with everything you want. You can do anything you desire. What would the world be like for you?"

I felt the weight of the momentary silence. Opening my eyes timidly, I gazed around. The principal was a middle-aged man who bared his protruding upper teeth when he spoke. His spit flew when he shouted for emphasis. Considering his question, my mind went blank. I'd never thought such a thing would be possible. But his question seduced me into deep thought. That blissful house, if it exists, must be a heavenly place on earth.

"Class, don't underestimate the power of this question. The vision it generates is mightier than an atom bomb," the principal exclaimed. "This vision helped our party conquer the Japanese, defeat the Nationalist Party, build a new China."

I dropped my jaw. The whole class looked bewildered. The principal seemed to understand the confusion on our faces.

"Let me give you an example," he replied, waving his hand. "I'm sure all of you have heard the story of quenching thirst by visualizing plums."

The whole class grinned; a three-year-old baby would know this well-known tale.

One day, as the legend goes, the famed General Cao led his army up a huge mountain to make a surprise attack on the enemy. The sun scorched the land and the exhausted soldiers, who had been journeying for nights and days, were parched. Some had already died of thirst; others lay on the road, gasping. The general's order to march on fell on deaf ears. Then, the general had an idea.

"Attention, soldiers," the general exclaimed, galloping to the head of his struggling army, waving his horsewhip in the air.

"Not far ahead of us, I've found a forest of plums. They're ripe and plump, sweet and sour. They make my mouth water. How about you?"

All the soldiers cheered. Saliva flowed from the corners of their mouths. They were all in high spirits because of an imaginary forest of plums! Spurred by their desire to pluck the fruit, the soldiers marched faster, accelerating their speed until they had climbed up the mountain in the shortest time possible. In the end, they ambushed their enemies and crushed them.

But they never found the forest, I told myself the first time I'd heard the story. But who cared? They won the battle, which was the most important thing.

Now, this familiar example illuminated our eyes and minds; truly, imagination works miracles.

"Unlike China," I heard the principal saying, "the rest of the world is drowning in the deep waters of bitterness. It's the Party's destiny to liberate humanity and free mankind; this is the dream of our country. And, fortunately, you are the lucky generation that will become part of that big dream."

The principal's passion was contagious.

A wave of excitement swept over the class. My heart was hammering; my face was flushed. I'd never reckoned I could be a person important enough to change the world. This newfound pride dwelled inside me for a long time.

Through my childish reverie, I heard Principal Jia announcing rules and directives. There were many and most were familiar, such as "obey your teachers." But none was more important than this: love the Party with all your mind and heart because the Party is dearer than your parents.

A stray dog barked outside the schoolroom, watching us enviously, its eyebrows twitching.

Sweating with excitement, I felt lucky that my left-handedness had been righted. With my fractured left elbow in a sling for six weeks, I had no choice but to use my right hand. It had been awkward at first but my parents regarded the incident as a "lost horse"—a blessing in disguise.

If the fracture hadn't occurred, I could not imagine how I would have redeemed myself for being abnormal. Still, I would raise a left hand to ask a question while my classmates used their right hands. If I forgot to use my right hand and wrote with my left, my left elbow would collide with Moon's right arm, and my embarrassment would be doubled.

Being jeered at and mocked by one's peers is the last thing a six-year-old can withstand. *I would prefer losing my mind rather than losing face,* I thought. This was a revelation for a boy with a reckless streak like mine, as I would discover later.

By this time, Principal Jia had stepped away and Master Fu had moved to the centre of the platform. He spoke about his past bitterness regarding the old China. He shed tears but smiled through his teary eyes when he spoke of the new China.

Tears are contagious too.

"In the past, we were s … s … s … lave; now we are ma … ma … master," he stuttered. We found out that when Master Fu became excited, he began to slip into this old habit. I admit I was moved to tears by Master Fu's broken words, deeply convinced that without our saviour, Chairman Mao, there would never have been a new China, and without a new China my father would never have drunk from my mother's bowl. In the end, I would not have existed! In the past, I had obediently sung the popular patriotic songs, the familiar words forming easily on my lips, but this day my heart was singing too.

By now, logic and passion had joined hands. This line of

reasoning was so compelling that all doubt was dispelled. Their words had conquered my heart and my little mind as well. Of course, all of this took place subconsciously, so I did not know this at the time.

Pride filled my chest as I listened. I still remember the moment I resolved to devote my life to the revolutionary cause. I fell into deep reflection, my face reddened; I was so ashamed of every self-ish—even evil—thought I had ever entertained. For example, I had wanted to enjoy fish and pork every day, not just on the New Year's Eve feast.

Just then, the principal gestured for the class to applaud Master Fu and the tremulous group stood and saluted the ever-watchful eyes of the Chairman Mao portrait high on the whitewashed wall.

Principal Jia wiped his tears with the back of his hand. Then the master removed the cover from the basin that contained "a taste of the old society" that he distributed to the class: a bowl of grain chaff cakes mixed with bitter herbs. I'd eaten chaff cakes before but Mother never mixed them with bitter herbs. Master Fu took the lead and gulped down his portion.

Swallowing my first bite, I had to fight the urge to throw up. That would be the wrong thing to do; I would lose face in front of my classmates.

Moon, however, immediately vomited. I clamped my mouth tightly but my stomach contents were rushing uphill toward the only immediate exit. I ran from the classroom and spat the mouthful of bitterness onto the ground. Tears blurred my eyes as I searched desperately for a way to atone for my transgression.

Overcome with shame, I hung my head and returned to my seat.

When everyone had returned to the classroom, I dared not lift my eyes toward the faces of the authorities, which were over-shadowed with shocked disappointment and indignation. That I wasn't alone in my predicament gave me some relief.

The punishment for those who had not managed to choke

down the chaff cake, thus failing the first class, was to confess the secret sins hidden in our hearts and minds before the entire class so we could redeem ourselves. When class was dismissed, I was thankful to see that the same stray dog who had barked earlier had licked up my vomit from the dirty ground.

I shook my head in disgust and ran off.

When I got home, Father was fiddling with a handgun. It felt cold when I touched it, so I knew it was real and not a plastic stage pistol like I used to carry. To say I was surprised was an understatement. *This is a golden opportunity for me to play with a real pistol,* was my first thought.

My thoughts must have been visible on my face. "Like father, like son," Papa mumbled with a smile.

One evening, Uncle Wang came to speak to my father, rushing in as though a wolf were chasing him. He closed the door quickly behind him. Smoke was seeping through the cracks between the planks of the wooden door.

I strained my ear against the bedroom door but could hear only muffled voices. The whispers rose and fell in intensity and urgency and I heard shouted curses from both.

A good hour later I heard them open the outside door and hurry out of the house.

"Where's Papa going?" I asked my mother, who looked stunned.

"Don't know," she replied, sitting at the table, and passing her hand through my hair to smooth it down. "You finished your homework?" she asked, bending down to read what I'd written in my exercise book.

"How do you write the word 'confession,' Mama?"

Startled, she asked, "Today you learned what in class, son?"

I told her about what had occurred.

Mama paled and fell silent.

I instantly regretted opening my mouth. The words I'd spoken were weighing heavily on her mind, I could tell from her worried eyes.

I still wanted to know how to write the word "confession" but stayed silent. The more things I began to understand, the more I wanted to reduce the burden of worry on our family; I knew that, like me, they could not soothe anyone's anxieties.

Mother heaved a sigh and scribbled the word for me.

My father didn't return for three whole days.

By then, news of skirmishes among twenty-four strong men against "all the bastards" in the neighbouring Li Family village flew across the town. The fight began after a fatal accident in which a small boy from the Li Family village was crushed behind the huge tires of the tractor driven by a young fellow from our town.

The young driver had been driving uphill when the engine had choked and stuttered. This caused the tractor to slip backward, hitting the boy and rolling over his body. He was killed instantly. The villagers soon tracked down the driver, demanding divine justice and compensation: an eye for an eye, a life for a life.

Accompanying his men to the Li Family village, Uncle Wang brought with him a slaughtered pig, a case of wine, and ten cartons of the best cigarettes in town, to redeem the young man's dangerous and fatal mistake. The driver's father even dropped to his knees before the whole village, begging for his son's life. All his efforts were in vain and his plea was denied.

Three days later, the young driver was summoned to the boy's funeral. The four pallbearers were just beginning to lower the coffin when the unsuspecting driver was hit with a spade and pushed into the hole. The coffin crashed down onto his body.

Justice had been served for the Li Family village.

The driver's father was overwhelmed with fury and sorrow. He knelt before Uncle Wang, begging for revenge. Uncle Wang was moved to tears. "Get up, old man. Now your matter is mine!" he vowed, then transported his rejected gifts to the house of Lin Valley's headman.

As a result, twenty-four strong men from our town assembled

and set siege upon the Li Family village. My father led the men with his pistol. They fought for three days and three nights before the battle ended and the enemies surrendered. During the siege, the dead boy's father was stoned to death and Headman Li fatally shot. People believed it had been Li who had tried to force the marriage of that poor lady who had jumped into the river with her lover many years back.

Justice for all.

People saw this battle as a great victory for us. From then on, no other villages would dare challenge the famed town of Phoenix. This thought pleased me.

It was not until much later that I knew the battle my father had waged was a prelude to the endless series of fierce conflicts among dissenting factions during the period that historians now call the Great Cultural Revolution.

✧✦✧

8

REPETITION IS IN the blood of our culture. Waves in the river rise and fall and are repeated endlessly by other waves. All four winds blow repeatedly, despite their differing directions. All mountains are called mountains, whether they are lushly forested or completely bald.

The core tenet of our school curriculum was also repetition. A thousand-year-old poem is memorized and recited from the right to the left and from up to down. (Our classic books used to begin from the right, to be read vertically.) When you have read something and heard something a thousand times, we were told, it will become a part of you and your eyes will gaze on the world like those of a poet and your ears will reverberate with poetic rhythms. I later learned that our school instructions were inspired by our cultural addiction to foods. When I ate a chicken leg on New Year's Eve, I first licked it with my tongue, peeled the skin with my lips, bit on the flesh with my teeth and, lastly, chewed on the jagged bones until there was nothing to spit out.

A complete absorption. And digestion.

As for the question of "truth," it was not our job to think about this or find an answer. The truth was spooned into us via every word uttered by our beloved Chairman. (Of course, I did not know that some lies were sweeter than nectar at that time.) In those days, all pupils were graded on their ability to memorize Chairman Mao's three major essays and selected poems, such as:

> *Dare to ascend the ninth heaven to pluck the moon,*
> *Dare to dive under the five oceans to catch turtles.*

In the Beijing dialect, a turtle is a tortoise, but in our local dialect, "turtle" sounds the same as the word "cunt." For Principal Jia, this was a big embarrassment. When he read Mao's verses aloud to the class, muffled giggles broke out, causing him to fan his perspiring face with a notebook as if to shoo away his embarrassment. To avoid risking his own uncontrollable laughter, he turned his back to us and wrote the verses down, his white chalk squeaking against the blank blackboard.

After repeating the verses, Ear blurted: "Principal, we don't need to dive into the oceans; we can pick up cunts on Turtle Beach." Immediately laughter exploded like a boulder thrown into a pond.

One day in class, the sound of a loud fart came from one of the middle rows, sending a foul smell over the entire classroom. I held my breath as if I were diving in the water. Meanwhile, Bubble lost no time in yelling out: "Do not fart!" The whole class roared; Bubble had pretended to recite a line from Chairman Mao's poem *A Bird's Q & A:*

> *We have food to eat.*
> *When potatoes are cooked,*
> *Beef is added.*
> *Do not fart!*
> *Behold, the earth and sky are upside down.*

This happened so quickly, it was beyond the principal's ability to respond. More importantly, no one knew how to discipline someone for reciting the words of Chairman Mao. "Quiet!" he shouted. "I said silence!" His spit flew toward my face. Then he vented his anger on Ear. "You! Come forward. Stand here. Bow your head." He grabbed the poor boy's only ear, yelling: "Do you have no ears?"

More chuckles from the class.

In the end, Principal Jia punished the whole class by forcing us to recite the well-known fable *The Farmer and the Serpent*. "And copy it verbatim three times!" he ordered.

At recess, girls skipped rope while boys played marbles. In the schoolyard, there were also three or four ping-pong tables made of cement. Ping-pong, my favourite pastime, was named for the sound the round white ball makes when it bounces. Sounds, like sights, play an important part in our language. We have lucky sounds; we have ominous sounds. For example, the number 8 is the sound of prosperity but the number 4 is the utterance of death, as is the mentioning of a clock. But why are sounds sinister? Are they as innocent as the mind of a child?

Bubble, who sat in the back row of our class, had been my friend since I was a young boy. Originally, his name was Li Biao. However, his given name, *Biao* (meaning a strong tiger) was the same as that of our beloved Vice-Chairman, Lin Biao. This was no small matter. Principal Jia would not allow him to register unless his name was changed. Obediently, his parents changed his name to Li Hu (When *biao* loses its symbolic stroke of paws, it turns into *hu,* which means a tiger) on the spot, but we always called him Bubble because he had a reputation for blowing bubbles. Once, he taught me the trick: purse your lips, gather saliva with your tongue so that a bubble is formed from within, then gently release it with the tip of your tongue. This way, your bubbles resemble small balloons flying in midair, then pop in the sunshine after dancing for a few seconds.

I thought having two names was an advantage, like having two sets of clothing. Bubble was proud of his nickname and of his unique bubble-making know-how. "Let's have a competition," he suggested one day. But no one dared accept his challenge.

At that time, morning exercises and noon naps were part of the curriculum. Apparently, this was proof our country cared for the physical well-being of our "morning sun generation," the principal explained.

But for a boy like me, forced napping was like being locked in a prison.

The afternoon session began with a two-hour naptime immediately after our lunch break. Teachers would patrol the schoolrooms to ensure that all the students were asleep by checking whether we had placed our heads on our arms on the desk. They also scanned to see whether our eyes were open and sometimes checked whether we were faking sleep by knocking at our heads with their sharp index fingers.

Humans are creatures of habit, people say, and they are right. Like opium capturing an addict, a habit paralyzes your thinking when it climbs into your mind, declares it to be your master and enslaves you, causing you to fall into the trap without consciously knowing it. (I heard Father mention in passing that his father was addicted to opium and as a result squandered his fortune.) In no time, your mind becomes the slave of your habit; you are not yourself anymore. Once you have fallen into the habit of napping, you cannot break from it. Even years later, slumber assails me at noon if I fail to rendezvous with this old friend.

One day, my arms became numb from the weight of my head, so I fake-napped on one elbow while using the free hand to thumb the pages of *Dream of the Red Chamber.* The vigilant patroller discovered me and demanded that I stand in front of the blackboard for two hours. The book was seized, of course. I had no idea at the time this dream book was touted as among the four best classic novels in the history of Chinese literature.

As a result of being disciplined, I decided to nap on a newspaper that I'd laid on the ground beneath my desk. I tilted my head Red's way, and spotted her buckled shoes with their embroidered flowers on the tips. Her white cotton socks reached above her ankles and her bare legs below a white skirt that covered her knees. The need for secrecy meant I intentionally avoided Red in public to escape gossip coupled with mocking remarks and ridicule. But any time her eyes cast out the bait, my heart would flip-flop like a fish on a hook. We expressed our feelings with our eyes so that our classmates couldn't hear or even recognize what we were doing. For example, when she glanced down at the tip of her shoes while holding the book *The Monkey King* in her left hand, I knew right away that she was saying: "Let's read the novel together after class."

Looking at her legs, I wondered to myself, *what is lying between her naked thighs?* Then I looked around wildly in case anyone could see my thoughts. My aroused body trembled; my face got hot and red. As if holding the reins of a galloping horse, I grabbed my wandering thoughts with the hands of my faint will and held them tight. But the temptation to let them run wild was powerful and I challenged my eyes to look closer and my head to think further. But they were as timid as a pair of mice.

Trembling with longing and its partner, fear, I tried to pull off her clothes in my head. Sweat trickled down my spine and wetted the newspaper crumpled under the weight and heat of my burning body. But my head lost its way and plunged into a deep pit. Like a whirlwind, the force of my stare peeled off Red's underwear. At last, she stood naked before me, revealing her hint of a bosom. I forced my eyes closed for a few moments, then for much longer. I was fantasizing about the making of "cloud and rain," the intimacy experienced by the young protagonist Bao Yu (or Jade) in the Dream Book during his first sexual encounter. (His name literally means jade, and he abandoned his outdated dreams when he grew up. By now Jade was more than 200 years old.)

That scene in the Dream Book remained indelible in my memory. My mind had hungered for more details, but my eyes saw nothing but the many dry words of the gossips that filled the 120-chapter book that bored me to death.

Why the two male authors of this great timeless Dream Book were so obsessed with the minute intricacies of human gossiping and small talk was a mystery. This must be an important human act, I supposed, although I had been taught that it was usually females who succumbed to it. Why was I so confused about this part of the adult world? Perhaps they lived in a different universe.

The bell buzzed abruptly, shattering my fantasy.

I climbed out of my reverie, ashamed of my lewd thoughts, which had vanished. But I did not rue the moments when I had savoured these thoughts, just as I savoured the chicken leg at the extravagant table on New Year's Eve. For days, I cherished my new-found excitement without telling a soul. Not even my right hand.

However, I had to clean up my thoughts before misfortune befell me. Or so I reckoned.

9

MOTHER WAS PLEASED when electricity arrived to light our house. After so many years her dream came true, even though it was the first one of the three—we still had no stairs in our bungalow house and no telephone. But Mother's dreams continued to support and sustain her life.

That year, at age eleven, I discovered the pleasure of reading by the light of a kerosene lamp. But books were as rare as meat. Almost all books—other than those of Chairman Mao—were regarded as poisonous plants. To utter the word "library" was as horrifying as the word "graveyard." There was one exception, though. Tons of seized poisonous plants (meaning books) were piled up in the town's only junk recycling depot, which became my summer library.

One summer day, Uncle Wu was there, sitting at his table beside a large standing weight scale, listening to the radio. A female voice was forecasting that the Yangtze would flood and reported on the water's rise or fall from the head to the tail of the river flowing through Phoenix Town, which was too small to appear on any map. The Yangtze begins in the mysterious, cloudy mountains near Tibet. Like a gigantic dragon, it circles around mountains, crosses plains, flows through valleys before meandering through the heart of the yellow-earth land until it wags its tail at the mouth of the East China Sea.

I had known Uncle Wu since I was little, as he was a colleague of my mother (and not my real uncle). He had an elder brother who'd escaped to Taiwan in 1949, which caused big trouble. Uncle Wu was pleased when I handed over a pack of Flying Horse cigarettes I'd stolen from my father's drawer and I was then free to wander through the worlds of Charles Dickens, Robinson Crusoe, and the like. From time to time, just before leaving, I would squeeze a book into my pocket while Uncle Wu was busy weighing the incoming bundles of old newspapers and banned books. Often, he would pretend to update his daily charts with more pluses and minuses, turning a blind eye to the square bulge protruding from my trousers.

One day, a middle-aged female director caught me red-handed and forced me to reveal the yellowed *Arabian Nights* in my trousers pocket. She reported me, which caused an uproar at my school. I say *my* school now out of habit but at the time it belonged to the Party, like everything else in the country, including its people. A school was a training camp for future soldiers—whom the Party called "successors"—to fight for our great country, both literally and politically. As such, stealing public assets from the Party was a serious crime. On top of that, eating fruit forbidden by the Party meant a double penalty.

I still remember imagining the consequences in my head and tossing in bed as moonlight flooded the floor of my bedroom while I mentally rehearsed my confession essay over and over. Principal Jia had ordered me to expose the roots of the evil thoughts that had prompted my crime. After a long night of searching, I discovered the roots: my thoughts had obviously been poisoned by the banned books. This outrageous lie, a huge insult to the great authors I admired, saddened me deeply. The more I thought about what I would have to do, the more terrified I became; I was even scared of my own thoughts.

The next morning, the students were assembled in the schoolyard to perform the daily exercise ritual. Then Principal Jia announced the commencement of the "criticizing meeting," which meant it was my turn to stand on the platform and read my confession aloud in front of my disapproving peers. I had hardly finished when Bubble jumped onto the platform, pointed his finger at me and turned to the crowd: "This bad egg, he also stole *The Monkey King* book from me! Worst of all, he told me that he entertained three Aladdin wishes that are contrary to our Party's wishes."

What? His accusation shocked me.

Now I'd become a real thief, like the boy who had stolen the eggs. And a real contrarian, too. If I'd had a thousand mouths, no one would have listened to my protestations of innocence. I could do nothing but lower my head, tears trickling silently down my cheeks and into my mouth, salty and bitter. Trembling, I stood there, overwhelmed with dread.

The next day, my confession essay was posted on the wall at the back of the classroom where a new "self-criticism" zone had been created. An identical copy was also affixed permanently on the wall of my memory and is still visible today. As a reward for his lie, Bubble earned a red necktie. I didn't speak to him for a long time and now viewed him as a stranger. He shunned me, as well, as though I were a leper. Later, I decided to forgive him because, in those days, lying was not only a tactic but also a necessity.

Gradually, my lying tongue and I became friends again. *I cannot lag behind my peers like a stray dog,* I mused. *I must catch up; I must redeem myself.*

One day, a math teacher wrote a quiz on the blackboard, which read as follows:

> *Train A left a station at 10 a.m. at a speed of 40 km per hour.*
> *Train B started 2 hours later at the same station at a speed of 50 km per hour.*
> *Train C started 4 hours later at a speed of 60 km per hour.*
> *Now work out the following solutions:*
> *1. When will train B catch up and pass Train A?*
> *2. When will train C catch up and pass Train B?*

A strange but shrewd thought entered my head, and I boldly raised my left hand.

"Did you figure out the formula?" the teacher queried.

I nodded my head, declaring: "A stands for America, B for Britain, and C for China. Both the A train and the B train are imperialists. We'll board the C-train to surpass the Americans and the British and entomb all the imperialists. No one can slow down or block the wheels of the C-train."

The teacher looked shocked but also pleased. The tidings of my abrupt awakening also pleased Principal Jia, who applauded my politically—if not mathematically—correct solution. That night, I lay awake, fidgeting with pleasure. Listening to the industrious crickets chirping in the dark outside my window, I finally fell into a deep sleep.

But I did not bask in my success. After school, I roamed the streets with Ear, hunting for opportunities to do good deeds like our national icon, Comrade Lei Feng. When no opportunities presented themselves, I would steal a few pennies from home to report them to Principal Jia as a lost find. One night, Ear and I captured a sad, undocumented vagrant who was smoking at the wharf. We forced the poor man to go to the local public security office. My heroic act pleased the director, who wrote a letter to the school complimenting my heightened awareness of order and security.

One day when Master Fu came to class, I stealthily approached him from behind and quietly informed him about Landlady Liu. "She fed sparrows in her backyard; she had swallows nesting under the eaves of her house," I told him. "Most importantly, she lent me books that had poisoned my mind."

I had learned to lie without blinking an eye.

Consequently, a school meeting was held, and the teachers concluded that the attempts of our old enemy to poison our young generation had never died. I later found out that all of Landlady Liu's original lands and buildings were confiscated in the 1950s and her complex became our walled-in Phoenix Elementary.

The next evening, Jia summoned the school's Red Guards to search the landlady's old brick house, which stood alone at the end of the street near an embankment. They seized boxes of books from the house and piled them in the school's sports field, where all the students soon gathered.

Holding a torch dipped in kerosene, Master Fu declared, "Monsters and demons are still roaming around to destroy our new generation with sugar-coated bullets and bombs." Then he cast his torch onto the confiscated piles.

With a roar, the flames leapt up in the dark, enveloped in ghostly smoke. The evening wind blew the dark cloud away from the school into the sky.

That term, I too was awarded a red necktie. With pride, I adjusted the tie around my neck and showed it to my mother. When the tie was too tight, it would choke me, and now my face felt red and hot. I saw the redness reflected in her eyes. For a moment, mirth took hold of her; her furrowed eyebrows eased and she appeared to be very proud of her son. This, however, disturbed me even more as I'd obtained her approval through deception. Disgust rose inside me, protesting, but I bit my lip and forced myself to swallow it.

Telling lies was a learned skill, one I had mastered.

10

YEARS WENT BY silently.

Phoenix Elementary became Phoenix Secondary.

Now our weekly curriculum mandated at least three days of physical labour. We learned how to plant rice seedlings in the water fields, how to pull weeds from the wheat fields and how to build terraced gardens in the mountainside.

"Countryside is our classroom," our teachers told us.

By now, most of my classmates had learned to smoke under the open sky, like our fathers. Lying on the wild grass with smoke swirling above my head, I thought that it was manual labour that made us human. Our ancestors, we were told, were descendants of human-like apes, but it was their use of tools that made them evolve. Thus, without physical labour, we would lose our humanity.

Our labour class was graded each week.

When we rolled up our sleeves and trousers cuffs and stepped into a rice field, leeches would often sting our legs and arms. If we screamed in pain, the teachers would scold us, telling us that we were "bourgeois," the meaning of which we didn't understand.

One day Moon fainted in the field after she saw tiny bloodsuckers swarming over her legs. After they were ripped off her body, blood from tiny pinholes began to ooze out.

Moon failed miserably.

I was frequently reprimanded for mistaking seedlings for weeds. To me, they looked the same and I couldn't tell one from the other. "That's why we need to learn from the farmers," the teacher told the class, citing me as a bad example.

I failed too.

In class, we studied the fable *The Old Man and the Mountain*. An allegory about an elderly man, his children, and his children's children, who never stop digging and shoveling until they move the mountain that blocks their way.

"The old man has shown us the way, so let's follow suit," Principal Jia proclaimed one day. Hence, the middle school added to the curriculum a two-year mountain-digging program. On labour-class days, students would bring spades, pickaxes and lunch bowls in preparation for an entire day on the mountainside.

The pickaxe was heavy on my soft hands. Before lifting it high I spat onto my hands. When it thudded, clouds of dust exploded into our eyes.

On the second day, I had blisters which quickly burst open and bled. Afraid of failing the class, I concealed the pain. Soon, though, the skin over the blisters thickened and hardened, becoming calluses, gradually turning our hands into those of farmers. These were the hands the Party needed to build our new China. Such words of courage and comfort were fed to our tired and troubled souls.

One day, Red was about to hop down from a stone slope. "Someone help!" Her eyes were seeking mine, both of her hands reached out in the air.

But I did not extend my hand. Whether I was afraid she would feel the calluses, or I was too shy to take her hand in public, I don't know. Instead, Ear offered his open arms with a big smile on his face. Down she jumped, landing on a loose hillock of earth, and losing her balance. Ear seized the opportunity to catch and hold her tightly. Realizing what had happened, she struggled to break loose from his embrace, pushing him away with all her might. In a second, she broke into a run, away from us, leaving me with my mouth agape.

Afterward, I replayed this scene in my mind again and again when I lay in bed, regretting my inaction. I had missed a golden opportunity to hold Red in my arms. I began to despise my own timidity and mentally yelled at my tear-filled self, "Next time, be bold. What're you afraid of? Girls? You poor little hypocrite! You think of girls day and night, but when a chance comes up, you're like a turtle hiding inside its shell."

After my shameful public confession, I began to criticize myself frequently and harshly to the point of self-condemnation.

At midday, our labour class was punctuated with a break where we would enjoy a pleasant two-hour respite. Those hours were memorable. Boys would hunt for wild rabbits, while girls would pluck wild roses to decorate their braided hair.

One day, some girls spotted a huge cobra hiding in the bushes near a half-dug terrace and screamed for help. Big Guy came to the rescue. We called him Big Guy because he was tall with huge hands. We saw him grabbing a pickaxe and swinging it at the cobra as it raised its head high, spitting out its spear-like tongue while Bubble threw rocks. Having killed the snake, Big Guy proclaimed he would cook the trophy for supper and asked Moon to share his table.

"How about me?" Bubble joined in.

"All of you are welcome. Tonight, we'll go catch green frogs in the rice fields so we can have a great feast," he announced.

Big Guy was the student head for our labour class and we envied his great physical prowess. Principal Jia had been a smart teacher to choose him. Big Guy would report all student activities, good and bad, directly to the principal. This structure of government saved our principal and teachers a significant amount of time and effort. I had made friends with him; I knew it was his job to assign tasks in labour classes.

Like the rest of us, Big Guy had picked up the habit of smoking cigarettes. All adult males smoked and drank; there were no exceptions. Exceptions were abnormal and abnormality was an enemy, so no one could risk it. I stole money from home and bought him cigarettes that we smoked together during the break. I enjoyed favoured treatment in labour classes, as intended. I hated labour class for obvious reasons, but I could not say that. I could not even think like that for fear that someone would spit out that "bourgeoisie" accusation.

By now, I'd learned many valuable lessons.

One day, we were digging in the mountain like the children of the silly old man in the fable. It was summer and the sun was beating down on us. During the break, Big Guy and I smoked in the bushes where the shade was deep, fanning ourselves with straw hats.

"Beautiful," he muttered.

"Yes, it's beautiful," I replied, watching the white cloud of smoke over my head.

"No. *She* is beautiful."

"She who?"

"Moon," he whispered, glancing around. "Really want to kiss her."

He confided that he liked Moon and asked me to keep a secret. I nodded. I did not tell him my own secret: that I liked Red. That was too risky. He carefully retrieved a piece of crumpled paper from his pocket, asking me to hand it to my former tablemate.

"Why don't you do it yourself?"

"Too afraid."

"What did you write?"

"Don't open it. Well, you can see it."

I opened the note. It was a pencilled "I love you." I giggled and called him a coward. When it came to Red, I was the real coward. But for unknown reasons, I did not have any fear speaking to Moon. Maybe love and fear walked hand in hand.

Big Guy got up and motioned me to follow. I thought he was going to pee in the bushes, so that's what I did. Instead, he ran to the shed made of straw and mud that was used as an outside toilet. There he gestured for me to wait outside.

"Come quick!" I heard him calling shortly. Inside the shed, Big Guy was holding his pants partway down his thighs, groaning, his right hand jerking on his erect penis. Suddenly, white foam shot from his penis. My nostrils filled with the heavy smell of cucumbers mixed with the stale odour of the shed.

I stood there with dropped jaw.

"Man's essence! You see it? I'm *man* now!" Big Guy proclaimed with joyful pride.

I did not tell anyone else about this scene.

Years later, however, when I read *Confessions* by Jean-Jacques Rousseau, who also amused himself with this innocent but guilty pleasure, I understood Big Guy was not an alien, and I was not an alien, either. Human experience is universal, regardless of where you live or whether you are a great man of letters, or a tiny figure like me.

Late that night, I hid under the quilt, and timidly reached out my hand to imitate Big Guy. Erect for the first time as I was massaging myself, I felt an excitement and thrill I had never experienced before. I could not stop rubbing my erect penis. Because I craved more.

But no foam ejected from my body, as I saw it ejecting from Big Guy.

When I was exhausted, I fancied myself strolling barefoot on the sparkling beach sand somewhere on the island, like a lonely Robinson Crusoe. My old dog Yellow (not Friday) chased me, wagging his tail. I looked up, a storm was brewing in the vast sky. Suddenly, I was swept up and thrown into the ocean. I could see myself sinking down and down, drowning in the waters.

When I woke up, I was still gasping.

11

OUR LABOUR CLASS continued well into the new year.

In 1971, Lin Biao, formerly a close friend of our beloved Chairman Mao who had tried but failed to overthrow him, died in a plane crash. When the news of his death was announced at a school meeting, all of us were more bewildered than shocked. After that, criticizing Lin Biao and Confucius was added to our curriculum. As part of a new government-led propaganda campaign, I guessed.

One cloudy morning, the students were assembled in the schoolyard for morning exercises, which used to embarrass me; ashamed because I could not follow instructions to turn either right or left. Forced to abandon my left-handedness, it was hard for me to tell left from right. I was always confused, and it took me a while to learn which side was which.

"If you continue to make such stupid mistakes, one day you'll be doomed, because you'll find yourself standing in the wrong line," our sports teacher scolded me multiple times for failing to follow such rudimentary directions.

After exercises, Principal Jia jumped onto the platform. He cursed Lin Biao as a traitor and declared that Bubble could change back to his rightful name. "To cleanse the poisonous remnants of this traitor and those of our ancient enemy, Confucius, will remain a revolutionary task for our school for years to come," he declared.

A name is a name; it does not think. It is an empty vessel unless you give it meaning.

At the time, I didn't know what Lin Biao had done, so I had no idea why he was connected to the saint of our ancestors, Confucius.

Nor did I care. By now, I understood my life's mission: follow the Party blindly whenever it called us. My mind did not generate questions anymore; it had stockpiled certainties, exclamation marks. Questioning meant doubt, and doubting was an anti-revolutionary crime.

Meanwhile, I noticed Bubble nodding, his tearful eyes wide open. He was thrilled that vindication had come at last. But since we had called him Bubble for so long, we continued to do so and he was happy about that as well.

At this point, Master Fu ran to the platform, throwing the tightly held fist of his right hand as far as he could toward the sky, shouting, "Down ... down ... down with Lin Biao!"

All the students followed suit, punching the air and yelling "beat down the great traitor!"

"Long live Chairman Mao!"

In the winter term, a new task set me on fire.

Principal Jia asked me to be responsible for writing big-character posters for the whole school. The task pleased me. My father read the *People's Daily* every day and I read it sometimes as well. Principal Jia believed I was good at catching the trends of the newspaper. So, when other students went out to axe the mountain, it was now my job to copy the articles manually from the newspaper with an ink brush, a legitimate duty to dodge the labour class I hated. Afterward, Principal Jia hinted he was pleased with my work. My recycling of the news won me a reputation at school.

One Friday in December, the weather was freezing.

The other students attended the labour class on the mountainside but I was left to work on the posters, which adorned the walls of every room on campus—even the walls of the toilets.

It turned out Moon had been asked to assist me by drawing cartoons. Under her gaze, I took off my gloves, laying bare my frostbitten hands, and brandished my Chinese brush-pen on the white paper as if swinging a sword on the battlefield. I pictured how I would feel as I wielded my sword while riding on horseback toward my retreating enemies. *The pen is mightier than the sword,* I told myself.

Words are more lethal than aimed bullets, my big uncle had told me. From time to time, I paused to blow a warm breath into my cupped hands. Moon finished her cartoons, which featured a gigantic, sword-like pen tip crushing a dog-shaped Lin Biao crawling over a cat-like Confucius. She asked me to add a caption. I was searching in my head for the obscenest swear words in our language.

"Your mother's cunt!" seemed most appropriate for this situation; those were the most salacious words boys of my age could use to crush the spirit of our challengers.

Just as I was about to draw the word with my brush, I paused. I couldn't find the official word in the library of my mind. I looked at Moon for assistance but I was unable to admit I was at a loss. After thumbing through the pages of the *New China Dictionary,* I still could not locate the entry. I thought of Chairman Mao's poem and decided to use the word *turtle* as a synonym for cunt.

After I glued all the posters on the outside wall of our classroom, I stood with both hands behind my back, gazing at the wall with satisfaction. In my mind, these were not posters, but flying bullets and firing cannons. *I am like a real soldier fighting against real enemies in a real war,* I reckoned.

In those days the emotional state of the nation was unstable. As was customary, obscene slang and swear words were fierce weapons fired from the mouths of zealots at the heads of our opponents.

The baffled Moon did not know what I was thinking, so she was about to go see Principal Jia for more work.

Before she left, I had a task to complete, I thought.

"Moon?"

"Yes?"

"This is for you," I said, handing her the note.

"What is it?"

"You'll see." I was still studying the dictionary.

From the corner of my eye, I saw Moon open the note, looking shocked and flushed.

"How dare you! I'll report you." She ran off.

"It's not me, Moon!" I stood there, speechless.

"It's from Big Guy!" I yelled after her, but it was too late. *How could I have made such a stupid blunder*? I scolded myself. My heart was racing. Was I in trouble again? I should tell the principal that it was a note from Big Guy. Would he believe me? My body was weakened by fear; my soul despaired. I could not keep working. The world began to spin before my eyes. I withdrew to a corner of the classroom, trembling like a mouse being hunted by a cat.

(Oh, I forgot to mention about Big Guy's first love note in the past summer. When I declined the task, he pleaded with me again to help him release "the burden in my heart," as he told me.)

It took a long while for me to convince myself not to worry about the note, sure that I could explain the trouble away.

At noon, I went to report to Principal Jia on the status of my work. Moving quietly, I went to his room in the upstairs corner of the two-storey wooden house at the centre of the school compound. The door was ajar, so I pushed it open. I did not find him, but saw Moon lying in his bed.

When Moon saw me, she looked mortified and pulled the quilt over her head, burying herself under the covers.

Principal Jia rushed in with a bowl of food.

"What you doing here?" he yelled at me, his face red with rage.

Petrified, my mind went blank. I did not know what to say and just hung my head.

"Get out, you little cunt!"

"No—come back!" he shouted after me. "She's in bed for a nap. If you dare tell anyone what you saw, you're expelled."

I ran back to my classroom, frightened near to death. My stomach hurt. I should've knocked and waited at the door. I should've said I was sorry. But, in my mind, uttering courtesies was "bourgeois."

From that day on, I dared not look Principal Jia in the eye, nor did I dare tell anyone what I had witnessed. The principal moved me to the back of the room, far away from Moon, who was in the second row. Whether it was because of the anonymous note or because of my startling discovery of the principal's closet and the skeleton within, I did not know.

12

IT WAS SPRING.

At the front of the class stood a beautiful young lady. She was our new English teacher. We called her Teacher Blue. Her face was pale but lovely; I could read deep sorrow in her eyes. You could tell right away she was not a country girl. She was curvaceous and taller than the average villager. When she looked at us, her gaze was as sweet as honey. But it was my heart, not my eyes, that first became aware of her beauty.

We boys graded beauty by gauging the shape of faces.

In the warmth of her presence in the classroom, thirty pairs of eyes were focused on her as she wrote down twenty-six letters on the blank blackboard. The creaking chalk sounded like a melody. She blushed when she noticed the furtive gazes of her wide-eyed admirers. We would soon learn to emulate her gestures, her tone, her elocution.

We pronounced the letters of this newfound alphabet in a loud, singsong tone, repeating each one after her at the top of our lungs. After several classes, our voices were hoarse, but this gladdened us because the twenty-six letters had ignited a fire in our minds. Taking in our passionate eagerness, she nodded with visible pride.

She began to teach us how to build English sentences starting with "I love." "I love Chairman Mao" was the first English sentence uttered from our Chinese mouths.

"Knowing a foreign language is our weapon against the imperialists," I remembered Principal Jia saying when he first introduced Teacher Blue.

One bone-chilling Monday morning, snowflakes began to fall during recess. We boys used sticks to knock down the long icicles hanging from the eaves of the dark grey roof tiles. Two pigs, one black, one white, sauntered into the schoolyard, ignoring the boisterous humans around them. That aroused Bubble's interest in building an appropriate English sentence. "I love pig," he proclaimed, licking the icicle in his hand.

Laughter burst out.

One afternoon, Master Fu scurried to the front of the class, followed by Principal Jia, who hushed the class with a wave of his right hand.

"We have just learned that a serious crime has been perpetrated against our beloved leader, Chairman Mao," he said, his face stern and his tone sad.

A pall of silence fell on the class, the students stunned into wordless surprise. It was as if death itself had dropped in on us.

A copy of the *People's Daily*—specifically, a column featuring a photograph of Chairman Mao—had been used as toilet paper in the boys' washroom. A vigilant student, later praised for his political awareness, had reported the crime. "This was a heinous blasphemy committed against our great leader, the worst sacrilege in the town's history," Master Fu shouted, as we looked at each other. Ear had his head down and was thumbing through his dictionary. "I wondered what the word 'blasphemy' means," he murmured.

An investigation followed. Girls were eliminated. Apparently, this crime had nothing to do with them since the scrap of paper had been found in the pit in the boys' toilet. Principal Jia indicated he encouraged self-reporting. Master Fu's long, searching stare seemed to pierce each of us in turn, like a flashlight searching through the darkness of a cave. Each boy was questioned, but no one confessed. I fidgeted when it was my turn to respond, bending my head to avoid his attack when his accusing glare focused on me. My face turned as pale as death and cold sweat began to drip along my spine. I worried I might become a suspect; we had the newspaper at home and I sometimes brought a copy to school.

Once again, I became afraid of my own thoughts. *Was I a collaborator?*

The boys were kept late for interviews with a public security officer.

"If you confess your crime, you'll be treated leniently; however, if you resist, your punishment will be severe," the officer announced ominously. My heart pounded. My insides writhed with a compulsion to confess; the words were on the tip of my tongue. But I could hear a small voice of warning urging me to hide inside my shell. In the end, in hopes of spurring a confession, the whole class was assigned to recite *The Farmer and the Serpent* the next morning.

"Tonight, I want all of you to put your hands on your chest while lying on bed and ask your heart one question, 'Who was that serpent?' Then, next morning, you'll have the answer," the principal declared.

My heart was still pounding when I got home, only to see a curious crowd in front of my house. Uncle Wang stood in the centre but his usual smile was absent and his face was still. I have heard people say that friendship is like birds perching on the same tree; upon hearing the first gunshot, all the birds fly away in different directions.

Beside him, three men were busy fishing something from inside a box. My father stood by silently. With a pale face and trembling hands he motioned me to go inside. Not daring to speak, I curled up in a corner of my room.

Some time later, I heard footsteps outside my door and cupboards and drawers opening and closing. All at once, the bedroom door shot open, the hinges screaming. A man turned on the light bulb and bent down to shine his flashlight under my bed, the place where I hid my marbles, my Chairman Mao badges and cigarette packs. He opened a box holding copies of *The Red Treasure Book* and *One Hundred Thousand Whys*. (I used to lie in bed and thumb through the pages, drawing a map of the universe in my mind to find where I was. Our teachers had told us that China is the only central kingdom under the sun with a lengthy history of civilization.)

The man picked up a volume displaying the sun, the moon, the constellations and the Milky Way, then tossed it away; he took everything else away for further investigation. A wave of regret washed over me. I should have listened to Grandma, who used to tell me her tricks of concealment, such as hiding her valuables in the ashes of the kitchen stove when they heard the Japanese were coming.

"I'm scared! Bleeding!" my elder sister burst out, crying. She was curled on the ground, her pants red and wet. "Did that bastard kick you?" I yelled, holding her hands. She shook her head and I stared at her in puzzlement.

Grandma ran to hold her. "No fear, no fear." She comforted my sister, wrapping her in a towel. At my questions, Grandma shooed me away, offering only the confusing observation that all women were victims of periodic melancholy.

When Uncle Wang and his men left, Mother told me the object of their search was evidence of my father's anti-revolutionary activities. The Party had received information that he had deceived the army when he enlisted by concealing his family background. (My father's deceased father was a landowner.) Later I learned my father's Soviet-made watch was viewed as a very important piece of evidence "proving" he had illegal connections with the Soviet Union which by then had become our enemy.

"The trees have eyes and the walls have ears. Guard your secrets in your heart," Grandma whispered in my ear.

That night, Father came to my bedside. "Do you want to hear a story?" he asked, which cheered me up. "Yes," I almost yelled.

He told me about a father who asked his son to climb to the top of the stairs, then jump down. "Come on, son, jump down. I'm going to catch you," the father said. Without further thought, his son jumped down, but his father stood there watching as the boy fell and sprained his ankle. "Why didn't you catch me, Father?" the son cried.

"Because I wanted you to learn a small lesson through the pain."

"What lesson?" the son asked in tears.

"If you want to survive in this land, son, trust no one," his father replied.

A small lesson for him, maybe, but a big one for me, as it turned out.

After that day, my father was tormented by his desire to find the name of his informer.

A few days later, a town meeting was held at People's Square at the very spot where Master Fu had cracked the actor's head open with a brick. My father stood on the platform together with Mr. Yi, Uncle Wu, and Landlady Liu. Each of them wore a tall, cone-shaped hat and a cardboard placard around their necks. I sat in the crowd with my mother and sisters. Fear held us still and I hung my head, afraid to look up at the platform.

Uncle Wang presided over the denunciation of the four people on the platform. He labelled my stoned-faced father a "counter-revolutionary," the most horrendous name one could be called. Our old fortune-teller, Mr. Yi, was a "demon." Uncle Wu was a "traitor and a snake" because he had an enemy brother in Taiwan. Landlady Liu was a "beast." These labels terrified, as intended, everyone watching. Father and Uncle Wang used to be drinking buddies but now Uncle treated Father like a shifty outsider.

The whole town reacted like these four people represented four different classes of enemies. This shattered my heart.

I heard hoarse shouts but in my mind I saw the actor lying in a pool of blood while the townspeople cheered. Anger rose in me. *How could Father bring such public humiliation and disgrace on me and on his family!* Unable to take any more, I slipped away unnoticed by my weeping mother, who hung her head as low as she could. Breaking into a run, I hid in a small hut just outside the square.

I still remember how I felt at that moment. I wished the earth would open wide enough that I could slide down into the abyss to hide from the angry crowd. With luck, I would disappear completely.

The fierce shouts were like poisonous arrows being shot at my father, the faces twisted by hatred. The air smelled of explosives.

I hid, dumbfounded, paralyzed, my mind blank in the ice-cold wind. I had buried everything—my heart, my hope, my home. I was grief-stricken, but my tears ran dry inside me.

People's Square would forever remind me of blood and torment, always evoking great sadness when I walked through it. But I blocked that period of my life. To this day, I can only vaguely recall the pain, remembering only that it was so much bigger than me.

After that date, wherever I went, the shadow of People's Square followed.

When I entered adulthood, I tended toward procrastination. Whenever I was about to finish an important project, I felt pain all over my body, which would force me to give up at the last moment. This current writing project commenced many years ago. After finishing ten chapters, I felt smothered by my feelings. So I stopped.

Years passed. After reading many books on psychology, I recognized my tendency to quit was associated with seeing my father exposed to unbearable public shame and humiliation. In my subconscious mind, I associated public attention with shame and humiliation. To avoid the feeling, my subconscious forced me to quit writing. My past unceasingly haunted me during those dormant years.

When I started this book, I treated it like someone else's story, nothing had happened to me. However, when I finally picked it back up where I left it, I decided to expose my heart and soul—choosing vulnerability—and tell my own story.

After that, it poured out of me as if a dam had broken.

Memory is a strange thing. I was filled with thoughts, feelings, reflections, and contemplations. I also imagined throwing myself at the feet of the master of my fate, begging for mercy. The master's heart, however, was made of stone; he was unmoved.

Who am I? I began to wonder when I started to examine my own thoughts.

When my father returned home that night, he was limping, his face swollen and caked with congealed blood. He sat down and drank a whole bottle of liquor. Late that night, Mother, sobbing, packed up his things.

"Don't forget my razor blades," Father mumbled, holding a small mirror in one hand. "They told me capitalist thoughts are like beards: if you don't erase them, they grow in your heart every day. Besides, don't bring my old army uniform, they said I have no right to wear uniforms."

When I woke up the next morning, Father had gone without saying goodbye. Mother said he went to a re-education camp somewhere; she did not know where. I did not see my father for many years.

At school, I was aware of the spiteful glares and felt ashamed. When the meddlesome boys tortured me by asking the whereabouts of my father, I replied with a trembling voice, "He's in the PLA."

"You're lying, little boy, your father was an anti-revolutionary. He's sitting in jail," the boys mocked. I was stunned by my inability to shed a single tear until I realized why. It was a desperate attempt to keep one last scrap of self-regard: dignity.

Our English class was short-lived. The following term, the authorities decided English was a capitalist tool and Chinese people should exhibit disdain, not passion, toward the capitalist tongue.

When news about the cancellation broke, the class greeted it with silence. Then Teacher Blue disappeared from our classroom. Some said she returned to her village. Others said she went to college. Others still said she was pregnant with her village leader's child and that she killed the child and ran away like the white-haired girl in the movie. Various tales were told and retold and, when no one had any more room for the gossip about our teacher, the town forgot about her. As you know and I know, most of the time, people just make stuff up. Did they make up the tale of the white-haired girl as well?

I found an unsettling humour in these absurdity tales, reminding me of the constant struggle in the war between fact and fiction, lies and truth: A struggle inherent in both history and life.

Devastated by the news, I felt miserable and lost. My memory of her and the language she taught stayed alive for a long time. The beautiful sound of a new tongue still flew rhythmically within my dreams, like the sound of waves.

13

ONE MORNING, I woke up in a cold sweat from a dream that had haunted me for years: I saw myself wafting to the bottom of the river after my boat capsized during a storm.

It was so intense; for a long time, I could not be sure if I was awake or dreaming. When my eyes examined the spaces around me, I recognized the predawn blackness, and drifted back to sleep.

To be human is hard; to live a human life is even harder, Mama used to say. She reigned over the kitchen as if she were managing an entire kingdom. For Grandma, bitterness and life were the same thing. Without eating bitterness, how do you know the taste of sweetness? This was the mysterious wisdom passed on to me by my grandmother.

After Father left, my younger sister also disappeared mysteriously from our house. When I asked Mama, she hesitated, then broke into sobs.

One evening, a neighbour came to see Mother in the kitchen.

"Your old head will never come back," I heard her whispering to my mother, who was quietly stoking the fire in the belly of the wood stove with dry branches. A hush fell between them; only the crackling sound of the fire broke the silence. Later, in the dead of night, I heard Mother's muffled cries and Grandma's wailing. I thought they were sad because of my father, so I buried my head under the quilt.

The next morning, Mother asked me to go with her to visit my sister in her adopted family. We walked several miles under the curling clouds until we arrived at a grey brick house with a big willow tree in front. My sister's white skirt was pinned on a branch, blowing in the wind. Mother pushed the door open without knocking. In the middle of the room, my younger sister sat at a table, eating her rice porridge. When she saw us, her face lit up with excitement. Then she rushed to Mother, encircling her waist with her little arms, and cried: "Mama, I want go home."

A middle-aged lady rushed in and glared at her unannounced visitors. What happened afterward I cannot fully recall, only vaguely remembering her saying that my sister used to sit under the willow tree for hours after dark, holding a pair of her shoes, waiting for her Mama to show up. From then on, my poor sister apparently learned to cry inwardly.

Taking my sister with us, we started the walk home. On the way there, Sister gingerly plucked something from her breast pocket. "For you, Mama," she murmured.

"What is it?" Mama asked. "Oh, it smells."

"Egg. I saved it for you on my first day."

Mother bent down in the middle of the dusty road, and held my sister close, crying. "I sorry, daughter. All my fault."

Trying hard not to, I cried too.

➤ One Saturday night, Mother told me the Co-op Store had been authorized to sell sixty-six packs of playing cards, and I was determined to get one. But I needed a plan.

Later that night, when I heard her snoring, I tiptoed into my grandmother's bedroom. Moonlight slanted into the room through the window, and I could see her lying in bed, her old cotton-padded jacket covering her like a blanket. She always wore this old jacket, even in summer. When I asked her why, she replied, "I don't know. But when I wear it, my stomach-ache goes away."

Grandma was telling only a part of the truth, however, because, one day, I had accidentally discovered there was an interior pocket in the jacket containing a small roll of cash.

Apparently, Grandma had been secretly saving money for an urgent situation. There was some precedent for this: Grandmother also used to keep a huge box containing paper currency used during the Nationalist Party's reign before 1949. "Who knows, one day, this money may be useful again," she told us. However, before Uncle Wang's men came to ransack our house, my grandma smelled something dangerous in the air and fed all the old paper money into the belly of the kitchen stove before it could be found.

Meanwhile, I gingerly pulled off her jacket, and when it slid to the floor, I bit the threads sealing the pocket, reached inside, and quickly extracted a ten-yuan note of the people's currency before slipping back to my room.

Before sunrise, I ran toward Ear's house without my conscious mind being aware of where I was headed. Arriving at his door, I paused; it seemed that I had thought of something urgent and shocking. I ran off. What was the fate awaiting my friend? Why did I suddenly and intentionally shun him? Oh, my dear reader, be patient with me. I will explain.

Then I knocked on the door of Bubble's house and revealed my secret.

"Really?" Bubble's eyes widened. He did not believe me until I pushed him into the corner of the room and showed him the crumpled currency clutched in my hand.

Bubble shrieked, jumping up and down. We scurried to the Co-op Store where we saw a crowd already assembled in front of the one-storey building. Cigarette smoke laced the air.

At about eight o'clock, the crowd began to bang on the door, yelling, "Open up!"

The director of the store stuck out his head from between the iron bars but, instead of opening the door, he pulled open a front window. "Line up here," he yelled to the impatient throng of people already squeezing their bodies against the window. Obeying the order, the crowd rushed the window like wasps swarming their next meal.

My mother came into view; she was one of the cashiers. I hid behind Bubble and pushed him ahead, inch by inch but there was a lot of commotion; the big crowd was restless. I felt helpless. So did Bubble, whose wrist was marked with red scratches. We cursed the crowd. About thirty minutes later, the window was slammed shut. No more product. But the people refused to disperse, stomping, cursing and spitting for a long time afterward. Eventually, everyone trudged away, indignant at their bad luck.

When Grandma saw the bruises on my arms caused by the crowd, I told her the secret. Not about stealing her money, but about my desire to possess a pack of playing cards. She went inside and closed the door behind her. A few minutes later, she brought out an old and yellowed deck of cards.

"Where did you hide these, Grandma?" My heart jumped with joy.

"I have my ways. Even the Japanese couldn't find them." Grandma's smile was proud. "Come, sit here. You know why the deck has fifty-two cards?"

"No. Why?"

Grandma told me one story that I still cannot unremember.

A long time ago in China, some government ministers were summoned before the King, who told them that an army of savages from a barbarian country had assembled on the border, ready to invade. These ruthless invaders were about to plunder and destroy China. The destiny of the entire nation rested on this moment.

The ministers proposed many solutions to preserve China's knowledge and wisdom. Some said the ancient scrolls and sacred writings should be hidden in Himalayan caves; others suggested they be buried in the artificial tombs. If not extremely well-hidden, the writings could eventually be lost.

Then one minister thought to visit the Master in the Grand Temple. When he arrived, the Master was meditating in his inner chamber. The minister asked him for his help. Finally, the Master opened his eyes, yawned, and stretched, saying, "Tao had already answered me: A picture is worth one thousand words." Then the Master told the minister of his grand plan.

All the artists in the land were then assembled in the palace where the Master initiated them into the mysteries of truth and instructed them to use their imagination to depict this truth in their artwork. The artists concealed all the symbols of natural powers, the divine qualities of Tao, in fifty-two picture cards. In this way, the inner teachings of our wisdom were preserved.

I stared at Grandma, my mouth open, my breath caught in my throat. I was dumbstruck.

"Why are there fifty-two cards, Grandma?"

"Year have 52 weeks, four seasons, thirteen lunar cycles, buried in these cards. Together, these cards symbolize the mysteries of the universe. Without imagination, our world is lost forever."

"Why four seasons, Grandma?"

"Spring, summer, autumn, and winter correspond to the four elements: air, fire, earth, and water. They also correspond to the four winds: east, south, west, and north. Each of the winds also corresponds to the four creatures at Creation: Dragon, Tiger, Bird, Tortoise. All things in the universe are interconnected."

We were both silent for a few moments. Grandma was waiting for something, and then a question came up to me.

"But, what ... *is* imagination?"

"It is many things. It is a firefly's light, a bird in the air with nine heads ..."

That night Mother came home late. She went straight to her room and shut the door behind her. It was dark in her room; the hour of electricity was over after 10 p.m. A few minutes later, I heard muffled sobbing. Holding an oil lamp, I tiptoed out of my bedroom and knocked on her door.

"What's wrong, Mama?"

My legs were trembling; my shadow was flickering. The door creaked open.

"Come in, son." Mother wiped her wet eyes with her right sleeve. "Have words to tell you."

She motioned me to sit on the edge of her bed. I sensed something terrible had befallen our family.

"Remember this, son: never get yourself entangled with numbers, because it brings disaster," she asserted.

Grandma rushed in. "What happened?" she asked. She had overheard and was worried.

Mother told her, in a calmer tone, that she was suspected of stealing cash because her books did not reconcile. This meant she would be sent to a re-education camp known as the May Seventh Cadre School.

My father was still in a camp somewhere and the officials would not disclose its location to us. Now, Mother would be sent to a camp as well.

In those days, our very language belonged to the Party and its words were dyed blood red like our national flag. (When the Party referred to a learning class or a study group, it did not pertain to studying but to brainwashing and forced confessions.) As we all knew, red was the colour of revolution, the soul of the Party; traffic lights in cities had been changed for some time so that a red light signalled "go" and green meant "stop."

Years later, Mother told me that being incarcerated in the camp was worse than being in prison; they would not give you food and water or allow you to sleep until you confessed your "crimes" and begged for food on your knees.

The rest of the conversation I do not remember, as my mother and her mother hugged each other through their tears and sobbing, sighing over their fate. "Old Heavens, your eyes are blind," Grandma protested.

Early the next morning, as the rain poured down on Phoenix Town, Mother stepped out with a plastic bag in one hand and an umbrella in the other, flanked by two men wearing hooded raincoats.

After a few steps, she paused and looked back. Her gaze met mine. Her face was wet; I was not sure whether it was the rain or her tears. Then, under the stern gazes of the two men, Mother turned and walked away. Her shoulders shook but her steps quickened. I stood trembling by the entrance, watching as Mother's shadow disappeared in the misty clouds of the rain. At that moment, I vowed to reinvent myself—to become another person who, in future, would elicit joyful smiles from Mother.

That fateful day was printed in indelible ink on my subconscious. I used to be proud of my innate talent for math but after that, when I looked at numbers, my mind misread them. When I saw 666, for example, the numbers swam before my eyes and my subconscious tricked me into seeing 999 instead. My mind overrode my eyes. Gradually, I gave in to feelings of terror during math classes until one day, my mind went entirely blank whenever I observed Arabic numbers written on the page.

As I grew older, lack of mathematical knack became a simple personal trait, one that needed no explanation. However, I later learned that behind each of my personality quirks lurked a significant amount of memory. These traits were only a tip of the iceberg hidden in the ocean of my brain.

For a long time, I was not able to understand why I was so weak and powerless when confronted by numbers. In math class, my head became dizzy, my heart thudded heavily. Many years later, it dawned on me that math class triggered emotions related to that fateful evening when my mother had told me never to associate myself with numbers; thus, my mind would automatically shut down at the sight of them. When you get physically hurt, the wound will usually heal over time and eventually, the hurt is forgotten unless you add emotion to your pain. But when you are emotionally hurt, there is no medication or remedy that can heal the unseen scars.

My mother's words went deep into my subconscious. When you are young, your mind is susceptible to suggestions in part because you lack the ability to assess the truth of them. When such words come while you are charged with emotion, they change you and become part of you. Thus, in later life, however you may struggle to change yourself, it is going to be futile unless you cure the root cause. When your will wrestles with your subconscious, the latter always wins.

As for the ten-yuan currency that I had stolen from Grandma, I used some to purchase cigarettes, some for wine. In those days, ten yuan was a lot of money. I wanted to smoke and drink like an adult. When I took my first sip of wine, I thought I was drinking the panacea for despair and unhappiness. How I squandered the rest of the money, I cannot recall. Some of my early memories have been blocked due to the emotional hurt, and this blockage helped me. For many years into my adulthood, I carried guilt on my heart because of this theft. My hand would tremble when I reached for my wallet. When paying a cashier, my heart would thrum like a galloping horse and I would race to the door, gasping for air.

Of course, all of this worked subconsciously without me knowing why this was happening. We are who we are and the reasons why we act as we do lie below the tip of that iceberg.

14

THE DRAGON BOAT Festival was as old as the mountains. The legend originated with an ancient poet, Qu Yuan (born in 340 B.C.), who ended his own life by drowning. Even though he lived in China before Jesus Christ, he still lives in the memory of the river and the land. In his famous poem *The Lament*, the whisper of the poet still echoed in the ears of the wind:

> *The road ahead is long and endless,*
> *Yet we will be searching far and wide.*

When I first heard those verses, they sounded other-worldly but indelible, albeit incomprehensible. Even still, from time to time the words seemed to shout at the entrance to my heart and I would search for that sound as if the memory of my soul was echoing the poet's mystic voice.

Why did he commit suicide, though? For a long time, I was unable to comprehend the forces behind his death. Even more mysterious was his dazzling, mind-spinning poem *Heavenly Questions,* in which the poet asked human souls endless questions about the mysteries of the universe and the fate of human existence. Did the mystic solve his own riddles, like Oedipus? This, I don't know. But no one seemed interested in solving these puzzles.

Perhaps our beloved leader Chairman Mao also pondered the same questions of the soul. In his poem *Changsha*, Mao wrote:

> *I ask, in this vast land,*
> *Who rules over the destiny of mankind?*

No other modern people in this land, except perhaps for Mao himself, could solve this centuries-old riddle.

What is the purpose of life? Who controls human fate in this mundane world? I began to ask myself such questions. The vision Principal Jia had described for us, of a life filled with everything we desire, began to float like patches of clouds before my eyes. But when clouds of doubt began to fill a corner of my mind, I was consumed by fear. *Life is like a book,* I thought, but who is the author of each page? At night I lay awake, this question echoing in my mind.

As is tradition, we call the Dragon Boat Festival "Rice Dumplings Day." On that day, not long after my mother was sent away, the crowd began to assemble in People's Square. I hurried to join those close to the platform. A few townsfolk were playing cards, laughing and yelling, many with cigarettes dangling at the corner of their mouths. The losers had to pay the winners by surrendering their best brand of cigarettes, which were concealed in their inside pockets. Among the yelling speculators closest to me was a man called Fool-the-Second. No one knew his real name. He was the only son of Landlady Liu, who had knelt beside my father on the platform at the denunciation meeting.

During the land reform movement in the 1950s, people believed Fool-the-Second swooned at the sight of his father being executed, gunned down and lying in a pool of blood. When he came to, he no longer knew who he was; people said he had lost his mind.

Soon after, he wandered away and no one knew where he went.

Many years later he was arrested as an illegal vagrant and sent back to town; there was no patch of earth in this enormous land he could call home. Like a drunkard, he sometimes lay on the ground crying and trembling. And, winter or summer, he wore the same worn black jacket.

After the players finished their cigarettes, they began to amuse themselves by arm-wrestling one another. Just then, an old farmer came into view, guiding an aging yellow cow across the square. One player jumped up from his seat and blocked the animal.

"Wait. Let's play a game with your beast," he suggested.

"I drive this poor animal to the butcher," the old man snapped, pointing to the red-brick slaughterhouse on the other side of the square.

"Let's have fun with the beast before it's slaughtered," another player added. Then the first player dragged over Fool-the-Second by the collar of his worn jacket, stinking of dog poo.

"Dare to lick the cow's ass?" he said to the vagrant. "I give you rice dumplings!"

The players and spectators applauded the idea, shouting, "Go, Fool-the-Second, go!"

One player bet a bundle of six steamed rice dumplings, which were lying on the makeshift gaming "table" in a bamboo basket. "See? You lick, yours!"

I do not know whether Fool-the-Second was sober or drunk at that moment. But he smirked and pulled aside the beast's long tail. He closed his eyes and stuck out his tongue, licking the cow's ass as though he were licking a bowl of melted ice cream on a hot summer day.

People exploded with laughter. Fool-the-Second had a big smile on his face. Then he limped away, holding his "trophy" tightly against his chest, and disappearing into the crowd.

By then the midday sun had hidden its smiling face, clouds drifted over the land. A storm was brewing; it was too late to cancel the race. *The weatherman is wrong again*, I thought.

The beating sounds of gongs and drums shook the earth and so did the crowd's enthusiasm; the boating race was about to begin.

People flooded the streets and ran toward the wharf. Ten dragon boats would soon depart in a race and cross the river against the rapids and the downstream currents.

Dressed in white shirt and black trousers, I took my place as the drummer on a dragon boat with my teammates, the gamblers who had played the trick on Fool-the-Second.

Crossing this section of the river can be dangerous. One legend tells the story of a fisherman's boat that was swept away in a storm by the roaring torrents. People searched for him along the river for three days, but without success. On the third day, however, the boat suddenly surfaced on the river, the fisherman alive inside. Later, he told people he'd been in a palace at the bottom of the river and had been arrested by the people there. In tears, he had begged for his release saying he had two children. Finally, he was let go after being fed noodles and meat. When told that he had been gone for three days, he shook his head in disbelief. Then he vomited out worms and frogs.

"Bang!"

The sound of the signal gun shattered my daydreams. As we paddled against four other boats, I pounded the drum in the middle of the dragon with all my might. "Fuel up, fuel up!" I shouted at the top of my lungs while hitting my instrument with two drumsticks, my words mingling with the shouts of the spectators craning their necks on the shore.

Our boat was leading the way, like a real dragon rushing to the middle of the river. Rolling waves swept over our boat and we were drenched. We thought of nothing but paddling, paddling, paddling. Just then, a boat that was trailing us suddenly turned its dragon head, hitting the right side of our boat. Our dragon head swivelled upon impact, colliding with the other boat. Both boats capsized and all of us were swept into the raging waves. Before I knew what was happening, I was swirling into the roaring waves and soon lost consciousness.

Somehow, I could feel my body hovering in the water, like a fish. I opened my eyes, and saw an exotic building that looked like a palace. Two guards with spears grabbed hold of me. I struggled and explained that my dragon boat had capsized but they wouldn't listen. They dragged me inside a small cell and shut the door behind, and I remained there for what seemed like three days and nights, although I lost track of the time. I was starving. On the morning of what I thought was the third day, my cell door was opened, and the same two guards ushered me to a big dining table heaped with crabs, lobsters, long noodles.

"Eat, please," whispered an old, bearded man sitting at one end of the table. His expressive eyes were speaking to me. My mind responded with "thank you" and the words could be heard without me opening my mouth. I discovered that we didn't need to use our words to communicate here; we sent out sound waves with our minds. When you think, you instantly stir the waves, which travel at a frequency that simultaneously carries your thoughts.

I was stuffing myself with as much of the seafood as I could when I heard a musical laugh ringing in the room. Suddenly, a girl was sitting before me. She was about my age and beautiful as a fairy. I do not have the words to describe her beauty. As I looked at her, dumbstruck, she seemed to understand what I was thinking and smiled at me kindly.

"You need to go back. You're missed on earth," she told me.

When I came to, I was lying on Turtle Beach, the same place where Red and I had spotted the dead bodies of the two lovers. Grandma was kneeling on the sand, crying. I felt someone pressing on my water-filled stomach. I vomited and vomited. Fortunately, no worms or frogs came out, only remnants of rice dumplings.

This mysterious, visceral experience convinced me that the tale about the fisherman was real; maybe the legend of our nine-headed bird was true as well. People refuse to believe these legends because they have never seen with their own eyes what these stories tell us.

Chairman Mao used to say, "If you want to know the taste of an apple, you have to eat it." I was not sure if his words were universally true anymore, but I was old enough to know I needed to keep this experience to myself. People would think I was insane if I told them. That alone didn't really bother me but spreading rumours like this would have constituted a crime that deserved serious punishment.

That night as I lay in bed, heat rose off my body as though I were floating in a vat of hot soup. Dr. Ma, the only barefoot doctor (who practiced medicine without medical training) at the town's clinic, came to inject something into my right arm but my fever did not abate and continued to burn for hours. Through my open bedroom door, I saw Grandma grab a bamboo rake and hurry outside into the night. Grandma's god lives in the mountain, and her god has many names.

"Little Bright, come back. Come home," I heard her cry.

Her cries soon faded until I heard nothing but the blowing wind. That night, I was sure the winds had carried her pleas to the edge of the sky and to the top of Phoenix Mountain.

After Grandma's small feet had carried her home, she told me she had been searching to find my lost soul. She was convinced that she had found it and had wrapped it in her handkerchief.

"See?" Retrieving the handkerchief from inside her breast pocket and holding it in her palm, she carefully unfolded the cloth to reveal the handful of soil inside. "See?" she repeated, as if she were showing me a glittering diamond. Then, she concealed it under my pillow.

Sometime after midnight, my fever disappeared and I awoke, although I still felt very weak.

"Where is my soul?" I asked Grandma, my curious eyes wide open.

"It went back into your body," she replied, closing her eyes for a few seconds.

"What do I do with my soul?"

"You fly like the nine-headed bird."

"What happens if people lose their souls?"

"They die; they become lonely ghosts."

"Do ghosts eat and drink, too?"

"Surely, they do. That's why living people offer them food sacrifices, burn hell money for them; they buy foods, place to live."

A few minutes later, she went out, closing the door gently behind her. The window was open and I could see fireflies fluttering in the dark. They kept themselves alive all winter, living underground so that, when spring came, they could fly out, generously sharing the essence of their body to spark their joyful light in the darkness. My confidantes.

Watching their shimmering dance, my eyes were wet and tears began to roll down my cheeks for no reason at all. I began to sob. As a silly child, I used to catch fireflies in the summertime, keeping them captive in a glass bottle. They glittered in their glass prison for hours before they faded when the day broke.

A strange feeling climbed up the back of my mind, making me feel at odds with the familiar world in which I'd grown up. The connection with the mysterious landscape of my inner mind became tangible. I was sure I could feel the *weight* of my soul and I hoped that one day I would be able to measure its depths.

That experience created a pathway of connections within my brain.

Although summer was still young, Phoenix Town was already sweating in the heat. When the river rose to the dangerous highwater mark, the townspeople would monitor the embankments around the clock. A watchman would beat his cymbal in the dead of night and shout, "All's peace ... and well!"

One August day, the entire town assembled in People's Square where Uncle Wang announced he had received a mandate from the Party. In his words, Phoenix had been chosen to shoulder our country's burden by receiving the water that was being diverted to rescue the big cities downriver from being flooded. It also meant that our whole town would be under water! The ensuing exclamations and protests from the assembled crowd were cut off quickly. "This is a glorious task," the mayor thundered, shocking everyone into a strange, hanging silence.

The silence continued over the square until Uncle Wang cleared his throat. "It is our mission to obey the words of the Party. We must sacrifice our lives gloriously for our country if called upon to do so."

On the day Uncle Wang detonated the explosives that would cause the river to inundate our town, rain poured from the sky, as if from an open mouth. In no time, the whole town was immersed in the engulfing waves from the great mother river. Standing at the foot of Mount Phoenix, overlooking the water-filled valley, the townsfolk knelt, calling loudly: "Open your eyes, good Heavens!"

Fourteen days later, the flood receded, revealing several decomposing corpses, one of which belonged to Landlady Liu. Some said she had refused to evacuate. Others said she had jumped into the thunderous waves when the dams exploded.

➤ For a long time afterward, people would say they saw "river ghosts" running along the shore. Some believed they saw a dishevelled old lady walking along the newly restored dams, others believed they spotted a ghostly figure running into our schoolroom.

In time, life returned to some form of normalcy, as if nothing had happened. The awakening sun still rose in the morning, the moon still shone on Main Street on a cloudless night, the river still flowed eastward. The ups and downs of fortune had long been a part of our people's blood. Townspeople continued to eat their morning porridge and drink their nightly glass of rice wine. Cigarette-puffing men still pissed on street corners—even in broad daylight. Women still went down to the marble steps to the riverbed to pound their laundry while savouring the current gossip.

"Zhang's daughter-in-law is ugly and, two years into marriage, her belly is still flat ... The wife of Li's family was beaten by her hubby's fists and kicked out for two nights because she refused to have sex during her period ... Old Wang was arrested and taken into custody because he had sneaked into a public toilet to peek at women's buttocks ... Zhao's wife had finally given birth to a son after three daughters ..." (The one-child-per-family policy would be implemented nationwide a few years later.)

And on went the gossip: "Now Zhao's incense can continue to burn. By the way, they are going to have a big celebration on the 30-day full-moon anniversary. Don't forget to go and drink wine. Not invited? Go ask the prick why he dishonoured you ..."

For the townspeople, the passage of time had ceased a long time ago. Only the river, with its ebb and flow, moved continuously, to the east. Despite the many vicissitudes of our world, the river continued to listen and watch, amassing its own memories. With voices speaking aloud and rumbling low, emotions buried in its waves, it presents a thousand faces: unpredictable, capricious and stubborn. Sometimes, it is peaceful and quiet. Sometimes, it is upset and angry. Other times, it is tearful and in pain. Sometimes, it acts like a tender-hearted mother baring her breast to nourish her children. Other times, it acts like a cruel tyrant or a dragon, devouring and destroying everything in its way.

When the sun laid its golden rays on the calm body of water, the river turned tender, baring its heaving breasts, inviting you with a golden smile, "Come, come dance with me to the winds from the east."

Until one fateful day when everything changed.

15

SEPTEMBER 9, 1976.

It was destined to be a lucky day in Phoenix Town because Uncle Wang's son, Steel, was to wed his beautiful bride.

The September sun was sad and lonely but still menacingly hot, a burning fireball hanging far away in the sky. In such heat, sleeping inside a brick house was akin to boiling an egg in a hot wok on the stove. The townspeople brought bamboo beds to the embankment so they could sleep in the coolness of the river breeze. Greedy mosquitoes swarmed human blood feasts in and out of the smoke from pest-dispelling herbs burning beneath the bamboo beds. Men lay half-naked, fanning away the smoke. Laughing, coughing and cursing filled the hot air.

That night, a huge crowd gathered in front of Uncle Wang's house. A big paper cutout representing "double happiness" was affixed on either side of the double doors. A large Chinese character symbolizing the arrival of fortune had been written in red ink and hung upside down in the middle of the entrance frame, meaning a reversal of fortune.

The next morning, a tractor was dispatched to fetch the bride from a neighbouring village. Meanwhile, a crowd assembled at Uncle Wang's house where tables were laid with bottles of wines and packs of Red Double Happiness cigarettes, which were considered lucky. A gong-drum team puffed cigarettes at the entrance, talking loudly among themselves.

Grandma was invited to drink the lucky wine. By that time, my mother had returned from the camp, but she had changed, worn down by humiliation. She refused to attend the wedding, so Grandma took me. Although I had urged her to get there earlier, she dismissed my eagerness as poor etiquette. "For meetings, you go as early as possible, but for eating, you come as late as you can," she told me.

Grandma clutched a red envelope in her hand containing the people's currency as a token of her congratulations. On this special occasion, which people regarded as an auspicious day, children were allowed to smoke lucky cigarettes like adults.

Although I had been born in the year of the tiger, that year I was thirteen because, in our traditional age-counting method, you are already one year old on the date of your birth. This is because our ancestors believed that life began not at zero but at one. (We still refer to daytime as "the sun," a month as "the moon," night as "late," and an hour as a "tiny piece of time.") People claimed smoking could stunt your growth. I was pale and skinny, mostly due to malnutrition, and was a head shorter than my peers. Grandma had exhausted all her old recipes to jumpstart the growth of my body, but the effect was apparently limited. *Maybe being short is in my genes,* I thought. People pointed at me behind my back, saying, "Look at this boy, his growth has stalled, but the eye of his heart has grown big." That saddened me, but I could not risk talking back so I just walked away, turning a deaf ear to the jeers.

Inside, Red was running around between the tables. Since middle-school, we'd avoided each other; being teased was the last thing we wanted. Despite our efforts, however, some still took pleasure in teasing us by imitating a popular tune from the local opera known as *A Heavenly Match*: "They returned home together as a couple." My face would blush and I would spit curses at my offenders and run off.

It would be more than embarrassing if I talked to Red during a wedding, of all things. So, when she spotted me, I pretended that I had to follow the noisy crowd. My ears still echoed with the gossip about Red's betrothal to me when she was in her mother's womb.

Now, her father had betrayed my father and my head was abuzz with plans of reprisal. *Friendship, let alone a love affair, can never happen between Red and me,* I thought.

After Father was taken away, Uncle Wang came to console my mother. "If our country asked me to sacrifice my only son," he exclaimed, "I'd obey without blinking."

After Mother left, the sight of Grandma's bound feet rescued my sisters and me from being bullied. "Look at my feet!" Grandma would yell to our tormentors, "Chairman Mao claimed poor peasants are the masters of the new China. I from poor peasant's family. You dare bully my grandchildren?" Then Grandma would stomp her feet on the dusty ground, glaring scathingly at the bully boys until they'd run, disappearing around the crook of the street.

In my mind, Grandma was not a little old lady; she was a giant full of courage, resilience and hope.

Just then, the clattering of cymbals and drums dragged my roaming thoughts back to the wedding. Firecrackers exploded in the distance, the sound getting louder near the bridegroom's bridal chamber. Amid the sound of trumpets, the bride stepped down from the tractor, veiled in a red silk scarf, accompanied by her well-dressed bridegroom. Guests showered candied peanuts over the couple's heads and the children swarmed to pick up the treats.

Once inside the house, Steel unveiled his bride. The couple was led toward the portrait of Chairman Mao hanging high in the centre of the whitewashed wall where they bowed.

The crowd applauded and shouted "good, good," when the ritual was over. Shouts of "May Chairman Mao live ten thousand years!" and "Long live our socialist new China!" echoed in the hot and crowded air.

The Chinese word "good" (好) denotes the union of a duality, such as the integration of *yin* (女) and *yang* (子), or the feminine and masculine. Hence, goodness is not fulfilled until both a son and a daughter are born to a family.

If yin and yang are GOOD for us, can we cut goodness into two separate halves? Like two bodies, or two minds? I wondered.

Uncle Wang was a genius at sniffing out the direction of political winds. On this occasion, he had put together a ten-course menu that perfectly converted people's food obsession into Party-loving propaganda. For example, the first dish was a bowl of pig's head, believed to symbolize leadership. The second was a bowl of steamed chicken, symbolic of the success of the four wings of China's modernization. The next one was ten hard-boiled eggs, representing perfection. A bowl of fried fish was the last course, synonymous with abundance.

After that day, Uncle Wang's famed menu spread by word of mouth far beyond Mount Phoenix and has since been used for other red (celebrating) days, like weddings and birthdays, and for white ceremonies like funerals.

Our stomachs were replete.

The ceremony progressed to its final event: apple biting. The bride and bridegroom would bite a swaying red apple hanging by a red thread between their mouths. The bride's face blushed. She cupped her face in both hands. The bridegroom encouraged his bride to be brave. A few seconds later, the couple stood face to face, ready to perform the ritual. A man stood up on a chair, to sway the apple between the two opening mouths. Both mouths struggled to bite. Like a fish gasping for air. They missed the moving target, resulting in a collision of lips and much laughter.

Meanwhile, I held my breath; my heart beat faster and blood rushed to my head. In my imagination, I was biting the red apple with Red as my bride, embracing her, ready to kiss. Ecstasy engulfed me. My body jerked.

"Kiss! Kiss! One more kiss!" Laughter exploded like a bomb. I opened my eyes and felt my face on fire. But Red had disappeared like a cloud. Also, I felt the wetness. A viscous substance had exuded from my body. I was afraid to move my legs.

I felt I was a man now, thanks to General Cao.

From then on, I went over my daydream repeatedly to experience the thrill and pleasure. Again and again.

Stuffed with the pleasure of devouring the ten-course banquet, a cluster of three or four guests and their bulging bellies followed each other to the direction of People's Square. A propaganda team was invited to perform *Eulogy of the Dragon River*. After the white-haired girl incident, I dreaded approaching the familiar square alone. Dread would crawl up my spine every time I neared it. Even on movie nights, I would hide in the crowd. "Once you've been bitten by a snake," the proverb says, "you'll fear a curled-up rope of straw for the rest of your life."

That day, when I sat down, the same old fear came over me, and I felt sure something awful was about to happen again, like the night when the actor was killed. In my mind, the shadow of a man was walking among the crowd like a ghost.

A few minutes before four o'clock, just as the performance was about to start, Uncle Wang hurried onto the stage, stopping to catch his breath before turning to address the audience. "All performances are cancelled immediately," he pronounced.

A hush fell over the crowd. All eyes were on Uncle Wang, who shouted: "The Central Party Committee will announce sad news at four o'clock sharp!"

A few minutes later, the loudspeakers around the square came to life: "It is with great sadness we announce to our nation that our great leader, Chairman Mao, passed away today."

The crowd was rendered mute by the shocking news. There was a momentary hush, as everyone weighed the enormity of the announcement.

Moments later, a young boy sobbed from within the silent crowd, "Daddy, I don't want to miss the show."

The man beside him slapped his cheek hard. The boy wailed, triggering the entire crowd, which began to emit sorrowful wails.

Some bent their heads down to their knees; others raised their heads heavenward, yelling, "God of the heavens!"

For many days and nights, all entertainment activities were strictly prohibited. Laughter was also banned. The whole town was awash with tears, misery, despair. When people met each other in public, their swollen eyes seemed to ask one pressing question: "What will be the future of our nation?"

Classes were cancelled for the duration of the mourning period. The whole school was draped in black as students watched the mourning procession in Beijing from a 14-inch, black-and-white TV on the only available channel. Adults and children wore black armbands. I took great care to shed tears when the occasion warranted, as it was a real crime not to be saddened by the sudden passing of our saviour. I laboured to enliven my tearless cries when my tears ran dry.

Strangely enough, when you fake it, tears come, then pour out like raindrops. To me, this was baffling. Years later, I learned that there is a great mystery hidden in human emotions: most of the time, we cannot distinguish which emotions are true and which are false.

For many days, the sky was weirdly dark and overcast with clouds. The loudspeaker lady announced that the sky was crying, too, over the loss of a great Eastern star. Then, one day, gusts of winds blew westward, and lightning flashed across the sky, followed by a deadly silence.

"Bang! Bang!"

Thunder boomed, followed by hailstones as big as ping-pong balls, which pelted down from the sky. I was overcome with fear, made more miserable by my troubled imagination.

Is the sky going to fall? What will our world be like without Chairman Mao?

As usual, the pendulum of life continued swaying in the old wall clock, although the ticking was drowned out from time to time, particularly on a windy or rainy day. Gradually, the rhythm of that sound drowns out all else, including time, space, human destiny.

PART TWO

The mind is like a river.
The thoughts are like the various droplets of water.
We are submerged in that water.
Stay on the bank and watch your mind.
—A.G. Mohan

16

As **WINTER WENT** by, greens sprang up; the earth looked moist and young in the mists shrouding the land. The mountains came alive with the sound of birds, and young leaves on willow trees sprouted to their fullest.

A new schoolbag flung over my shoulder, I began high school in September.

The newly built Phoenix High School sat at the foot of the mountains, a four-storey building constructed entirely of cement blocks. Each block contained two empty holes that looked like a square "8" when stood on end. When placed face down, it formed the shape of the Chinese word *hui* 回 (meaning return), like a circle within a circle, or a zero within a zero.

One day, all the students filed onto the sports field. There, the new middled-aged Party Secretary, Teacher Dai, waving his right hand, divided us into two.

Thus was this collection of students separated into two faculties: science and arts. The majority in science, a few in arts. Teacher Dai claimed that only science could rescue China and realize its dreams of modernization. Math, physics, and chemistry, known as MPC, constituted the three pillars of science, he said.

Since my math grades had been rather poor, I was chosen to sit with the minority arts camp, but I didn't complain. I had grown wings of imagination which, so far, had afforded me the pleasure of feeling free. However, Teacher Dai pointed out that imagination—which resides in the faculty of arts—was as useless as daydreaming and should be treated with disdain.

But how could humans fly without wings of imagination? I pondered.

Years later, I learned that our brains are divided into two hemispheres, left and right, with each in charge of different faculties. Scientists say imagination and intuition reside in the right hemisphere. We call it *yin* in Chinese because it is considered intuitive, receptive and feminine. On the other hand, the left hemisphere is viewed as having language, logical, analytical functions. We call it *yang,* the masculine.

Marxist theory had solved the chicken-and-egg mystery, Teacher Dai explained in his first politics class. Matter existed before mind! First, there was a chicken and it laid eggs. "Without chickens, where do you find eggs?" Teacher Dai asked rhetorically.

All of us nodded assent.

"But where did chickens come from in the first place?" I raised my left hand and asked timidly. I was surprised I was still left-handed when it came to questions.

"Through evolution," Teacher Dai replied. "As did humans. A long, long time ago, our ape-like ancestors crawled on the ground, as did other animals. But they finally stood up and walked like us, because manual work and the use of tools made us human. As a result, our minds evolved, and languages developed out of necessity. A lengthy process, though."

"So ... so, apes ... birthed humans?" Bacon, my seatmate, stammered.

We all laughed, jerking our heads from left to right, from front to back.

On the first day of school, Bacon and I had become buddies. He brought me novels to read.

"How come you have so many banned books?" I asked one day.

"My grandfather dug a hole in the backyard and hid them from the Red Guards," he said. When I asked about his westernized name, Bacon whispered, "Because my grandfather adores Francis Bacon's aphorisms."

"Knowledge is power," I blurted.

His grandfather used to be an accountant for his village. Now, Bacon was bringing his treasures to me. I began to realize the sky had changed; knowledge was not evil anymore. In fact, Teacher Dai had also emphasized in class: "Knowledge is *good* and China desperately needs power to move forward under new leadership."

"You're exactly right, Bacon, humans evolved from man-like apes." The declaration brought my mind back to the classroom when I saw Teacher Dai nodding his head, a grin cracking his lips. "They are our ancestors. At one time, we were all animals, but we survived by evolving and adapting to our surroundings, unlike other lazy animals, such as pigs and dogs."

Some of us were not as convinced. We looked around skeptically. I still had some doubts.

If Charles Darwin was right, could dogs become human, too? How are humans different from animals? Can animals speak and think? If mankind is deprived of these abilities, are we then animals?

Of course, I'd learned not to be stupid and openly voice thoughts different from those of our teachers. That would still be a crime, even though Chairman Mao had passed.

"Do you know why we call our roadway a 'horse-way'?" Teacher Dai asked. His question surprised us. We looked at each other, shaking our heads.

"Because we're walking on Marxist roads," he said, shrewdly answering his own question. What a smart answer! We all knew that the Chinese word *ma* means "horse" and is the first character used to spell *Ma*-rx.

By all standards, legal and moral, not bowing to authority was still a serious offence. Like always, the standard curriculum was rote learning, and passive obedience was the gauge used to grade all students. Our job was to upload the classroom inventory and store it in our minds. Thus, our minds became copy machines, processing mechanically without our own thoughts. I used to think my mind was a part of me and I owned it, but I later discovered I was wrong; the words I spoke were not my words, and the thoughts in my head were not my thoughts. Our country owned our minds. (Much later in life I became unsure whether our minds resided inside or outside of us.)

This thought frightened me profoundly. Did I own my soul, or did it belong to the Party?

And what happened to our souls? From my drowning experience, I knew I had a soul and that it could reside in another realm.

Despite the doubts, my head nodded in agreement with Teacher Dai.

After class, Teacher Dai summoned me to his office on the second floor of the new building. This room also constituted his living quarters where a table, two chairs and a bed were the only furniture.

In those days, thinking evil thoughts was labelled a counter-revolutionary act. The political life of the owner of those thoughts would be over, in the eyes of the Party. The more I thought, the more I was scared. I even began to feel angry with my own thoughts; they would be disastrous to my political well-being.

How could Teacher Dai possibly know what I was thinking? Do I have to confess my crime first to earn a credit for self-denunciation?

A hammer of fear drummed in my heart. My feet refused to move as I hesitated at the door, which was adorned with a red flag atop a hammer-and-sickle sign that read: Party Secretary's Office.

"Come in, Little Bright." Teacher Dai seemed to read my mind.

"Teacher, I ... I ... confess," I muttered while dragging my heavy feet along.

"Confess to what?" Teacher Dai asked, frowning, "Reading the *People's Daily* is far from a crime, but dodging your responsibility is."

While I was still panicking, Teacher Dai handed me a copy of the *People's Daily*, pointing at a two-page article entitled, "Goldbach's Conjectures."

To my great relief, Teacher Dai had found out nothing about my thoughts. He just wanted me to read the article to a loudspeaker broadcast live to the students assembled on the sports field. (In those days, loudspeaker broadcasting was the most popular media after newspaper reading.) I thought it was a good opportunity for me to parrot the tone of the announcer's voice that had been ringing in my ears for years on the loudspeaker placed in our house.

When I saw a picture of Deng Xiaoping on the front page, however, my hands trembled and my mind went blank. I tried to shake the memory out of my head, but the flashback refused to leave me.

I recalled with shame that after the night Uncle Wang had ransacked our house, I had gone to see Principal Jia to inform him that it was Ear who had torn out the article in the *People's Daily* in the toilet and disgraced Chairman Mao. As a result, Ear had been expelled from school and banned from attending any school in town. I now felt ashamed of what I had done. But I had believed I had to betray a friend to save myself, just as Uncle Wang had done to my father.

Friendship is nothing when it conflicts with loyalty to the Party, I mused.

Still, I was too ashamed to tell this secret to a soul.

The following morning, I read the article at the broadcasting studio for at least two hours, using the official dialect of the land. (No one taught me the official dialect; I learned to speak it from listening to the loudspeakers.) After I finished, I was drenched. Perhaps it was because I was afraid of mispronouncing something.

Perhaps it was because I felt as if I were reading riddles. All I remembered was 1 + 1. *The formula is so simple, even infantile,* I thought during my broadcast.

How can we prove 1 + 1?

Or 1 + 2 = 3?

Simple things must conceal a deep mystery.

The article claimed Professor Chen had spent a decade in a labour camp during the Cultural Revolution solving this mystery.

A child could solve 1 + 1; did we need a scientist to spend a decade on so simple an equation? However, if the Party glorified such a formula, it must be like the great mysteries of science, or the enigmatic riddles of Qu Yuan, the poet.

Shortly afterward, Teacher Dai began his address. I remember him saying that our country was in a "scientific spring" and that universities in China were opening their doors to embrace those who were willing to contribute to the great cause of scientific development. His emphatic speech, delivered in his high-pitched voice, was punctuated by long explosions of applause from the audience.

So, like all students, passing admission exams and studying at university became my high school dream and at the same time it became a tool for the development of our country. If I wanted a future far from the mountainside, going to university was the only path to get me there, I thought.

This reminded me of a tale Grandma told me.

There was a young man from a poor family with no money for lamp fuel. On summer nights, he would read books by moonlight and in wintertime, he would read beside the window using the snow's reflected brightness. When the poor man felt thirsty, he would scoop up a handful of snow. When he felt sleep invading his mind, he would use a rope to tie his braid to a beam on the ceiling so that if he dozed off while reading, his head would be jerked up.

In those days, both men and women grew their hair long. When the time for change came, men had to cut off their braids and many cried out in defiance; they would rather lose their heads than their hair. But in our time, standing against the political winds was like throwing yourself under the wheels of the train of history. "The mountains would never bow down to the wind," Grandma used to say.

In the story, the man believed reading could change his poverty-stricken fate. So, for more than a decade he continued to pore over the classics by icy-cold windows, as if sowing seeds of hope in the snow-covered ground, patiently waiting for the bamboo tree to break through. Then, one day, to everyone's surprise, the district governor dispatched a bamboo sedan chair carried on the shoulders of four servants and invited him to take the position of the new magistrate in the region. As it turned out, the poor man had secretly travelled to the country's capital to take the official selection exam and had the top score among hundreds of candidates. As a result, he had won great honour for his ancestors and family.

"If you can eat the bitterness of all bitterness," Grandma used to say, "then you become a man above all men."

This would get on my nerves. My political sensibility warned me of the dangers associated with this old-fashioned way of thinking, so I immediately dismissed Grandma's thoughts as politically backward. Our new communist ideals had long ago destroyed the traditional ideology.

"Grandma, do you remember your old earthen pot? The one you used to preserve your marinated vegetables, that was smashed to pieces by the team destroying the Four Olds? Old ideas, old culture, old habits, old customs?" I warned her.

Unlearning confused my mind, as it did Grandma's.

One day, a hunched old man appeared in our classroom accompanied by Teacher Dai. He was short and leathery. At least in his sixties. He was Teacher Hu, our new English teacher. He had graduated from Cambridge University and returned in the 1950s.

When the winds of the Cultural Revolution swept the land,

Teacher Hu had been denounced as a Rightist (or Right-Winger)[1] and received his re-education in the cow pen.

That was the official version of Teacher Hu's life story.

When prompted to tell his own account, Teacher Hu waved a hand, saying, "Let bygones be bygones," although we sensed much sorrow in his voice.

In addition to his personal story, which interested us enormously, Teacher Hu taught us international phonetic symbols, English texts, English grammar and usage.

One day, Teacher Hu dipped his brush into an inkwell and wrote down English words in large letters on a piece of window-sized white paper. In time, the whitewashed walls of our classroom were bedecked with these posters.

"Out of sight, out of mind," he muttered with a bitter smile. We were unsure whether he was thinking about his own life experience or just reminding us of this universal wisdom.

Occasionally, Teacher Hu would give in to students prodding him to talk about his Cambridge days. I will never forget one story he told about a quiz he took in economics class. Thinking he would achieve a high grade, to his surprise, he and everyone else got an F; the professor had made a false proposition on purpose, forcing the students to draw erroneous conclusions. His whole class had to retake the quiz. (We did not understand what a false proposition was in terms of logic. But our curiosity was aroused by his story.)

The lesson Teacher Hu learned from this failure was to not trust authority and to verify the truth by conducting one's own investigation. However, that experience proved to be a disaster for him when he received his re-education, and survival became his top priority. (In this sense, our great teacher Darwin was right.) The importance of staying alive was the first thing he learned from the pigs he fed, he told us.

---

1. Those intellectuals who favoured capitalism and opposed collectivization in the Anti-Rightist Movement.

Teacher Hu told us that the structures of the English language are based on time, order and logic.

"What is logic?" we asked almost in unison.

(There is no equivalent term in the Chinese language. It was author Lu Xun, a leading figure in modern Chinese literature, who first translated it as *Louji* in its homophonic Chinese.)

"Logic is a way of thinking based on a set of meaningful rules and principles," our teacher explained. "If you violate the rules, the result of your thinking—what we call conclusions—could be unsafe or false."

This was the very first time I had heard about rules of thinking that were not intended to control but to regulate our mind's activities. I began to sense the enormous difference between *what* to think and *how* to think.

Our teacher cited as an example a popular belief.

"All Chinese are shrewd, I am a Chinese, therefore, I am shrewd too."

Then, he asked if anyone agreed with him. Many raised hands. Then Teacher Hu asked if any of us thought this was a false proposition. We looked at each other, shaking our heads adamantly.

Gazing around the classroom, Teacher Hu sighed. "Unfortunately, we're wrong," he remarked. Then he explained the difference between universality and specificity.

"*All* is a very dangerous word. Very dangerous. Because it encompasses everything under the sun. So is another word: *only*. We must use both words sparingly and carefully. We must understand the falsehood of 'all for one and one for all,' which was the very root cause of the notorious Cultural Revolution. Do you appreciate the gravity now? Otherwise, we will lose *all*, including our humanity."

Never had I thought like this before. The weight of the resulting silence crashed on our heads.

"When the assumption you begin with is false, everything generated from that must be false. Failing to see that is an example of flawed reasoning. Incorrect conclusions can produce nonsense, absurdity, chaos and even disasters."

This thing called *logic* was fresh and fascinating to us. Teacher Hu called it the "highest science."

"Education is not about accepting everything without question—like ducks being fed—it's about learning how to think critically," Teacher Hu said. "We must verify and analyze what is true and what is false as part of our learning process. A teacher's job is not to provide answers but to inspire students to search for their own."

This provoked the class's interest in the subject. Buoyed by Teacher Hu's explanation, I was lost in thought. *The purpose of our life is to search for truth. Like Qu Yuan said in his poem?* I used to think we had already found the answers to Qu Yuan's cosmic riddles. Was logic like a magic wand, the waving of which brings order to my life?

What Teacher Hu taught in class was like throwing a boulder into a quiet pond but his words got him into trouble when they reached the ears of the leaders. He later professed to both the students and teachers that he was wrong to spread a capitalist idea of education and that he would not dare to open his mouth to talk like this again.

Fortunately, his seemingly heartfelt confession quelled the criticism, and he pretended that he was in good spirits and accustomed to being treated as an inferior. Still, I imagined him whispering that, without logical thinking, our mind is like that of a drunkard, chaotic and unfocused.

Logic made my head spin; I was weighed down by my thoughts.

Were our thoughts under the control of our minds? If logic is the highest form of science, does it supply answers to the mystery of human fate and explain why I am who I am?

That day, I began to search for the logical pattern to my life.

17

BY NOW, THE labour camp had closed.

One day, my father staggered home, as if he had dropped from a cloud. But I was dismayed that he was as inebriated as the drunkard I'd seen on the street corner. He dropped onto the bed and did not open his eyes for three days and nights, neither eating a bite nor sipping water. He slept as deeply as death, to the point that Mother had to get up in the middle of the night and put her finger beneath his nose to feel for his breath.

Mother had been delighted to see Father return but his catatonic state threw her into a deep hole. On the fourth morning, however, the loudspeaker in our house finally woke him up, whereupon he jumped out of bed and shouted at me: "You hear it, son? You hear it?"

"Hear what?" I asked.

"Listen! We are no longer labelled as landowners."

Father was clearly excited by the words of the male voice emanating from the loudspeaker as it announced the Party's decision to abolish this hated Maoist classification.

"I just woke up from a nightmare," Father whispered.

He poured himself a bowl of wine, drinking it down in one long gulp. He was elated. However, it seemed his life was destined to be a wet one.

The words from the loudspeaker meant that my dreams were a certainty. No more labelling. The future had become a bright, wide road. Of course, if I could pass the university entrance exams, life would be even better. But it seemed to me that I could finally be the master of my own destiny, carrying my life in my own hands.

In that night's dream I kissed a girl who looked familiar but whom I had never met. It was not Red or Moon. Moon had moved away. Red, along with Bubble, were in the science class, and we avoided each other. If we happened to meet on campus, Red would lower her head and turn away, as if I did not exist. This saddened me; I felt I was walking in a desert, longing for water.

In the night, I fantasized about the pleasure of kissing girls. *What would it taste like? Better than eating chicken?* I wondered. *What would it be like if I kissed a girl on the mouth and pulled off her clothes so we could have sex?* I thought of Robinson Crusoe, lying alone on the beach of an uninhabited island. *What would it be like if I were stranded on an island with Red? Just the two of us, the whole island.* It would be lovely. We could lie naked and have sex all day long without fear.

My fears were constant and numerous, however. I feared my angry father; I feared my surly teachers; I feared blank walls; I feared hungry mosquitoes; I feared roaring water; I feared the face-less talking poles on the street—I even feared myself. I was the fear.

What is a fear-free world like? That would be a paradise on earth.

Did our hero Jade in the *Dream Book* have fears, as well? What happened to him when surrounded by pretty girls, playing flirting games with the breast-sprouting young women of his choice?

When I was fantasizing, an erection would ensue. Then I would masturbate to have a release.

I was burning with desire. My fevered imagination kept me awake, fluttering in the night like a startled bat. I liked to compare myself to bats or nocturnal cats that found freedom and solace in the dark. But when morning dawned, I felt tired and ashamed, and I wanted to turn away from the sun.

In the front row of my class sat a girl named Lily. She had a head of long black hair. I did not know why but her presence reminded me of the girl I saw at the long table on the day I nearly drowned. When I breathed, my nostrils filled with the fragrance of her hair. The smell hastened my heartbeat, incited my imagination and produced an unbearably embarrassing erection that bulged beneath my summer trousers. Standing up was out of the question.

One day, Lily was bending over her desk reading *Fortress Besieged*[2]. I had heard about the novel; it was about a Mr. Fang who returned to China from studying in France in the 1930s. Our hero became a professor but, later, people discovered he had secretly bought a bogus diploma from a fake American university.

In those days, speaking with a girl openly was considered shameful. I was about 16 years old; fantasies about kissing and touching always knocked on the door of my mind. In my young life, I could not recall ever seeing any members of the opposite sex kissing or touching each other. Not even in our movies or in any present-day books. Only in my dreams did I see myself kissing the same unnamed beauty and trying to open her legs with my eyes.

I had heard about a 400-year-old book called *The Golden Lotus* that was filled with lively details of sex scenes. It had been banned and burned during the Cultural Revolution. Self-discipline through abstinence is called self-oppression, which causes tremendous pain.

As you think, so it happens. Once again, a General Cao trick!

Borrowing a book from a pretty girl would be a beautiful excuse for an initial interaction, I thought. So I waited nervously for an opportunity to make my move.

To my dismay, Bacon stole my chance. "When you finish, can I borrow it?" he asked Lily.

"Can I?" I jumped in, without waiting for her to respond. My face burned, but I didn't want my rival to win. Lily nodded with a small smile.

---

2. A Chinese satirical novel about Chinese intellectuals, written by Qian Zhongshu in 1947.

I had been afraid she'd treat me with cold-eyed indifference but she did not seem hard at all. Perhaps she was equally eager for this moment, I thought.

"How about we three read together during our noon break?" she suggested. "A threesome?"

Jealousy rose in my heart, and I wanted to reject this idea right away, but Bacon nodded eagerly.

Romance was possessive, love was exclusive, so I glared at him, cursing him silently. I wanted to be alone with Lily without him hovering.

But I heard myself saying, "GOOD!"

"You can read for us, Little Bright," I heard Lily say, which pleased me. It was a golden opportunity for me to hold my affection in the palms of my hands and show it to Lily.

"1 + 2," Lily claimed, giving me a mysterious wink.

Anyway, it's better than the Gang of Four, which had included Chairman Mao's widow. The group had eventually been beaten down by Deng Xiaoping, who became China's de facto new leader.

I understood her equation, but not what it implied. Did she mean she needed both Bacon and me?

My heart drummed.

I also knew she was teasing me about my recent reading of the article on Goldbach's conjectures over the loudspeaker. When she smiled her face was suffused with sweetness. In return, I forced my lips into a smile.

During the two-hour noon break, we regrouped on the lawn behind the building. By now, the new leadership had abolished napping so we could learn more quickly.

We sat under the shade of some willow trees in a spot where Bacon and I used to hide out. When the wind rose, leaves fell on us.

"Only a leaf, not an apple," Bacon remarked, retrieving a leaf from his head and showed it to Lily, who smiled. "Otherwise, you would've discovered the fourth law of motion, after Newton," I replied with a sneer born of jealousy. "You should be in the science class, Bacon."

"Indeed, Little Bright, I now stand on the shoulders of the giant," Bacon said, still holding the leaf on his palm.

"You stood on the crown of my head, Bacon."

Lily blinked, looking puzzled.

"When Isaac Newton was sitting under an apple tree, a fallen apple inspired him to discover the law of gravity," I said, trying to impress Lily.

She seemed impressed, sending waves of euphoria through my heart. I had won! My eyes went to Bacon, who was toying half-heartedly with some blades of grass.

Lily nodded her understanding, causing a strand of hair to bounce in front of her face.

Sunlight shone down, warming my cheeks, while the noon breeze stirred the grass and gently lifted her long hair.

I opened the book and caressed the page, touching the words with my hand as if kissing the face of my fate.

"Do you want me to read or not?" I could not wait to show off my reading ability.

"Go ahead."

"Quick."

Both replied in unison.

Lying elbows down on the grass, Lily twisted her body toward me, her hands cupping her cheeks in an "I am listening" pose, her knees bent and her legs scissoring up and down, as if she were swimming in a river of joy. That was all the encouragement I needed.

I began to read.

Our hero, Mr. Fang, was standing on the deck of a steamship as it crossed the ocean, returning to China. There, he had a chance encounter with Miss Bao, and they flirted, the ocean winds blowing her hair and cooling her face. I continued:

"Embrace me," she murmured in English. "Embrace me now."

My voice was almost inaudible, my breathing became quick, and something in my throat was choking me like a fish bone. I paused, looking at Lily. She turned her head to avoid my gaze.

But I smiled secretly at the wishes of my heart.

Meanwhile, Bacon was still lying on the grass, his eyes closed. Perhaps his mind was on the deck of the ocean steamer. Like mine.

Silence fell. Time seemed frozen and my heart leapt up and down like a rabbit trying to knock open the door of its cage with its head.

The phrase "Embrace me" ran around my head like a trapped animal. My lips quivered with desire. I was in some sort of a trance.

The book, which had slipped from my grasp, was now lying open on the grass. I felt like I was alone on an island, like Robinson Crusoe.

I continued to bask in the sensual joys of my daydream until the warning bell broke my reverie and my lovely world collided with reality.

Lily jumped up as if just waking from a dream.

"Quick. Let's review some exam questions," she said, breaking the silence.

"What is the seventh wonder of the world?"

"The spine of the ancient dragon," Bacon said. "Er, I mean, the Great Wall of China."

"No legend is as enduring as the tears of the widow whose cries toppled part of that great controversial project," I said, referring to a famous folktale.

"That topic is not on the exam," Lily said. "What are the four great inventions of China?"

"Paper-making, printing, gunpowder, the compass," I said. "But wait a minute. The teachers must have got it wrong. How can we claim a glorious history of 5,000 years but have only four inventions? The ominous 4?"

"That's what it says in the history book. We can't make it more unless the textbook says so," Lily insisted.

"Something must be wrong," I said.

"The more, the better, I guess," Lily said.

"Of course. That way, we can claim we are No. 1 under the sun."

"What does idiomatic wisdom say about that mindset?" Lily asked.

"In order to cheat others, you must first fool yourself," I replied. For some reason, I felt disappointed and sad.

"We're far off topic now. Let's get back," Bacon said.

"What did First Emperor of China do after he united China?" Lily said, continuing with her quiz cards.

"He burned the classic books and buried Confucian scholars," I replied.

"What was the most popular slogan for the Party?"

"A regime originates in the barrel of a gun."

"What is the main reason for learning a foreign language?"

"To use it as a weapon and take advantage of foreign things to serve China."

Just then, the class bell rang, as if in agreement. No questions left unasked, we smiled with self-satisfaction.

After that day, the hideout became our rendezvous place. Bacon continued to bring books retrieved from his grandfather's cave and we continued to read together until the day my dream was destroyed.

On that day, Bacon had excused himself from the noon reading. My heart jumped with a thousand raptures, encouraging me to pluck the fruit of my toil. My favourite fantasy in *How the Steel Was Tempered*[3] would best fit this lovely scene.

As I read, my longing for intimacy spilled into the flow of the words.

"Beautiful!" Lily said when she heard the love story of our heroes, Pavel and Tonia. She was twirling with the strands of hair ruffled by the whispering wind. Sometimes she pressed her fingers

---

3. A socialist realist novel, also called the *Making of a Hero*, written by Nikolai Ostrovsky (1904–1936).

115

to her lips. I was utterly disoriented both by the beauty of her words and the warmth of her breath.

I paused; I told her that *she* was like Tonia, which made her smile and blush.

"You're so pretty!" I wanted to say, but I could not squeeze the words out of my mouth. I continued reading.

When our protagonist broke up with his lover, Lily sighed. "She used to be so pure and pretty," said she of our heroine, Tonia.

"A great shame."

The rising and falling tones of my voice as I read seemed to make Lily drowsy. Of course, I did all this intentionally. When Uncle Wu listened to the rise and fall of the river, he felt drowsy, so I tried to mimic the effect.

There she was, lying before me, her breasts rising up and down. My mind drifted off at the sound of my own reading. A wave of desire rose inside me. My mouth went so dry I licked my lips, wanting desperately to touch the sweet tenderness of her flesh with my hungry eyes and gentle hands.

Mind utterly blank. Without thinking I rolled over to her and kissed her on the lips.

Lily's eyes snapped open. She looked shocked, disbelieving.

She slapped my face, hard, then jumped up. "You bad egg!" she spat.

How words hurt! They hit my heart even harder than her slapping hit my face. They were like arrows. Those horrible words left me holding my cheek. My heart was wounded, bleeding in despair. My face burned with shame and anger.

Those words echoed in my head for a long time.

After that, we tried to avoid each other's gaze in class. But when I closed my eyes at night, I saw her lying on the grass. I wanted to write her a note to say, "I love you," but the idea sent cold shivers down my spine as I recalled Big Guy's note to Moon, who ran off to Principal Jia's office. Did she tell him that I sent her the note, or did she just give the note to the principal? How did she end up in the principal's bed for a "nap"?

I had no clue.

Although I lacked the courage to do so, there were moments when I wanted to say "I like you" instead of "I love you" to her face. I was thinking of her every day and imagining her returning my words with a smile on her blushing face or even "I love you too, Little Bright."

But soon that urge faded. "You're such a coward!" I rebuked myself as whatever courage I had ebbed like a retreating wave. When I thought of her, I felt pain. I was lovesick; it hammered inside my head constantly. Feigning indifference in class masked my humiliation and helped bandage my wounded heart.

Once I asked Father: "What is love?" He gave me a baffled look. I'm not sure if he was confounded by the illusiveness of love, or at my question about love. Maybe both.

In my mother's album of yellowed photographs, I noticed a young lady with long hair cascading over her shoulders. When she smiled, her cheeks were marked by two charming dimples.

No matter how often I asked him, Father never told me about how he'd fallen in love with Mother. When I pressed, he just grinned and waved the question away. Later, I filled in my father's silence with my own idea. Here is what I figured out by myself: You don't need a reason to love; love is born from the heart or, rather, from the eyes of the beholder. When your gaze is beautiful, your lover is beautified and vice versa. Whether or not that is true, I did not know. I was not so sure that love is blind, as people like to say, but I felt that love was sorrow.

Now I fell into a pit of sorrow as deep as that of young Werther,[4] if not deeper.

---

4. *The Sorrows of Young Werther,* a novel about unrequited love by Johann Wolfgang von Goethe.

Even worse, I failed some of the mock exams, including Chinese History. My sorrow dug a deep, dark pit of pain, and I jumped into it. I seemed to have lost everything including the long-cherished dream of going to college.

18

MOTHER NEVER WENT back to work after returning from the camp.

Sometimes, on dark, rainy days, she would pack up her old nylon bag, muttering, "I must go now. They awaiting me. To question me books. I didn't steal money!"

On such occasions, Grandma would lay Mama down on her bed, rush for a kitchen knife, chop on the edge of the old, battered bench beside Mama's bed, shouting "Kill you ... kill you ... you evil spirit!" until Mama relaxed and slept.

The violent rhythm of chopping that cured Grandma's constipation now seemed to work miracles on my mother's melancholy.

The next morning, when the sun rose, Mama would get up and make her way to the kitchen. She started the fire in the stove, then cooked red yams for breakfast, acting as if nothing had happened. None of us dared ask her about the day before, afraid the question would trigger horrifying and painful memories. It was better for us to bury the old memories in the dust of the past.

When Father was still at the camp, Mama would send him cartons of cigarettes and bottles of rice wine from time to time. My older sister and I asked if we could visit him, but Mama would always dismiss the idea, saying that Father was in a faraway place and that children's visits were prohibited. Eventually, we gave up.

One summer day, my desire to see my father grew so strong that I hatched a plan. I told Mama that our class would be attending a labour class in another village and would stay there for the night. She believed me. Early the next morning, at about six o'clock, I boarded a bus that travelled along a bumpy, dusty road for a good three hours to a bus depot. Then, I transferred to a bus that carried me to a remote area where I walked for another three hours along a muddy path to a small, mountainside village. People there told me the labour camp—groups of makeshift shelters that housed political contrarians—sat at the foot of a mountain.

Though I could see men working in vegetable fields, I could not find a figure that looked like my father. By now, the aggressive sun had retired behind the mountains. I sat in an opposite field, watching the trails of the reddened clouds. There was no sign of my father. I had begun to wonder if I had the correct information from Uncle Wang, when I saw a man approach from a distance, balancing a creaking bamboo pole across his shoulders that carried two identical buckets. My heart began to beat rapidly.

That man was my father.

I slid down, hiding. Father set down the buckets and stooped to spread their contents with a scoop. Shortly afterward, the wind blew in my direction and a burst of foul air filled my nostrils. I could tell right away the buckets contained animal excrement, which the people in the villages used to fertilize their vegetable gardens. Before long, Father went away, carrying the empty buckets. About fifteen minutes later, he came back, carrying the same heavy buckets and slowly walked toward the fields, his eyes gazing at the ground, a white towel on his shoulders beneath the pole.

I wanted to see my father but I dared not run to him. I don't remember how I came up with the decision to stay hidden; I only remember that I was too embarrassed to approach him. Perhaps it was because I refused to admit that I was the son of a counter revolutionary. When the sky became dark, I went back to the bus depot and slept alone on a bench for the night, like a sad old vagrant.

I never told Father that I had visited him, even after he came home. I never told a soul, folding up the hurt inside my heart. I couldn't tell whether I was ashamed of myself, my father, or my country—perhaps all of them. On the other hand, my father never told me how he survived his camp life. Nor did I dare ask.

Those years changed Father. He no longer bothered shaving and had grown a beard. The sun had darkened his face, etching bitter lines around his mouth and dark circles around his eyes, somehow evoking the hardness of the yellow earth. Harshness, stubbornness and indignation seemed to swirl around him, filling me with fear. When the excitement over the news of my family's "landowner" declassification had died down, Father grumbled, "They only changed the soup, but not the herbs." The endless monotony of his days and nights seemed to be too much for him and he was tormented by the incessant ticking of the wall clock.

His Soviet-made wristwatch had been confiscated, so when he went outside, he lost track of time. He would listen intently to the loudspeakers on the streets as they announced the morning, lunchtime, suppertime and bedtime news. It was always the same news but read by different male and female broadcasters, so the news became new every time you listened. The news became a dish we consumed at the dining table. Every time he sat at that table, he would hold a bowl of rice wine in his trembling hand, smoking incessantly and complaining about his fate.

"Why don't you seek help from your old captain?" Mama whispered to him one day.

"No—no!" he barked, shocking us into silence.

It seemed that almost everyone in the village came to bang on our back door. But Father adamantly refused to answer it. He had lost his prized wristwatch, he had lost his dignity, and he was willing to submit to his fate. But he was not willing to lose face.

"I dare not shed tears. I'm not qualified to shed tears," he said.

That was now my father. The father of my childhood had disappeared without leaving a trace.

While eating, Father would also listen to the long-wave low-frequency radio that he had bought from the Co-op Store after the sale of this new type of radio had become legal.

In those days, you would go to jail if you listened to any of the enemy radio stations; the Party wanted to protect the minds of the people from being poisoned. Father also resumed his habit of reading the *People's Daily* every morning, never missing a day.

The "new father" would yell at us for the slightest thing and slap us if we did not listen. He would also argue with Mama when a fit of rage hit him. Sitting at the dining table, he would yell, sometimes smashing his empty bowl on the ground and shouting angrily, "I've never tasted such awful wine before."

Mama never dared talk back. Sometimes, I would see her sitting on the corner of her bed, crying. If we came in, she pretended she had a severe headache, muttering through her tears, "My head killing me."

We became scared of Father when he flared up in anger; we would tiptoe around the house and speak in whispers, finding a place to hide if he became enraged.

One morning, Father stormed into the front room, yelling at my mother, "Give me a bowl of wine!"

"Not until breakfast," Mama muttered.

"No, I said right now!"

Mama obeyed.

Father sat at the table, lifted his bowl and then poured the wine down his throat. He began wailing. Mama scurried over to wipe the wine and tears from his face with a white towel, muttering, "It's all right. It's all right."

"You hear the news?" Father burst out, grabbing the towel, and pushing Mama away. "Our great leader saying the Cultural Revolution was wrong!"

My father put his head down on the table, muffling his cries with his arms. "Finally vindicated."

Sometime later, Father went back to work at the same Grain and Oil Depot in town.

At school, my "relationship" with Lily veered from strained to nonexistent, while Bacon seemed to be on good terms with her, making my jealousy surge from time to time. *I would never regret it if I could do something to make him disappear*, I thought. I wrote her a note, then crumpled it and threw it away, vowing in my head to forget her now and forever. As time went by, I did forget about Lily, although we saw each other every day in class. I had decided to force her out of my mind because my lovesickness would impact my performance on the looming college entrance exams.

About a month before the big event, the pressure began to build. We had to sit for mock exams again and again. Fear of failing weighed heavily on me and sometimes, I would panic for no reason. I could not go to sleep at night after I had written an exam. My destiny hung on my ability to memorize, which was essential to passing. For instance, you had to stuff your brain with the histories of countless dynasties and kingdoms in the country's 5,000-year-old river of glory. Most significant was First Emperor of China, who had united the warring states for the first time, while also burning all classics and killing millions of scholars.

I had carefully prepared notes in a Q & A format for each of the six subjects. As if sharpening my sword before a big battle, I put aside all other thoughts—no more thinking about Lily or being jealous of Bacon. I was amazed at the power of the human mind; when you concentrate on a task with all your heart, insignificant matters are squeezed out. When you entertain great expectations, you can skip food and sleep for three days. That was my mental state prior to the exams, and I did well during our mock exams. Teacher Dai claimed I was a good candidate for a respectable university.

One morning, only three days before the big event, my history notes and preparatory books disappeared from my drawer in class. I began to panic. Then a student spotted them in the pit of the toilet. Apparently, some bastard had stolen my exam notes to destroy my future. I was infuriated.

It must have been Bacon, I thought. My indignation grew. I went up to Bacon, grabbed his collar and, summoning my strength, pushed him to the ground.

Lily came over to intervene. When my angry eyes met hers, I almost burst into tears. I do not know why I felt like crying. Was it because of my lovesick heart? Or because of despair? Still, my tears rolled down, which softened my indignation. The next morning, Lily handed me a thick stack of notes, her eyes weary. I said nothing, accepting them silently, my head hanging down.

When I went home that day, Grandma wiped my tears with her apron.

"Fortunately, you left all your other notes at home," Grandma said calmly. "However hard you have prepared yourself, something unexpected always happens in life. When rowing down the river, you don't know when the tidal waves will roll into you. Just smile and let your boat dance with the waves of life. No need to panic."

On the eve of my English exam, she boiled ten eggs. "Ten symbolizes perfection. Eating these eggs brings you good luck," she said.

That night, I stuffed myself with six of the hard-boiled eggs, which was all I could manage. Grandma watched me consume them, encouraging me to eat more. And she was right. I should have listened to her.

The next morning, I gingerly unsealed our English exam paper, which was filled with multiple-choice questions. I still remember the first question:

The Great Cultural Revolution was a _____ movement.
    A. mess
    B. mass
    C. madness
    D. magic

I remember I picked A.

(However, the correct answer is B.)

My brain turned blank suddenly; my head became dizzy. Never in my life was I given any options, and I never could practice making choices. We accepted whatever was presented, like an unthinking child being spoon-fed. What would life be like if I was given multiple choices before? I did not know. I felt like a baby eating a bowl of rice for the very first time.

Later we were told that China had learned the multiple-choice tests from American schools and tested them at the 1978 college entrance exams for the first time in its educational history.

But my fate was almost crushed by the wheel of the history.

When I finished, I was filled with terror and, that night, I could not fall asleep. My heart was heavy, as if weighed down by a big stone. I tiptoed to the kitchen and poured myself a bowl of rice wine, drank it straight down, then went back to bed so that I did not need to think about my future, my hope, my dream.

A recurring nightmare in which I have fallen into a deep shaft haunted me again that night.

On the day I took the math exam, I felt my pulse beating in my temples. After scanning the first few questions, my brain went blank again. My heart was pounding fast, blood rushing to my head. All the formulas I had stored in the tank of my memory vanished without a trace. My brain seemed to belong to someone else, and I was trying to steal something from it. I felt as though I were falling into a dark pit, gasping for air. The image of my mother's tear-filled eyes on the rainy day when she was flanked by two guards flashed before me, her frightened words torn from her mouth and dispersed by the wind. The numbers on the paper loomed in front of my face like ghosts holding my brain steady so it could be stamped with a round red seal.

I was so scared. I felt a rush of wetness oozing out between my thighs, soiling my trousers. When I walked out of the exam room, I still felt I was followed by an invisible, malevolent shadow.

I have no idea why my mind continued to go blank but it was not my fault, nor my mother's. I pondered if memory had done something to harm my brain. I was not dependent on my brain but on my memory.

19

FATE AWAITED ME silently in October 1978 as I soldiered on upstream of the river. My life book turned to a new chapter as I entered Red Cliff College.

In the first class, Secretary Yin came in, his eyes travelling from desk to desk; he seemed to gather data from our faces to calculate the accuracy of his expectations. He spoke with apparent pride, as he welcomed us into the "cradle of the engineers of human souls."

His high-pitched voice rambled on. He spoke English with a strong accent, which offended my ears. When he said "a beautiful country," we heard him saying "a beauty-fool-cunty." Often, he placed emphases on the wrong syllables.

Without glancing at his register, he began to call each of us by name. We looked at him with our jaws dropping. This was not a simple skill. You'd need a photographic memory and the eyes of an eagle.

Within minutes, however, his accented English grew charming to our ears.

As always, I waited for the punchline. It finally came.

"In four years, you will be walking out of here, filled with knowledge, pride, understanding of your privileges and responsibilities, marching on to achieve the lofty cause ordained by the Party."

Enthusiastic clapping ensued.

Then he wrote twenty English names on the blackboard in two columns: ten male and ten female. "You need English names," he told us, "because speaking English in class is mandatory." This was an order, we were told. When my turn came, there was only one name remaining. So, I picked it, and called myself "Victor."

Our self-intros took much longer than expected.

Apparently, our newly acquired tongue was foreign to our brains. It twisted and turned untamed inside our mouths. When a slip of the tongue or mispronunciation occurred, we all chuckled. One student, a tall handsome boy named John, remarked, "I'm sorry, class, I cannot talk long like some of you, because I have a bad cough today." However, we heard him say, "I had a bad *cow* today." We all laughed at the "cow" sitting in class. John realized at once that he'd made a "cow" out of himself.

John was a coveted city boy. City boys and country boys are different in looks and accents. They also smile differently. A country boy doesn't smile. He does not look in your eyes, but at your feet, while a city boy looks you in the face, saying, "Hey, who are you?"

A fair-skinned young woman, newly named Helen, stood up. She was slim, tall, generous with her smile. From her face, we could tell she was from a city too. Her choice of words was even more laughable; when she opened her mouth to describe her feelings, she blurted in a singsong voice, "I'm happy. I'm gay. I am happy and gay."

Some chuckled, unsure, then laughter erupted from everyone.

Emotions are contagious, and you cannot help but express them. We kept laughing until tears rolled down our cheeks.

Helen blinked, blushed, but still looked confounded, unable to figure out what the heck had gone awry with her "gay" mood.

Before my turn came, I wrestled with my limited mental inventory so that I wouldn't make a fool of myself. Despite my best effort, though, I slipped too. I wanted to say, "I came from Temple County" but instead I said, "I came from temple cunt."

All of a sudden, I heard a weird silence fall in the class. They gazed around, but no one dared to laugh. Just then, the bell rang, and finally we broke for the morning.

Then, laughter broke out in the hallway.

"Little Bright? Little Bright!"

A familiar female voice called out my old name from the hallway. I turned toward the sound.

"Teacher Blue!" I exclaimed.

To my great surprise, even after so many years, I recognized my primary school English teacher immediately. The years have changed Teacher Blue, and now her face was more relaxed, and the anxiety we spotted in our elementary school class disappeared.

"I knew it was you," she said, smiling.

"I'm so glad to see you, Teacher! Are you teaching here?"

"Yes, a long story short: teaching educational psychology."

"That's great! Are you going to be our teacher?"

"Yes, for sophomores. I live at the teachers' residence. Drop by when you need help."

"I will."

"You take care, Little Bright. See you soon."

"Thank you. Victor's my new name, now."

"Really? A new child is born!"

"Not a child anymore."

"Still a child. See you again, Victor." Giggling, she walked away swiftly, as if rushing toward her destiny.

I was unsure whether I should be happy or sad when Teacher Blue called me a child. Perhaps I would always be a child in her eyes. But I wanted to be a man!

What qualities do I need to possess before I become a man? I mused.

Is it about size? Is it about age? Is it about a job? Or is it about having sex with girls?

I knew not.

Despite this, the unexpected encounter with Teacher Blue delighted me and afforded me some relief from the self-loathing weighing on my heart after my poor performance on the admissions exams. (Luckily, my math result did not count because I chose to be an English major.) I wanted to be reassured by her voice, because she had experienced her share of bitterness in the shadow of Mount Phoenix.

I had scolded myself for not performing well for the entrance exams. Now I decided to stop thinking about it and give myself over to the endless road of fate ahead of me.

Lily failed the exams. Did she blame me due to my impulsive mistake? Perhaps. Perhaps not. Maybe it was the trigger for a chain of events but I didn't care anymore. We did not even say goodbye when we left Phoenix High. Now I could only search for her smile in the recesses of my memory or in the class portrait that had been taken at graduation.

Deep in thought, I followed a crowd of freshmen to the west campus and stopped at a new five-storey library building. The English-language section was on the third floor. For the first time, I caressed the dusty shelves filled with Shakespeare, Joyce, Dickens, Hugo, Tolstoy. In the right wing was the department's language laboratory. I gently touched the headphones and cassettes. What is in the Voice of America? What is contained in the *New Concept English*? I wondered.

When we went to the second floor, we were ushered into a big conference hall with large-screen TVs mounted on the walls. I joined the group watching a Japanese film, *Sandakan Number 8*, the title of which was translated into Chinese as *Watching My Hometown*. The first foreign film shown in China, thanks to Deng Xiaoping's first official visit to Japan. Of course, all the "indecent" scenes had been cut out, as they were deemed unfit for Chinese audiences.

The translation course was my favourite class.

Professor Yang was in his early forties. He always wore a grey Western-style suit with a red tie, which reminded me of the hard-earned red necktie I wore as a symbol of honour years ago.

"When a woman is beautiful, she may not be faithful. In contrast, a woman may be homely, but she is faithful. Which would you prefer?" the professor asked the class one day.

Our professor's simple question proved to be challenging. Some hesitatingly chose the former, some the latter. After a few rounds of emotional struggling, the majority concurred that a beautiful woman is the better choice. A minority still dissented.

"Why?" the professor asked.

"Because the heart of a beauty you can change, but not the face of an ugly."

That was the best answer we could come up with.

It reminded me of the most famous Chinese dilemma. To this day, no one in Phoenix Town could provide a satisfying answer to this century-old puzzle. The riddle asks:

> *If both your mother and wife fall into a river at the same time,*
> *and you can save only one life,*
> *who do you save, mother or wife?*

We had been boxed inside riddles forever, but it is more complicated than simply solving a Chinese riddle box. We are buried alive in that box. And suffocated. I was not a smart-ass type. I had no idea how to answer.

(Many years later, I solved the old riddle by reading a book on reasoning: the riddle is a double bind fallacy that should not have been proffered!)

Then our professor chalked up Hamlet's famous soliloquy on the blackboard:

> *To be, or not to be, that is the question.*

He asked us to translate. Almost all of us rendered "to be or not to be" to mean "to exist or to die" in Chinese.

It seems that no equivalent is to be found between the two languages.

"To exist or die does not capture the connotations of 'to be.'

Death is life's twin—mortality or immortality, human existence. This is not a simple question, but a question about the human soul," the professor said.

"Can you give us another real-life example?" Sam, who sat beside me, asked. "Say, how to accurately translate Deng's reform policy of 'crossing the river by groping for the stones'?"

"Class, what do you think?" the professor said, kicking the ball back to us.

A heated discussion ensued. Many preferred a liberal rather literal translation of Deng's famous statement. Such as, to find our ways by moving forward.

"Translation is an art," the professor stated. "Sometimes, when we translate foreign concepts, there is no linguistic equivalent. Then we are faced choosing either the literal rendition of the original concept or a liberal interpretation. Something being lost in translation is a real risk. The trap is that, during translation, there are three major pitfalls to avoid. I call them the three Ds: deletion, distortion, and delusion. The three Ds are fatal in translation; it's not about semantics, or a play on words, because you create a delusion when you do not create a faithful translation. As Leonardo da Vinci stated, 'Many have made a trade of delusions and false miracles, deceiving the stupid multitude.'"

"What does delusion mean, professor?" the pimpled faced Peter asked.

"Delusion means the unshakable belief that the false is true," our professor stated. Pausing for a moment, he continued. "I'm going to give you a better example. When you sit in a dark prison, but you believe you're in Heaven, then what you believe is a delusion. This is the best way to prevent prisoners from escaping, so to speak, because they don't know where they really are. Now, class, it's your turn to give me some examples."

Our class came up with numerous examples.

When you build a sandcastle, you believe it to be a palace.

One day, a soldier journeyed on a boat, accidentally losing his sword in the river. He carved an arrow sign into the side of the wooden boat that points to the place where he lost his sword. When the boat reached the bank of the river, he embarked on his search according to the arrow sign.

One day, a farmer rested under a tree. A running rabbit accidentally crashed into the tree and died, which pleased the farmer. This is a magic tree that kills rabbits, he concluded. So he waited for another rabbit. He waited for one day. Then another day. In the end, however, no more rabbits hit the tree.

A frog that lived in a well looked up at the patch of sky he could see. "Wow, how beautiful is the vast sky," he exclaimed.

"That's called a self-contradiction," our professor said, when we cited an example of the man who claimed to sell the best sword and shield at the same time.

Change will eventually suffer a tragic end, as reform brings chaos and stagnation brings stability.

Insanity is not crazy; it's crowd wisdom.

"We've had enough delusion now. Let's move on."

Then Helen raised her hand.

"Deng Xiaoping claimed, 'No matter whether it is a white cat or black, as long as it catches mice, it's a good cat.' Professor, do you think a literal translation is more appropriate to catch the spirit of Deng's words?"

"I think so." The professor nodded. "Here, cats and mice are only metaphors illustrating two important concepts in achieving a goal: means and ends. Deng meant this: to achieve an end, you can use whatever means you desire. In other words, the ends are the ultimate goals, no matter what means you use."

I looked dubious. But Helen smiled smugly. She looked like a smart-ass.

My time on campus flew by fast.

One day, Professor Yang asked the class to prepare for the term final by reading the *China Daily* article "Joint Communiqué on the Establishment of Diplomatic Relations between the U.S. and China."

Shortly after that, Secretary Yin appeared, freshly shaved, his hair smoothly combed. He also was dressed in a new Western style suit we had never seen before. He announced three American professors had been invited to lecture on campus.

A historic event on campus.

"Did you know the suit jacket was invented in China a long time ago?" he asked. We all nodded in apparent agreement. "We have historical records to prove it."

Then, he spoke to the class about appropriate mannerisms during the visit, including dress code and conversation etiquette. "This type of academic exchange benefits both China and America. Important beyond words," he said.

"Don't be humble or arrogant before foreigners. We will teach them how to make dumplings, they will teach us how to make atom bombs." Then, he retrieved a picture of the late Premier Zhou showing President Nixon how to use chopsticks.

Secretary Yin delegated the responsibility to John, who appointed a welcome team, for the smooth operation of the great event. I was chosen for the interpretation team. My roommate, Sam, and I had to sit up late to translate the poem *Gone with the Waves,* which had been composed by the renowned ancient poet, Su Dongpo (born 1037 A.D.) after his exile from the capital to the Red Cliffs. Unlike Qu Yuan, however, Su did not throw himself into the roaring river. At the Red Cliffs, he composed a famous poem that began with these words, which I translated for our American scholars:

> *To the east,*
> *The great river flows;*
> *Gone with the waves,*
> *Are all ancient heroes.*

The poet sought pleasure, peace and satisfaction in nature while immersing himself in poems and calligraphy. For this reason, Su's place of exile was turned into the now-famous Red Cliffs Park, featuring erected stones carved with his cloud-like calligraphy.

A Dr. Smith would come to lecture to us on the U.S. presidency. On the day of the event, the all-girl hospitality team sat in the front row in the conference hall. One girl was told to leave for dressing too humbly. "The face of our whole nation would be lost before the eyes of foreigners," Secretary Yin said, reprimanding her, causing the poor girl to run off in tears.

During the Q & A session, I stood up and read my rehearsed question from a crumpled note.

"We heard that in America, which is translated as 'the Beautiful Country' in Chinese, everyone is qualified to become a candidate for U.S. president. But only rich people become U.S. presidents. Do you think Americans are hypocrites?" My voice trembled.

"That's a good question," Dr. Smith said, smiling. "Yes, you're right. No country is perfect, and we have inequalities. However, it is a fact that any American-born citizen is free to register to become a presidential candidate. *Any* citizen."

I was stricken mute by the reply and a silence fell on the big hall. Obviously, this shocked his audience. Secretary Yin, seated in the centre of the stage, raised his eyebrows. Everyone looked skeptical. The professor looked around uneasily, apparently realizing something was amiss.

What type of country would that be?

I couldn't absorb the idea that every citizen in the country had the chance to become the king or emperor. "Oh, not a king—a president," Dr. Smith explained.

We had been taught that the emperors of our country were sons of Heaven and that Chairman Mao was the chosen saviour, comparable to the sun in the sky. Could anyone in the U.S. become a sun of the sky then? I wondered.

"Does that mean all people in your country are treated as children of Heaven?" Now I rephrased my question.

"Certainly! Everyone, including you and me, is a child of God," Dr. Smith replied.

I didn't understand what he was talking about. I had said "Heaven," but he spoke of "God." But I was too scared to ask another question and I doubted that such a place existed on earth.

Sam lifted his hand and read his script.

"America has only existed for over two centuries. Your governing document, the U.S. Constitution, is believed to protect freedoms, including freedom of speech, freedom of religion, and the right to keep and bear arms. However, these widespread freedoms and so-called rights have created chaos in the U.S. and the murder rate in your country is one of the highest in the world. How can you say freedoms are good to America?"

The professor looked concerned.

"What you presupposed about these freedoms is not accurate. Freedom is a desire—like a heartbeat, pulsing in every human heart. The problems are not caused by freedoms and rights, but by other issues, such as poverty and lack of education. No one can claim America is free from social problems, but that does not negate what we have achieved because of the freedoms and rights we enjoy."

During a break that afternoon, I overheard a discussion between Secretary Yin and Helen, the hospitality team leader. The question of how to accommodate the three American professors, two men and one woman, had become a headache. They had only booked two double rooms for the three professors. Who would stay in which room became a debate. At last, Secretary Yin decided that the hospitality team should just usher the three to the doors of the rooms and let them decide for themselves.

"It's their freedom, after all," Yin said, jeering.

By now, the conference hall was alive with the sounds of laughter and English, as we conversed in that language. John led a choreographed performance of *Kuafu,* named after the legendary hero who chased the ten scorching suns. Finally, Kuafu shot down nine suns with his arrows, saved the land and its people, but died of thirst, after drinking all the water from the rivers.

I was one of six students chosen to perform the fabled *Six Blind Men and the Elephant.* I played the blind man who groped in the darkness and happened to touch the trunk of the elephant made of flanks.

"What an elephant looks like? It's like a *spear,*" I claimed.

"No. It's like a *wall,*" another blind man argued, touching the body of the huge wooden animal.

"Wrong, wrong, wrong," another blind man joined in. "An elephant is like a *rope.* If you don't believe it, touch it here," the man argued, holding the rope-like tail of the beast.

Tonight, inside the dimly lit conference hall, trapped in blindness, the six of us fought each other with arguments, like a blind lunatic yelling into the darkness. "Not fair. You can't open your eyes." One blind man cried, fumbling in the blackness.

"How do you know I'm not blind if you don't open *your* eyes?" the other blind man retorted.

For a few moments a silence hung in the great hall. But soon laughter pierced the black veil.

In our language, the word *argument* means shouting and calling names, which would be a mistranslation if you are referring to reasoning. Here, passion overrules reasoning.

"Now class, let's turn on the lights so we can all see," Dr. Smith remarked.

Dr. Smith gestured with his right hand. His hairy forearm, exposed by his short sleeves, startled us. In the eyes of the Chinese, foreigners are "barbarians." They are still as hairy as the man-like apes. Well, at least, we thought, the Chinese are more advanced after 5,000 years of civilization.

"Which blind man is right, and which is wrong?" he asked.

The weight of the question crushed the class. Everyone fell silent; no one spoke up.

"All of them are wrong," Dr. Smith exclaimed, after a long silence. "But at the same time, all of them are right."

What had been darkness was now confusion. Our minds had blinded our eyes. But I felt the clarity of vision for the first time in my life.

When we touched the body of the elephant, we thought the *wall* was the truth. When we caught the tail of the elephant, we thought the *rope* was the truth. So, truth-telling, I realized, depended on how you perceived the reality of your experience. In that sense, all humans are like the six blind men and all of us can be wrong in the process of truth discovery. Most of the time, like the blind men, we are trapped in a reality. What we see may not be the truth but instead a perception or even an illusion.

How can we discover the truth? It again reminded me of Qu Yuan's famous quote (now translated by me):

> *The road ahead is long and endless,*
> *Yet I will be searching up and down.*

That night, I had stepped into a new unknown; I had no idea what I should believe anymore but I could never again close my mind. Like a blind man who now sees, I could not unlearn.

20

ONE DAY TEACHER Blue had a question for the class. "Which dog was the most famous in the world?"

Silence fell. No one had an answer.

"Did anyone ever raise a dog at home?" She eyed us from the platform.

I raised my right hand.

"So, tell us about your dog, Victor."

"It was torn to pieces by human mouths."

My answer was flat but the class laughed.

"I'm sorry for your loss." Teacher Blue waved her hand to hush the class.

"All humans, including you and me, are like dogs in some aspect. A Russian physiologist proved that theory. His name was Ivan Petrovich Pavlov. He won the Nobel Prize because he was inspired by the dogs in his laboratory."

Teacher Blue then related the story of how something Pavlov observed led to a discovery that shocked the world. First, he noticed the dogs in his lab were salivating when offered food at the sound of a bell. Then his dogs were salivating at the mere sight of him entering the room, without food. (He had forgotten the dog food that day.) After being conditioned to salivate at the sound of a bell, the animal would then exhibit the same response to a similar stimulus.

That is exactly how human brains are conditioned to react to a triggering cue by way of association.

I was amazed by Pavlov's classic conditioning theory and how it came to affect our understanding of human behaviour. This discovery was like a window being opened, and the light invading the space began to shine in the corner of my mind.

Now, I suddenly understood why our schools used bells! The Party had learned it from Dr. Pavlov.

Thanks to Pavlov's dogs, I also began to dig deeper into myself.

By the end of the term, we were asked to submit a short essay about the childhood events that had contributed significantly to shaping our behaviour or influencing our personality traits.

I thought of what had happened during my math examination. I had reacted to the subject of math exactly the way my mother had unwittingly conditioned me to react when she had told me her misery about accounting. I believed my mother and took her words to heart. Those words then dwelled inside of me. My subconscious jumped to the conclusion that math was dangerous. So when I worked with numbers later on, I would be emotionally thrown off; I was reacting automatically, of course. Once the fight-flight-freeze response in my subconscious was triggered, my mind blocked the threats of imminent danger.

I now understand that our subconscious works deductively, rather than inductively.

Later in life, I also displayed a sort of stage fright when confronted with public opposition or challenges. What about that fear? Now I realize the fear was associated in my subconscious with a vision of my father's painful public humiliation. This is how my subconscious works. My father was exposed and humiliated before the eyes of the public when he was thrown onto the stage. At that time, my trembling feet sent emergency messages to my brain to signify imminent dangers associated with the stage and the public. Then, my subconscious concluded that being exposed in public is humiliating, painful and dangerous. Next time, once a similar cue is triggered, the fear will automatically jump out from inside of me.

In those days, I still sometimes thought of Lily at night. I thought of the rhythm of her breath, the dancing of her hair in the breeze. But it seemed like all of that had happened a very long time ago.

In my subconscious, I feared failure, rejection, or love itself. Love is a very scary thing, like a monster hiding under your bed. But I couldn't help but love the monster.

I parted ways with that monster; I wanted to escape. I wanted to avoid pain and suffering. I ran away from Lily and from myself; I'd been terrified of my own low self-esteem.

However, now I had a better understanding of my inner being.

One day the following year, my roommate Peter handed me a letter before he'd stripped the Monkey stamp from its envelope. To my surprise, it was from Lily. "You keep your heart; I keep your monkey," Peter said, teasing. "You're as inquisitive as a monkey," I retorted.

This is another General Cao moment: when you think of General Cao, he stands before your eyes.

As you believe, so it happens.

When you think of something deep enough, hard enough, something often happens, something associated with that something or someone. This is the magic power of the human brain. I couldn't wait to tear the envelope open and extract the letter from it. The letter read:

Little Bright,

How are you?
Time flies, and the day we parted was like yesterday. But the time we spent under the canopy of the blue sky became the dearest moments of my life. I know I've hurt you, for which I have hated myself for a long time. Maybe I will for the rest of my life. I beg you to forgive my ignorance.

When we were born, we were printed—like a black-and-white photo stripped of colours—pure love and innocent imagination. We thought that kissing would rob girls of their virginity and make them pregnant. I was terrorized by this thought. I carried hunger, thirst, and silence within me in those days. I'm talking about my soul, not my body. Maybe you don't understand the horror that weighed down my limbs when I struggled to spread my wings and embrace my virgin dream. The sound of your words—"embrace me"—still rings in the inner ear of my heart.

Now I am awakened, mature enough to understand: kissing would impregnate me with hope, love, dreams. And much more!

Anyway, as our English teacher used to say, let bygones be bygones. Now we can open our arms to embrace the hope of a new era.

Your old classmate,
Lily

At nightfall, the moon rose high in the silent sky. When the dorm lights were switched off, the campus quieted down. As sleep drifted slowly over the students, I seemed to enter another state of solitude.

A true secret is always buried in silence, I thought. So, I switched on a flashlight to read Lily's elegant script under my blanket, again and again.

It was then that I discovered her deeper message.

She had not dated the letter. So, did that mean it was written yesterday?

I almost burst out laughing when I realized why she was mad when I kissed her. I liked the way she said she was pregnant with new hope.

How naive was she? Or rather, how naive we were in the past. *Was she still thinking of me?*

"The dearest moment of my life ..." revealed the secrets of her heart. *Did she regret that she had hurt me so deeply?*

Yes, of course, she hated herself and she was begging me for forgiveness. *Does she want me to embrace her and kiss her now?* This part of the message was ambiguous. But she hinted let's embrace each other with new love. *Did she mean that?* I thought so. It was implied in her last sentence.

In the meantime, Peter, who was sleeping in the bottom bunk, was groaning breathlessly.

"Are you masturbating, Peter?" I asked one night.

"No, silly. It's not masturbation; it's called the iron crotch practice, like Kungfu." He practiced iron crotch every night before falling asleep, saying, "You have to master your breathing to desensitize your penis by rubbing it."

When I asked him the reason for such practice, he replied, "To increase stamina, to be more manly."

Like me, Peter was a country boy from Red Peace County, which was a mountainside cradle that had proudly produced numerous army generals, including a Vice-Chairman of our country. In Peter's eyes, I seemed to be an innocent, silly boy. When he had handed me Lily's letter, he'd joked: "From a high school lover?"

When I shook my head, he spoke, "I tell you the truth, Victor: between the opposite sexes, there is only love or lust. Nothing in between."

"Is it also true that love is fed by desire?" I fired back.

He did not care to answer.

Helen was considered a class beauty, admired by boys, envied by girls. Similar, in some ways, to Helen in the Trojan War story. John was attractive, but Peter was more skillful. There was a wager among us about who would win Helen's heart. At last, Peter won Helen's heart. Yet their love affair had been buried and turned into an underground secret.

In those days, campus love affairs were strictly against the rules, for two reasons, I guess. First and foremost, our relationship with the Party should be heartfelt and exclusive. Secondly, our studies required undivided attention. Falling in love posed a danger to both the Party and students. Private life should yield to the great cause of the Party, we were told. Violators could face expulsion. To enforce this policy, an old lady guarded the entrance to the female dormitories 24/7. A boy needed a special permit (or excuse) to enter the zone.

For instance, you could say, "I'm going to see my sister on the second floor." Occasionally, if you kept begging and saying nice things to bribe the old lady, her heart might soften. On such occasions, she would just close her eyes and pretend to doze off so that you could sneak in on your tiptoes.

The fervor of love could burn your head.

Peter wore jeans and hung his sunglasses on the neck of his T-shirt on sunny days. The rumour was that Peter possessed the luck of having two influential uncles, one in Taiwan and one who was a high-level army official in Nanjing. Sometimes, on the weekend, an army jeep would pick him up at the college entrance. Peter was the only student who wore a Western-style suit when he posed for photos. We would borrow his suit for picture-taking on campus.

One day, his Taiwanese uncle called our chancellor's office long distance to speak to Peter, but he was nowhere to be found. When the rumour spread about his wealthy Taiwanese uncle, I asked him, "Why didn't you tell us you had a rich uncle in Taiwan?"

To which he replied, "I didn't think it was worth mentioning."

What a humble guy he was.

He claimed his Taiwanese uncle was willing to sponsor him to study in the U.S. but that he would wait. Because of Helen. The rest was a secret.

"Is it love or lust between you and Helen?" I asked him once.

He just smiled mysteriously.

"If your secret is exposed, just call your uncle in Nanjing."

"Do you think I'd bother him with such an inconsequential matter?"

➤ The summer sun rose early on campus, turning scorching hot when it ascended high in the sky. The river was unusually elevated that summer and the city authority was monitoring its rise and fall very closely.

To prepare finals, I usually busied myself in the library, reviewing class notes and reading references. One Saturday, Helen tapped me on the back.

"Victor, a beauty's waiting for you outside."

Lily was standing at the entrance, wearing a summer skirt.

"May I present our handsome Victor to you!" Helen giggled as she left.

I had said a lot of things to Lily in my head, but when she stood before me, I did not know how to open my lips.

Lily broke the embarrassing silence. "Surprised, Little Bright?" She looked me in the eye. "I can find you wherever you are."

"I ... I ... received your letter," I said, returning the grin, still thinking this must be a dream.

"My family recently moved to this city, so I decided to pay you a visit."

"Congrats! Now a city gal." My heart was racing, but I tried hard to stay calm.

"I'm here now, just take a ferry to cross the river," she said, gazing down her new pair of white runners.

"I know."

"Are you going to stay in the city? I mean after graduation."

"I hope, but it's not up to me to decide."

"Who decides then?"

"Of course, it's the Party Secretary of the English Department." I said.

"You know, Bacon's studying Chinese Literature at a college near Shanghai."

"How do you know that?" I blurted, casting a cold gaze at her. Suddenly the green monster crept up my spine.

"He … he … wrote …" she stammered, struggling to change the subject after realizing the weight of the old feud. "Shall we go enjoy the Red Cliffs?"

We fell into a long silence. But our eyes talked. People say secrets are shrouded in silence, which could be open to many interpretations, either literal or liberal, or a mixture of both.

The sky was clear and lovely and the wind gentle. I could feel the warmth of her gaze, but I kept looking away. I searched for the right words, a mixture of anxiety and desire stirred inside me, which made me shudder. *Perhaps the sound of the roaring river could crush the silence and bridge the distance that has separated us for so long. And to dispel the ghost of Bacon*, I thought.

We strolled to Red Cliffs Park, which overlooks the river as it flows eastward. This was a place where you didn't need language. In the cafeteria, tourists savoured the delicate and crispy Dongpo cakes, cooked from the poet's private recipe, as much as they'd savoured the poet's wave-like calligraphy.

As we walked on the stone steps, I picked up a heart-shaped leaf.

We sat on the bench at the hilltop pavilion, watching the gulls trailing the passing ships. In their wake, the rolling waves beat against the broken rocks and the red cliffs, splashing into myriad shimmering droplets, trying to cross the river's boundary to reach as far as they could. We listened to the sound of them crashing, as if they were revealing a secret. Flocks of birds wheeled in the sky above our heads. Here, time lost its dutiful count. As darkness fell, the other park visitors began to disperse. From time to time, ships' horns punctuated my thoughts.

My mind went back to the willow tree where I had seen her lying with her hands cupped under her cheeks.

"Embrace me, embrace me," my heart murmured. But my lips couldn't move.

"Embrace me," I heard a whisper.

"Beautiful!" I heard another whisper.

I could not believe my ears; I thought I was still daydreaming. I was unsure whether I was under the willow tree or on the red cliffs.

"Embrace me," I heard the whisper again, so low only a mouse could hear it.

I was not sure if it had been Lily who had whispered the words or if it was my imagination. I turned to look at her. Her eyes were closed, her breasts heaving up and down like gentle waves. The only sound I could hear was the rhythmic surging of the river below.

Suddenly, like a rogue wave rolling joyfully high, I pulled her toward me and embraced her whole body tightly in my arms.

I smelled the fragrance of her hair again. I took a deep breath and tried to inhale all the air around me, as if I wanted to breathe her entire body into mine, then I exhaled a long, joyful breath of satisfaction.

Meanwhile, when my chin moved toward hers, my whole body began to tremble with desire. The warmth of her body sent shivers down my spine.

I looked deeply into her eyes as if staring into the depth of the sky.

I kissed her.

A first kiss! No, a second kiss.

My math improved. I closed my eyes, allowing my wings to glide toward the heart of the darkening sky. My whole body felt itself entering the white clouds above, heading for the top of the world.

21

"TO BE PATIENT (忍) is to tolerate a dagger (刀) penetrating your heart (心)," my grandma used to say. A proverbial wisdom I remembered whenever despair began to weigh down my mind. Our ancestors took up their century-old pain unblinkingly, in silence. Then they passed this great virtue down to us, hoping it would show itself. They had been waiting for so long, the mountains had turned sadly bald and the rivers wearily yellow, and the land became hunched under loads of pain. On days when I didn't need to study, I asked myself where I was headed.

To return to the town of sorrow was the last thing I wanted. And the only hope to stay in the city was to win the favour of the Party Secretary. But how? To be nominated as a triple-good student? It seemed that the road ahead of me was far and endless, like Qu Yuan's imaginary road.

"Be faithful to the Party, it holds your destiny in its hands," my father told me one day when he came to visit me on campus. Our country commanded us to achieve excellence in three aspects: virtue, intellect, and physical aptitude. I tried with all my might to follow the Party's commands. For all these years, I had been an A student in almost every subject, including politics. I also got up early to do physical exercises. Once, in a college track meet, I won the second prize in the 100-metre short track. This was a great feat for a skinny student like me; my astonishing feat shocked the whole college.

I thought I was among a few hopefuls for the year's triple-good student.

But I was wrong again.

On the night of nomination, Secretary Yin presided the meeting. "When you vote, bear in mind that red thoughts and excellent grades are the watermark," said he, his eyes scanning the class.

But how can you read the colour of people's thoughts? I began to reflect on it.

My train of thought was derailed by hearing my name uttered and put up on the blackboard. Excitement jumped inside me and choked my throat. I was nominated as were John, Rose, Helen and Sam. Then, voters declared our democracy by casting a ballot. By showing hands. Chairman Mao had been selected chairman by hand-showing. Millions of hands up in the air!

When my name was called for voting, up in the air was only one lonely hand (Sam's), which was withdrawn quickly into a desk drawer. I couldn't believe my own eyes. There must be something awry with me, or with my name.

I buried my head and closed my eyes. Tears filled, but I could not let shame drip with wet. Finally, John and Helen, Secretary Yin's favourites, won the day.

"Our democracy has spoken. A victory for our party," Yin said his final words, then left the classroom with a broad smile.

My quiet hope popped like a balloon in the sky.

However hard I tried, I could not seem to fit in; the Party still blocked me at the doorway. *I must have missed something*, I thought. *But what was it?*

One June evening, I went to see Teacher Blue, who was pleased to receive me. I sat in the chair opposite her. She poured me a cup of tea.

"How do you feel, Victor?"

Her question surprised me. No one ever asked me how I felt. Feelings and emotions were rare commodities in those days. For example, "I love you," the three sweetest words in any language, is the exclusive property of the Party. We dared not utter them to our parents in fear that the Party would become jealous and offended. If you utter them to your lovers, that will bring trouble too.

So far, no one had cared about my emotions or how I felt. In my parents' eyes, emotions are thirst and hunger, cold and heat. In the eyes of the Party, emotions are the red bricks, cement blocks, stones, and steel that our country needs to build a great kingdom.

"It's okay to release your emotions, Victor."

Do I have emotions? I had been told they belonged to capitalism.

My eyes filled with tears, and I had an uncontrollable desire to cry. Wordlessly, Teacher Blue handed me her pocket handkerchief.

In a choked voice, my tears running down like a river, I poured out my disappointment in failing to become one of the triple-good students.

"Once there was a goat who wanted to become a lion. Do you know how to turn a goat into a lion?" she asked. I shook my head. "You can't. A goat can never turn into a lion, even though he might wear a lion's skin."

"I understand the moral of the fable," I said. "But I'm scared that I'll be forced to go home after graduation. I don't want to go back to a place where time and despair stand still."

Then the sorrowful images of my deeply bruised mother and inebriated father kept playing in my mind like a movie.

"What choice do you have, Victor?" she said, heaving a long sigh. "When our country needs a brick, a brick fills a hole. Each of us is only a brick. Do you remember the vows you made when you wore that red necktie?"

"What vows?" I'd totally forgotten what I repeated on the platform when I was crowned with the red necktie.

"The vows are still in the air, Victor."

"I don't recall any vows I made. I only remember one question ringing in my ear."

"What is it?"

"How can I win the favour of the Party?"

"Now you want to turn a goat into a lion again," Teacher Blue said. "Phoenix Town is my mountain of grief too. What do the rumours say about me?"

"There were a few versions, but I don't know which is true."

"Which do you think is true? Do you know?"

I shook my head. In the middle of the desk, I noticed a framed picture of a grey-haired woman holding a smiling girl on her lap. But I dared not ask who they were, for fear of stirring up old hurts.

"Truth is not facts; truth is what people say it is. If you repeat a lie for a thousand years, the lie becomes truth. People believe it without giving it the slightest thought. Our truths are the food our ancestors chewed up, spat onto the spoons and shovelled into our open mouths. When you want to find out what's true, it's like one blind man arguing with another blind man. If you sow seeds of myth, don't expect to reap the fruit of truth." She became agitated.

Suddenly, I remembered Principal Jia, whose surname could be translated as "falsehood" in English. This realization sent shivers down to my spine.

"That's true," I said. "But things are much better now. Our country has opened the doors to reform."

"Do you believe that, Victor? Do you have faith in a surgeon who is operating on herself?"

"I really don't know. But I cannot give up hope. For me, hope is the essence of my life."

"You can't eradicate social ills by using the same mindset that created the problems. Because when you resolve one issue, you create another. If we are truly committed to changing our country, we need to build a new social system. Otherwise ..."

Seeing perplexity on my face, she opened a small bottle of black ink, then poured it into her cup. Within seconds, the water cup turned black. She poured more water into the cup.

"See it now? Look at the water in this cup. If you want to clean the water, you need to pour it to the river. By the same token, if you want to cure the muddy water in the river, you must let it flow into the ocean. You can't just add more water to the dirty water to clean the water. As a social order is mirrored in our consciousness, change must be initiated from within, not without. It is futile just to change the mirror, we need to change the face reflected in the mirror."

I nodded in understanding, adding, "How to change the face in the mirror, then?"

"That's exactly how the human mind works," she said. "Learning new things will not change your old way of thinking. You must renew your mind and change your perspective."

"To unlearn the old things first?"

"Exactly. You need to pour all the dirty water out of the cup. When Chairman Mao came to power, he wanted to build socialism. What did he do? Well, you got an A in the History of the Party: Mao destroyed the old world."

I blinked my eyes, again and again, as if cleaning the fog on a window with a dry cloth.

Still, I was puzzled.

Teacher Blue sipped her tea. "Look, the Chinese word *education* consists of a symbol of two words: *loyalty* on the left, and a *father* on the right. It literally means, 'be filial to your father.' The whole purpose of our education is to teach our children to be loyal to our fathers and forefathers. Got it now? Our people were hypnotized. Our land is now under a deep spell."

She paused.

"Most people doubt the truth but believe in lies. When you reveal the truth, they will call you a liar and spit on you because of our conditioning to believe in lies. For instance, people say time cures all ills. That's untrue. When you are hurt, that hurt will follow you wherever you go, like your shadow. When it's triggered, the old wound will open its mouth to swallow you again."

This sounded titanic to me. Now the gigantic ship did not sink to the bottom of the Atlantic Ocean, but to the bottom of my mind. I did not know when Teacher Blue came to be so profound. She must have buried tons of books in her belly. Her words resonated in my mind.

"You have a plan?" she asked, looking into my eyes.

I shook my head.

"What is the number 36 of our ancestor's 36 strategies?"

"Retreat? Or exile?" I blurted.

"Not exile, but *exodus*. You can be in exile even in your home-land. Like Qu Yuan. Like Su Dongpo. You can still move your feet when you cannot change the ground. We were told that we 'belong' to this place because we were born here. They said humans are trees and when we uproot them, we die like trees do. A great Chinese idea! One famous writer said, 'A person does not belong to a place until they are dead and in the ground.'[5]"

I nodded my head.

"Retreat is not defeat, but surrender is," she remarked. "If all else fails, retreat is a way for self-redemption."

"Similarly, the centuries-old virtue of patience, a symbol of a dagger in our heart, is a curse," I observed.

While listening, I was drifting outside what I saw as my own time and space, which were deeply rooted inside me. Out of the blue, I was being thrown into uncharted territory.

Upon leaving, Teacher Blue handed me an English novel to read: George Orwell's *1984*.

By the time I walked out, the scorching sun had died beyond the horizon. I walked alone along the poplar-lined campus path like an invisible shadow painfully resisting the crushing weight of the dark. I walked as if my body had stepped out of me. There was not a soul in sight on the path. Tonight, nothing felt the same, because now I could see my world from a new perspective. Had I just awoken from a deep sleep?

But soon I slipped into another dream. This dream was bigger than me. This dream would unleash my soul beyond the rivers, mountains, the world. The stars appeared in the dark sky, and the

---

5. Attributed to Colombian author Gabriel García Márquez.

light of the stars penetrated the dark veil, which pressed down on me, penetrating the most inner part of my being.

The summer breeze blowing in the dark felt impregnated with freedom. For the first time in my life, my pent-up soul was venturing out into the open air. How beautiful freedom was, how important it was for our souls—as important as breathing. I gazed at the sky, looking at the universe as if through a stranger's eyes, eyes that belonged to someone other than me. I felt as if I no longer belonged to this land that grounded my feet.

I thought about what Nietzsche had said: "Madness is something rare in individuals—but in the groups, parties, peoples, and ages, it is the rule."

I felt as if I had suddenly grown up. The verses I had learned in English literature class from Wordsworth's *The Prelude* filled my mind like waves slashing against the cliffs:

> *I had melancholy thoughts ...*
> *a strangeness in my mind,*
> *A feeling that I was not for that hour,*
> *Nor for that place.*

When I reached my dorm, I was still holding Teacher Blue's handkerchief, saturated with the fragrance of wild lilies of the valley.

22

ONE NIGHT, MY thinking became unbearable. Tossing, turning and sweating heavily in bed, I was tormented by the pain of my suppressed emotions.

After a great deal of thinking, I concluded that my fate was now foreseeable. To remain unchanged would be akin to political suicide: drowning myself in the river.

(Not all thinking is good.)

I could reveal what I thought publicly, but I would lose the thread of hope needed to live in this land. I did not want to live a life like an animal, or like Grandma, my mother, my father.

Is there a difference between man and animal? We have two legs rather than four. We can think and speak; without this, we would resemble animals.

We don't know who we are; our identity is still a thousand-year-old riddle—the Sphinx riddle: we embraced with pleasure and passionately admired the animal kingdom because we are identical to animals. A dog is not repulsed by its owner's poverty; a son is not repulsed by his mother's wrinkled face. As is tradition, our culture always compares us to plants, trees and beasts as an analogy to expound the so-called truths. Such as:

> *A tree's leaf falls inevitably to its roots on the ground,*
> *as do humans.*
> *(The moral: You, like all humans, are rooted to the land.)*
> *No dog disdains its poor owners; no son scorns his*
> *ugly mother.*

(The moral: You cannot escape your fate.)
It is easier to change dynasties than human nature.
(The moral: You cannot change! All attempts to change
will be in vain.)
If a king asks an official to kill himself, the official
must obey. In the same way, if a father orders his son
to commit suicide, the son must die.
(The moral: The king's subjects must live in terror
because they are dependent on his mercy.)
The fate of all good men is: they are always doomed to
be short-lived.
(The moral: It's tragic to be a good man.)

The examples ran on and on. The land where our ancestors dwelled was filled with cursed animals, wild plants and forests of spells. All these ancient spells kept pulsing through our minds and ringing the bells in our ears, for thousands of years. Eventually, your head spun, and you became drowsy. By and by, we all became spellbound.

Are humans really plants or animals? I pondered.

Am I the first desperate person to penetrate the bottom of these dreadful thousand-year-old mysteries in the hope of breaking the spells? Certainly not! There is so much that should have been revealed. So much that should have been done. So much that should have changed. However, tradition ensured no person could reveal their true thoughts publicly. Tradition is so heavily loaded with tears and blood that it had crushed the land into a cold, dark silence.

That night, I had a dream in which I turned into a dog.

Time quickly slipped through my fingers. So did space.

When my English vocabulary grew richer in size and complexity, I became more sensitive to the plots, perspectives, allegorical meanings and emotion-laden words in English novels.

One day, I happened to pick up *The Adventures of Sherlock Holmes,* and it transformed my life forever. My fascination with

Sherlock Holmes was beyond description; inductive reasoning left me spellbound. I was excited; I wanted to unearth all the mysteries facing me and my life.

Our professors never taught us induction or deduction in class. There was no such course offered at college in China. Since I knew that my grades wouldn't help me in the future, I decided to skip classes and immerse myself in the pleasure of finding mind-boggling books hidden in the dusty corners of the library. A new window opened in my mind and its morning rays lit my steps as I ascended the spiralling staircase leading to the classic tower.

Yes, life is full of mysteries. But if I could learn Holmes' reasoning, it might help me resolve some of them.

So far, my life was surrounded by hearsay, speculation, conjecture, rumours—even lies. But we called them truths or facts. For my people, facts are truths and truths are facts, fact is fiction and fiction is fact. We jumped to conclusions without examining or verifying the facts. I was like a blind man, groping his way out of the building when he hears someone shout "fire!"

In addition, there was nothing more deceptive than an obvious fact, Sherlock Holmes whispered in my ear as I began my apprenticeship.

The first light that shone on me was the light of elimination. We must verify facts by eliminating the impossible.

I heard Holmes talking to me in the night: "When you have eliminated the impossible, whatever remains, however improbable, must be the truth."

One day I asked myself: *Can I solve the "to be or not to be" question by using Holmes' inductive reasoning?*

This fork in the path made me question everything about my own thinking. To examine decisions and their correlated events. As if the first light pierced the dawn.

An example. The night before the 100-metre race at the sports meet last summer, John and his secret girlfriend, Rose, had mysteriously disappeared. Was it a coincidence or a planned escape? If I said they were escaping the world, running into the night, it would be a conjecture with no evidence. *I must gather evidence and eliminate the impossible before I draw a conclusion,* I reasoned.

How about Bacon and my notes? Did he steal and toss them into the pit? Out of jealousy? Clouds of doubt began to clog my head.

As for my roommate, Peter, I'd long had suspicions about his claim of having two powerful uncles. I'd believed him because, in the past, I did not possess the ability to think through a complex maze. Now, I had acquired new analytical tools that I could utilize to resolve this mystery.

Like Sherlock Holmes, I reasoned from back to front.

Peter came from Red Peace, known as the county of generals, and it was true that many of them were high officials in Beijing. However, not all people from Red Peace were generals or high officials. Hence, it was highly possible Peter might have taken advantage of a false assumption to fabricate a deceptive story.

My townspeople were still struggling to tell the difference between one individual Chinese and all Chinese. "One for all and all for one," the Musketeers' motto, was very much alive in our minds and on our lips.

If Peter were truly the nephew of two famous uncles, this essential information must appear on his family composition form, and Secretary Yin would have revealed this fact with pride. I still recall Secretary Yin being able to perfectly remember every person in the black-and-white class photo. He had studied the details of every student, I reasoned. He could not have missed such important information about Peter.

So far, I was pleased with my reasoning. I thought I'd made important discoveries, just like Sherlock Holmes.

I knew from personal experience in those days that America was our common enemy. If he had a brother in the U.S., most likely Peter's other uncle in Nanjing would not have survived the Cultural Revolution. This was a "you die, I live" scenario. Good and evil cannot co-exist. If Peter had an uncle who was a high official, he would have spent a long time in a cowshed, like Teacher Hu. Was it possible that his uncle was later promoted, like Sam's father? It was possible, but Peter never mentioned that when Sam told us of his father's liberation. Hence, this scenario was likely to be eliminated.

How about his jeans and the Sanyo stereo he said his uncle sent to him from the U.S.? What about the jeep from the local army office he used for his personal errands? How about those mysterious phone calls from his American uncle?

Before I could reach a satisfactory conclusion, however, I needed further investigation to verify evidence.

One more thing I almost forgot to mention: timing. When Peter boasted about his two uncles, it was before he won Helen's love. Based on my initial investigation, I inferred that Peter's motivation was only too obvious. My next step was to investigate this story further with questions and observations like Sherlock Holmes would have done.

I wanted to test my newly learned skill.

One afternoon, Secretary Yin sent word for me to come to his office. It was my first time being summoned. I became edgy. When I entered the Dean's office, a good-looking female secretary who was fitting a piece of paper into her typewriter attempted to cover the machine in a hurry.

She looked at me and said, "Typing final exam paper."

A few moments later, Secretary Yin, who had been promoted, came in.

"Hi, Victor." He pulled out a chair opposite him, motioning me to sit down. "Need to talk to you about Peter. I know you're his good friend and roommate. Did he tell you about his two uncles?"

What happened to his two uncles? I wondered. *Maybe all my inductive reasoning about Peter was wrong?*

Dean Yin then told me he just returned from an investigative trip to Red Peace. I was startled, although my suspicions might prove correct.

"Do you know anything about a love affair between Peter and Helen?" Dean Yin asked.

"All I saw was friendship but no love lost between them, I believe," I said, applying the idiom just learned in class.

All at once my old memory of the toilet incident flashed back to my mind. I had secretly reported Ear, who was ultimately expelled. The very thought this could happen again frightened me. Cold sweat began to run down my spine.

I told Dean Yin that I really knew nothing about Peter's uncles or Rose. (I meant Helen.)

"Really?" Yin cast his suspicious gaze at me.

I hesitated, but still nodded yes.

"It's a shame, Victor. You're book smart, but not people smart." He sighed.

"People smart? I don't understand, Dean Yin."

Suddenly I fell down Alice's dark rabbit hole.

"Yes, I know you don't understand. You should've had a bright future, but your talent is used in the wrong place." He shook his head. "Holmes screwed you up, Victor. Even Newton's law of gravity does not apply here in our country, let alone Holmes or Shakespeare. China has its own laws. I do recommend that you hold your horse on the edge of the steep cliff, before falling down."

"I ... I ..." I stammered.

How did he know I read too much Holmes and Shakespeare? He must have checked my library loan records. Suddenly my mind went blank; I did not dare to ask more questions; I just lowered my head and kept nodding at his sounds. Seeing my silence, the dean waved his impatient hand before my eyes, as if guarding any state secrets from leaking out.

I know it was my time to step out.

People smart? But how?

The riddle haunted me since I was at elementary school; still I was struggling to comprehend it. *Too loose, too slippery, yet too deep.* This thought sent shudders to my spine.

For a few nights, I tossed in bed, pondering Dean Yin's motive behind seeing me when he obviously knew everything about Peter. Why me? Oh, it suddenly dawned on me that he wanted to use this opportunity to see if I was loyal to the Party. That's it! That was the whole import of the meeting. Now I lost a golden opportunity to show my loyalty to the Party. Once again, good grades for academic subjects paled next to me failing the Party's test.

I had to return to where I belonged. This pained me tremendously.

Prior to the final exams, Peter stood up in class and read his confession paper, which he held calmly with his left hand while picking, with his other hand, at the pimples that blossomed on his face. He admitted that his thoughts were dirty and evil and that he had wanted to ride on capitalist waves of thought. His voice turned high-pitched when he vowed to redeem himself by sacrificing everything and going to the remotest area after graduation to "serve the Party with all my heart and mind."

Helen had changed too. Walking to the front of the class, she spat on Peter, cursed him, then proceeded to count his sins. "I have been blind," she said, her voice cracking. She appeared tormented by shame. "Thanks to the Party, I was rescued from the grip of an ugly lying beast. From now on, my life belongs to the Party. And my heart, too." Her eyes were earnestly searching for support from Dean Yin, who was sitting in the front row scribbling indecipherable notes in his notebook.

The Dean's face was flushed, betraying his feigned annoyance. I suspected his blood was boiling. At that moment, Helen seemed willing to give up everything to redeem herself. Soon, she broke into heartbreaking sobs.

The classroom turned disdainful eyes toward Peter, while a rare wave of compassion for Helen swept over us and drowned our resentment. Apparently, Helen knew how to divest herself of shame. Finally, before the hot blush had departed from her cheeks, I could see from the tender way Yin looked at her that the sight of the regretful tears rolling down her fair complexion had softened the Dean's heart and wrapped her in a protective shield.

From his gaze, I could sense the portent of my own fate. I was not sure if time could erase bad memories and mitigate pain.

Soon after that class, Helen regained her radiant glow. If we met by chance, however, she would hang her head and step sideways as if she didn't know me. As I anticipated, good luck continued to favour her. The last I heard, she had worked as a secretary to Dean Yin after graduation and later served as a political supervisor for the English freshmen.

Conformity was the pandemic of our time.

"Those who submit your will to me will prosper but those who resist will perish." Those were the Party's commandments. Life was filled with endless, difficult exams, which I failed. When I copied answers from others, thinking that they were supposed to be right for everyone, I failed. Coming up with my own answers also led to failure.

"It's the people who are the masters of China," we were told. According to deductive reasoning, however, the conclusion of the statement in the following syllogism must also be true:

> *People are masters of China,*
> *I am one individual person*
> *(and I belong to the crowd called people).*
> *Therefore, I am a master of China.*

In our language, a person (人) is not people; two persons (从) is a follower. Three persons (众) is a human pyramid or crowd, and crowds become mass (or people). The word *people* does not exist independently at all; it is like a ghostly shadow. This linguistic twist determined the destiny of our people. It was as though our life goal was to climb to the peak of the pyramid and be a man on top of all men. By stepping on the bodies, shoulders, necks and heads of the masses at the bottom. People are like sand washing away in the river of history, and I was just one grain of sand washed away in the waves, I reasoned.

How about the following:

> *All men are mortal,*
> *Chairman Mao is a man,*
> *Therefore, Chairman Mao is mortal.*
> *(What happened to Long live Chairman Mao? Are we crazy?)*

Or:

> *All humans make mistakes,*
> *Deng Xiaoping is a human,*
> *Therefore, Deng Xiaoping makes mistakes.*
> *(Can we say thoughts aloud?)*

Are the above statements true or false? I had been told that, if the premise is true, then the conclusion must be true. Then I discovered that making deductive statements is like playing God: you speak from God's perspective to declare the truth.

How powerful are these premises!

But the reverse is sadly true. By insulting reasoning, we insulted God. We murdered God by mutilating reasoning. Therefore, a universal truth does not seem true in Phoenix Town; we make our own exceptions to the rules: we make man God.

What about Pavlov's dogs? Did they appreciate deductive reasoning?

I guess not.

But most of the time, I suspect our human minds tend to think more deductively than inductively. I myself was such an example.

Now, another fragment of my past intruded at the edge of my memory. I remembered my mother's sad tears, as many as raindrops. Her eyes seemed to plead with me. "Playing with numbers is like playing with fire—they are dangerous, son. Stay away."

My mind received her whispers loud and clear. A mother wouldn't harm her son; therefore, everything she told me must be correct. Clearly, my subconscious mind worked deductively! The consequence? When my eyes set upon its enemy, my mind automatically guarded me, its master, by shielding it from attack. Our minds exercise their power without discretion to eradicate our enemies.

Bingo!

After all the events of her life, my grandma's only hope was to survive. Thus, for her, troubled times *are* life. It was only logical. My mother propped up her life in the kitchen; to cook happiness for her children was her only dream. That was her unbeatable logic, too. Both Grandma and Mother believed that fate is unchangeable and you are a victim of life, for life.

But I had been born with a birthmark. A birthright! I learned to possess a bigger dream. I refused to accept my role as a victim. I wanted to be a victor! I wanted to find myself in the lost universe.

That was my logic. My fate.

By now, Sherlock Holmes had toppled my old familiar world. I could not imagine my thoughts could ever build my world back to the way it was. However, my peers saw me as having placed myself on an island of isolation, which bewildered me. *He has lost his head!* I was beside myself. Now, here I was shipwrecked and marooned on an unpopulated island. Like Robinson Crusoe, unable to return to the continent.

All thanks to Sherlock Holmes.

23

THE EAST IS *Red* bellowed three long blasts of its horns as it cruised downstream. Standing on the unsheltered deck I craned my neck as the old white cliffs came into view. Gradually, the ship aimed its bow toward the dock. The gulls, hunting for prey in the ship's wake, glided back up to the open sky.

"The moon is always brighter in your hometown," I recalled the verse from a seventeenth-century poet. Under the moonlight, while savouring mooncakes, anything is possible, save for clear thinking, because the moon looks different in every corner of the land. Like a moonlit illusion. Emotion poses a great threat to rationality. But this bias is hardwired into our brains.

Now, I found myself bathed in the same moonlight, a place where I could remember the smell of the grass, the colour of fallen leaves, the whispers of the wind, the cries of the waves. Most of all, I missed the marinated vegetables from Grandma's old earthenware pot.

The East is Red cut its engines and slid to a silent stop at the pier. I disembarked.

Father spotted me in the crush of people. Stepping on his cigarette butt, he took my luggage with his trembling hands, smiling at me from his wrinkled face. I was saddened to see how much he'd aged in the past few years. His eyes looked unhappy and defeated.

He was still wearing the faded army uniform with a fountain pen clinging to the edge of the top right pocket. He still had his habits. "It's easier to move a mountain than change habits," so said the axiom.

"You won't need to wait until the big feast night to savour

chicken legs," Father said. "Your mother got up to start cooking before the rooster crowed this morning. Still remember Uncle Wu?"

"Yes, I do."

"He's now a deputy at the People's Congress. Uncle Wu's brother from Taiwan had wanted to visit him. The county authority granted his petition but imposed two conditions."

"What conditions?" I asked.

"First, the Town Committee had to convert the street shitholes into public toilets. Then, a pipe with running water had to be installed. Thanks to Uncle Wu, no need to scoop water from the river anymore."

At dinnertime, Grandma set the table and covered it with all my favourite dishes. The fast motion of my parents' competing chopsticks should have spurred my appetite. Strangely, however, I'd lost my passion for childhood favourites. Maybe it was the fatigue caused by staying up on the ship reading George Orwell. I tried to relax and enjoy the food.

Earlier that day, toward noon, the August sun had shone directly into my eyes through my window. After it went down beneath the horizon, the heat still baked the red earth. When the veils of night began to shroud the sky, I saw the same familiar stars dispersed and sparkling overhead. I saw the shadow of me in the moonlight.

At noon, I wanted to hear the old songs of the cicadas, but the willow trees along the embankment had been felled. In the night, I wanted to see the dancing fireflies but I waited and waited, and saw nothing but dust bouncing in the light of streetlamps. I felt like a stranger in my familiar world. The cobbled streets seemed to reject my feet. I compared the sight with my memories. The world as I remembered it was not there waiting for me anymore. *Did I change or did the world?* The place of my childhood passion had been crushed into pieces by the waves of time. I had stopped belonging to the town, but I felt relieved because I had finally freed myself from being a captive in the trap of home-bound nostalgia. I was haunted by a shadow that I wanted to reject.

"Little Bright, Little Bright!" Our front door was pushed open and before me stood a man dressed in a Western style suit.

"You recognize me?" the man asked.

I looked at him under the yellow rays of the 60-watt lightbulb hanging from the white concrete ceiling. The old wall clock was clicking listlessly. Finally, I shook my head, hoping it might shake off my embarrassment.

"Fool-the-Second," he shouted, grasping then releasing both my sweaty hands.

"Oh, it's you. You've changed. Like a different person." I was still confused, unable to convince myself that the man before me was the same Fool-the-Second who'd kissed the ass of the cow to win six rice dumplings.

"No longer called Fool-the-Second; now called Ten-Thousand-Yuan Householder," my father said as he stepped out from the kitchen to fetch our visitor a cup of hot water.

"Wow," I said, unable to think of anything else to say.

"Surprised? Before telling you my story, help me read letter."

Then he handed me an envelope and took off his jacket. "Your father said you know Japanese."

The letter was from a Mr. Yamada in Japan who owned a pearl-culturing farm. He said he saw some pearl samples at the Canton Fair that Mr. Fu—his real surname—had produced and wanted to form a partnership with him to culture and produce freshwater pearls in Phoenix Town. The letter then concluded by asking Mr. Fu to visit him in Japan to discuss this further.

(Fu literally means fortune or wealth in Chinese; this is the first time I heard a Chinese man being addressed as a mister—except our village seer Mr. Yi—that used to be a capitalist name.)

Fool-the-Second jumped up, clapping his hands, then wiped his sweaty forehead with his sleeve. He handed me a 555 cigarette, a British brand.

I shook my head.

"But I saw you eat cigarette butts before."

"Yes, I was very mischievous as a child," I replied, embarrassed.

Although not standing close by, Grandma overheard our conversation. She couldn't help herself; she had to intervene. "Doing business with Japanese ghosts?" she shouted. "They murdered tens of thousands of us Chinese. You forget?" She sounded furious.

"You still living in the past, Grandma," Fool-the-Second shouted back, presumably so Grandma could hear him clearly.

My apologetic mother coaxed her mother back to her room. After exhaling a lungful of smoke from his nostrils, Mr. Fu began to tell me his story.

When the Cultural Revolution began, he foresaw the tragic signs of his own fate, so he fled. He wandered about the coastal cities in the south with the goal of smuggling himself into colonial Hong Kong. He slept on benches in the parks. When he was hungry, he begged for food. Costal guards accompanied by angry dogs patrolled the borders with loaded rifles. If they suspected that someone was trying to cross the strait in the dark, they would shoot the escapee. He saw corpses floating in the water with his own eyes, he said.

He paused to sip from the cup and lit another 555.

"One night, I starving near to death. Hadn't eat over three days. I lay down on street bench near Luohu Customs; I could see glimpse of Kowloon in the night. I lost last ray of hope then, no longer want live my horrible life. So me thinking about how to end my misery.

"Then, a middle-aged man approached me, spoke to me in Cantonese. I couldn't understand him. So, we wrote on paper. I wrote, I starving, I want dead than alive. He bought me some food. Ate with bare hands, like wolf. Then he gave me a piece, chocolate—the first time in my life had tasted such, such sweetness. I guess freedom as sweet as chocolate taste. Then I told him how my father executed, how my mother drowned. He listened, shed tears

for me. Until then, throughout arduous life, saw nothing but coldness, hatred, on people face. People had stone heart, but this man
had heart of Buddha. His tears softened me; was one person cried
for me. Me so moved, so excited, so content.

"This good-heart man told me he leaving for Hong Kong, accept inheritance. His aunt passed away, recently, left him estate. His
aunt owned shop, sold pearl necklaces, had no own children.

"He told committing suicide is most miserable thing on earth.
'As long as you have a breath, you shouldn't give up breathing. Life
is given by Heaven, and we must not take it away with our own
hands. To kill yourself is to eat your own body and soul alive,
which is the worst thing for a human being to do.' He said he suffered a lot because his aunt. But he toughed it out. The sun rise no
matter how dark the night, he said."

He lit another cigarette and exhaled a deep long breath.

"Moved by his sympathetic words," he said. "If can see spar-
row, that is sign I should live, told myself. I open my eye, saw spar-
row perched palm tree, tweeting at me. Is my mother's soul. I cried.

"I decide continue my journey into the future, that's bravest
thing I ever done in my life. My parents would proud of me. Before
leaving, this good man gave me paper with his Hong Kong contact,
I keep as last ray of hope.

"Sealed it in plastic bag, hide it in my worn jacket. Since that
day, have never left that jacket unattended.

"In my head, chanted verse, 'If winter is here, can spring be far
behind?' People think I gone crazy. Fine, I crazy then. Who is not?
Had already die once in this world.

"Deng Xiaoping began his reign, doors opened, I thought about
my benefactor in Hong Kong. Wrote to him, he replies, ask me see
him at the Canton Fair. Following year, went to Guangzhou, I with
loaded basket of local produce. Met him, he showed me how to
culture freshwater pearls. Numerous trials and much testing, I success raised cultured pearls in our local ponds and lagoons, sold

them to jewellers in Hong Kong, Japan. Went to the Expo, showcase my pearls. Orders begin pour in.

"Then town's mayor reported my home-grown business, to county leader, audited my bank accounts. I earned lots of money, almost ten thousand yuan, but our Party volunteered fill in the shortage, made me first ten-thousand-yuan householder, as an example."

His cigarette had burned out; ashes fell on his pants. But he still held the filter between his index and middle finger. He stared at the window as though he had been talking to someone standing outside.

He fell silent.

Suddenly, I thought of his mother, Landlady Liu, who had loaned me books to read. I had an urge to confess to him that I'd reported his mother to Principal Jia. But I decided to keep quiet. I looked away in fear that he might have seen the secret on my face.

"Donated half ten thousand yuan to Phoenix Elementary, build library, rename school Hope Elementary, in honour my deceased mother," he said.

He went silent again. My heart was heavy as a rock. I did not know what to say to him. Should I compliment him, console him, or congratulate him on his wonderful reversal of fortune? I didn't know which was more appropriate now. *Silence expresses that which cannot be said and it is more powerful than what can be said,* I thought.

Nevertheless, I wanted to ask him more about his kind-hearted benefactor, but I could not utter a word, as my mind was busy thinking about what he had said. I thought of Victor Hugo's comment in *Les Misérables:* "Even the darkest night will end, and the sun will rise." In the darkest of times, there are always some pearls somewhere that shine and give light to people in despair. Pearls are beautiful and treasured, and so are the kind hearts of strangers, especially in a lost world of darkness.

That night, while I was still tossing around in bed, Father came to sit at the edge of it and said, "You know Uncle Wang finally received retribution?"

"What?"

"You know Steel was called to join the Sino-Vietnamese War? A coward, this bastard! Like father, like son." I heard his teeth clanking.

"What're you talking about, Dad?"

"Let me tell you slowly." Father lit a cigarette and continued: "When Steel came back from the War, the Party issued him a Certificate of Gloriously Wounded on his wall. But it soon turned out the guy was coward."

"How so?"

"He shot his own leg in order to avoid fighting in the front. When this came to light later on, the Party withdrew his certificate and sent him to jail."

There was a lengthy silence.

"You still think Uncle Wang betrayed you back then?" I asked.

"He was only one I shared my secret. Save for your uncles."

I'd not heard from or seen my uncles in years. Several years ago, I heard they had declared to the Party that they had severed all ties with their mother—my grandma—and my family. Was it possible that my uncles had reported Father to the Party to protect themselves? In those days, all things were possible. I heard stories about children publicly denouncing their parents, severing their ties with their biological parents, and accepting the Party as their guardians.

I gave up on the sudden urge to play Sherlock Holmes the second it occurred to me. I did not want to excavate the dusty earth of the past, to ring the bell of my desires just to solve a mystery. Nor did I want to be permanently haunted by the old hungry ghosts who wanted to possess us. I would just be reopening old wounds.

"Dad, it's no use going back to yesterday, because yesterday does not exist anymore," I said, yawning. "Tomorrow's going to be another sunny day."

Those words were the best medication I could have prescribed to Father and myself at that point in my life.

The wall clock chimed twelve times. Slowly and relentlessly.

In our language, the sense of time does not exist on earth. The sun never gets tired; the moon never gets old. Time chimes only in our head; it is only a remembrance. Time is a misnomer. When we say "Do you have the time?" we meant "wristwatch," like my father's confiscated U.S.S.R.-made timepiece. Time was invented and created by human minds. Our will is the force behind the movement of time. If we can kill time in our minds, there is no time; it is empty without our thoughts. It is us. We die; it dies. After all, time is a die-hard illusion.

24

ALTHOUGH IT WAS still early when the rooster crowed for a third time, I knew it was time to get up. I decided I needed a tour of my old memories before the streets got crowded, so I dragged myself out of bed. Outside, the belly of the sky began to turn red.

I strolled along Main Street in search of the past. A small crowd stood scattered in front of a brick house recently renovated with a new left wing. Walking closer, I saw a dozen townspeople burning early-morning incense before an altar, leaving eddies of smoke dancing in the air. One elder lady prostrated herself before the altar while holding a bundle of burning incense with both of her hands, murmuring something I couldn't hear. A traditional yin-yang egg hung on the front door of the brick house, symbolizing the harmony between female and male. It was the house of the fortune-teller Mr. Yi, I suddenly recalled. Yi means change, as I now understood. It originated from the classic *Yi Jing*, or *I Ching*. Still, I was startled that his once illegitimate trade had come alive and was a well-to-do business today. An urge to meet him rose inside of me, so I joined the lineup outside his house.

When an old man emerged, a young lady approached anxiously and asked: "Dad, Mr. Yi find our pig?"

"Yes, he said the beast wandered off to the valley. Let's hurry."

After a while, a giggling young couple came out. The man, holding the woman's waist with one hand, was gently stroking her bulging belly with the other.

Then it was my turn to enter.

Clad in a long black cloak, the bespectacled Mr. Yi signalled me to sit opposite him at a round table covered with a cloth.

"What wind brought you here, young man?" he asked.

"Please read my future, Mr. Yi, as you did for me when I was born."

"Did I?" He eyed me for a few seconds and closed his eyes.

"About twenty years ago?" he asked, opening his eyes.

When he saw me nod, he paused and closed his eyes again.

"Eagles belong to the sky, tigers crouch in the mountains, snakes hide in the bushes. But you can change the unchangeable if you are willing to change your fate." Mr. Yi opened his eyes and grabbed both my hands firmly. "Welcome back, Little Bright."

Amazingly, he still remembered that I was born in the Year of the Tiger. After so many years.

How he found out who I was I did not know. Suddenly I felt a mysterious power pulsating inside my body, leaving me speechless.

He resumed: "As a river flows uninterrupted to reach its goal, the superior man walks in lasting integrity by carrying his purpose in his heart."

I was baffled. "What ... what do you mean, Mr. Yi?"

"What's the fate of a river?"

I shook my head and cupped my cheeks to hide my embarrassment.

"You'll need to search for your own answer. But one last counsel. Don't lie on bed thinking of your fate, think FROM your fate."

"Is there a difference?"

"Yes, like night and day. When you think of your future, you are daydreaming; when you think *from* your future, you are in the future, in the spirit, in the faith."

Still, I looked perplexed, unable to comprehend the deeper meaning buried in his words. Mr. Yi simpered. Obviously, he had anticipated my confusion. I thanked him with a donation, then rose to leave, as the crowd outside had already grown impatient.

Walking in the street, I ruminated on Mr. Yi's riddle-like prophesy. The thought of the Sphinx riddle suddenly struck me. Every human would pass before the beast. If you don't have your answer ready, you will be devoured. That is the tragedy of life. Now I seemed to understand the allegory of the twists of fate in Sophocles' *Oedipus Rex.*

Just then, I heard the screeching of wheels. I turned. A green jeep halted beside me. A handsome young man jumped off, shouting at me, "Little Bright, Little Bright!" It was Bubble, my childhood friend.

"What brings you back?" he asked, smiling.

"Eastern wind, I guess."

"No. It's the west wind that's now blowing."

"You're right, Comrade Mayor. Oh, no. Honourable Mr. Mayor." I chuckled.

"You remember our old friend Ear?" he asked.

"Of course."

"Let's go see him. Hop in." He waved for me to get in his dusty jeep.

He asked me to hold the bag on the passenger seat and we drove off.

"Where's Ear?" I asked.

"Sleeping in the mountain."

The jeep turned onto a dusty, unpaved road leading to the mountainside.

Bubble was silent, only nodding or shaking his head to answer my questions. He smoked a cigarette as he drove. Some twenty minutes later we stopped and he took back the bag. We walked toward the tombs halfway up the mountain. A bad feeling climbed up my spine and worked its way into my brain.

We pushed aside the thistles and stepped through the overgrown bushes, finally stopping before a tombstone with an inscription, *Home of Aiguo*. Aiguo literally means "loving my country."

We always used his nickname and I had almost forgotten his real name, Aiguo. Then Bubble, through his tears, told me what had happened. Ear had been a diligent worker at the cement factory in town. One day, when he was working at a quarry, the foreman ordered the workers to evacuate due to an impending explosion, but Ear did not hear the order. The mine exploded and caved in on him.

Bubble choked, unable to continue. I burst out crying, my tears streaming down my cheeks. Bubble patted my shoulder. Using his teeth, he bit open a bottle of liquor and poured half of it on the ground in front of Ear's headstone, then drank a mouthful before handing the bottle to me. Unthinking, I poured the liquor down my throat.

We huddled while I cried. "I'm sorry. I'm sorry, Ear. Please forgive me." My tears ran into the corner of my mouth. They tasted bitter. "I killed Ear, Bubble."

Bubble looked at me, puzzled.

"I told on Ear about the toilet newspaper and he was kicked out of school forever," I said, sobbing. "I killed him! If he had attended high school like us, he wouldn't have been working in the quarry."

"Not you, Little Bright. It's fate," Bubble said, sighing. "We are all victims of fate."

"But we can *change* it."

"We can only change ourselves. Not fate. No one can." Bubble shook his head.

I said nothing.

By then, the sun had risen high above the mountains. The wine on the ground began to evaporate quickly. Ear seemed to have overheard our conversation. Perhaps he was glad that I had confessed and asked for forgiveness. He drank up all we offered him.

The following evening, our old classmates were to be reunited at the Heavenly Eatery, a place close to the new market where the street vendors now assembled. Red had managed this restaurant since her brother went to prison. In the front hung a plaque with three words in golden embossed calligraphy: *Eating is Heavenly.* Beside the door frames were two posters with red-coloured writing:

On the left: *If humans cannot care for themselves*

On the right: *Heaven and earth will perish.*

Inside, teapots, cups, and china bowls were laid on wooden tables draped by a white cloth. Near the entrance, bikes stood in a horizontal line—brands like Everlast, Phoenix, Flying Pigeon. I paused in front of the menu affixed to the window:

Heavenly Eatery

10-COURSE MENU SERVED WITH WHITE RICE

1. *Leaping to Affluence (ten fried green frogs)* ¥5
2. *Spirit of Pigs (one BBQ baby pig)* ¥7
3. *Dragon Crossing the River (snake stew)* ¥5
4. *Buddha's Choice (fried tofu)* ¥3
5. *Hundred-Year Longevity (stewed turtle)* ¥7
6. *Wings of Dreams (ten chicken jaws and wings)* ¥6
7. *Everlasting Abundance (one sweet and sour fish)* ¥5
8. *Kuafu Chasing the Sun (ten 100-year-old preserved duck eggs)* ¥2
9. *Groping the Stones (ten fresh snails)* ¥5
10. *Ten Perfections + Ten Beautifications(pork over chives)* ¥6

CHOICE OF ALCOHOL

Bottle of Yellow Crane Tower Spirits ¥3
Bottle of Chinese-German Beer ¥1

While I was still studying the menu, a female voice called my name. It was Red, wearing a pink T-shirt over a white flowery skirt. Two smiling dimples still adorned her cheeks. Her ponytail was gone;

instead, a headful of long hair touched her shoulders. Her eyes shone but showed shadows of sadness.

"Long time no see, Red." I grabbed her right hand and felt calluses. I did not ask about Uncle Wang or her brother. She sat me down at a big round table in the centre of the room and poured me a cup of green tea.

"Why did you call it *Heavenly Eatery*?" I asked.

Her eyes reddened and filled. My heart sank, not knowing what to say to comfort her.

"My brother named it." She wiped at her tears. "He was a fan of *The Journey to the West*. He said Heaven is the mind, the earth is the body. The Monkey King is a symbol of the monkey mind, the Piggy, our flawed body."

"I'm so sorry about Brother Steel."

She nodded, biting her lip.

"Are you married?" I asked without thinking, but immediately regretted it.

She bowed her head, blushing. "I was betrothed once," she murmured, her eyes still filled with tears. I was embarrassed. The old days had fallen into the river, gone with the waves.

Just then, fits of loud laughter burst through the door. In came Bubble, followed by Big Guy.

"Hello, Little Bright. Welcome home." Big Guy came up to hold my extended hand firmly.

"Your hand grew bigger," I said, half-joking.

"Yes, we need big hands to open the doors of our country," Bubble said, laughing. He then drew out a pack of Great China cigarettes and offered one to me.

"I don't smoke."

"We're all uneducated commoners, except you." Bubble handed out more Great China to the men around him. Big Guy clicked open his lighter, lit Bubble's first and then his own, then puffed out a deep sigh.

"Little Bright, you remember the days when we inhaled Flying Horse cigarettes together while sipping rice wine and reciting poems beside the river?" Bubble asked.

"How could I forget?" Then I cleared my throat, assuming a boyish voice:

> *I live near the Yangtze's head,*
> *You reside at its tail,*
> *Day after day I pine after you,*
> *Only knowing we drink the same Yangtze water.*

"Then you peed into the waves," Big Guy said.

We all laughed. Red clapped her hands, breaking into a big smile.

Big Guy continued: "Chairman Mao used to smoke Great China. Remember the picture of him dressed in a bathrobe on the deck of a boat, holding a Great China between his fingers?"

Heads were nodding.

"Do you think the newspapers told us the truth about him swimming across the Yangtze? People said that never happened. He just dipped into the river for a while, then smoked on the deck," Big Guy said. "How stupid people were in those days!"

"We all were," Red said.

"Things are different now," Bubble replied. "The Party required us to liberate our minds and open the door to reform. Soon, China will leap into great affluence. Cars will be like streams flowing on the streets. We will eat bread, drink milk, say bye-bye to the bowl of porridge and pickles."

We felt the heat of excitement in the air. Those old days were gone with the waves. Soon, our urge to unearth the truth about our past subsided. Most of the time, you need to bury the truth; it is too painful to dig it out.

By now, ten perfect courses had been laid out sizzling and hissing on the table. Bubble offered a toast and proposed that we meet here again in ten years. "It's fun to talk about our past—to see what our future will be like." We all applauded, then drank up our first round of Yellow Crane Tower. When another round came, we all emptied our cups again without hesitation. To toast our future happiness.

Then another round came, to toast love and fortune.

I hesitated; my head had begun to spin.

"No, Little Bright. You have to empty your cup today," Bubble insisted. "We're so happy to be reunited, after so many years."

"If he can't drink, just let it pass," Red said, coming to my rescue.

"That's not in line with tradition," Big Guy said. "Remember the saying of our ancient saints? 'If you drink with a close friend who knows your heart, even a thousand cups of wine are not sufficient.' Come on, Little Bright."

If I protested again, that would be too embarrassing. So I drained my cup. Red used a spare pair of chopsticks to fetch some dried fish for me. I ate a mouthful, pleased she still remembered my favourite dish. But the fish was tasteless on my tongue.

Just then, a young man appeared from the kitchen, gingerly holding a rice bowl. "Who wants the vinegared snake bile?"

"Little Bright! Our honoured guest today," Bubble said.

"No. Not me." I pushed away the bowl.

"Still a coward, Little Bright?" Big Guy grabbed the bowl, then gulped it down. "My eyes are now opened, to see the unseen." He chuckled, wiping his mouth with the back of his hand. "Come on, Little Bright. You didn't have a chance to eat those green frogs when you were away."

"People say what you eat is what you become," Red said to me. "You can change your mind, or your heart, but you can't change your stomach."

I flushed, believing she was seizing an opportunity to chastise me. So, I changed the subject. "Do you guys know Big Guy's big secret?" I winked at Big Guy, who seemed puzzled at first, then laughed.

"You promised, remember? You said you would guard it for the rest of your life, Little Bright."

I laughed, too. Who was not guilty of enjoying guilty pleasures?

I still remembered the night when we ate frogs at Big Guy's house after labour class. But I lost my appetite. "No, no. I eat eggs and tofu," I replied.

"If we drink milk every day, do we grow white, like white guys?" Bubble asked jokingly.

"Confucius said all humans are the same, despite differences in habits," Red said.

"How come Chinese are so different from Americans, then?" Big Guy asked.

"Because we find pleasure in our stomachs, they find their happiness in their dreams," I said. "We have no stomach for their hot dogs, and they have no stomach for hearts that once belonged to pigs. We eat different foods; we think different thoughts."

"Americans eat dogs too?" Red asked.

"They eat man-made dogs, fake ones, silly," Bubble declared.

"In terms of thinking, I learned that Westerners use the left hemisphere; they call it intellectual thinking. We often use right-hemispheric thinking, known as intuitive thinking," I said, unable to resist showing off my knowledge.

"Too complicated." Big Guy shook his head.

"Remember seeing the TV series, *Man from the Bottom of the Atlantic*? Caucasians and Chinese seem like two different species," Bubble said, puffing on his cigarette.

"It's called *Man from Atlantis,* Bubble. Atlantis is a legendary, lost empire," I said.

"Same to me," Bubble said.

"What's the grand plan for our town, Mr. Mayor?" I asked, trying to change the subject.

"The government has approved the forming of the cement factory joint venture with Taiwanese investors. I've nominated Big Guy to hold a position as a vice director. I've sent our proposal for the expansion of the freight wharf. In a few years, you may not find your way home," Bubble said, draining his wine cup.

"Is it good or bad if we cannot find our way home?" Red asked.

"Of course, it's good. It's called reform. To change is to turn the heavens and earth upside down, we've been told," Bubble said, exhaling his Great China.

Swirls of smoke spiralled before us. Out of habit, Bubble began to purse his lips, skillfully blowing his Great China into proud swirls of circles chasing and dancing in midair.

"Congratulations, Big Guy, let's empty our cups." I proposed another round.

Big Guy was all smiles. Draining his cup, he said, "We've had enough politics today."

"You may want to escape politics, but politics will come after all of us," Bubble said.

This was so true! I thought.

"Little Bright, tell us about your girlfriend." Big Guy grinned, chewing some pork.

"Girlfriend? Who told you I had a girlfriend?" I said, stuffing a spoonful of eggs into my mouth. But in my mind, I was thinking of Lily. I did not even say goodbye to her when I left the city. Since she was a city girl now, I should return to where I had belonged without bothering her anymore. (In those days, country boys were belittled and despised everywhere in the country.)

Bubble shook his head, disbelieving. "Come on, we're all grown-ups now. Don't keep secrets from your old buddies."

"Red, are you still single too?" Big Guy said.

"You're drunk, Big Guy," Red snapped, pretending to be mad.

I blushed, too. My mind flashed back to the most joyful childhood moment. *Does Red still remember our vows at the beach?*

Suddenly, I thought I needed to provide some explanation to Red. "I was too busy studying. Love affairs were prohibited at college. Moreover, I'm still uncertain about my future."

"Aren't you going to teach at No. 1 High?" Red asked.

It seemed she was less interested in my words than in my inner thoughts.

"Yes, but I don't know whether I can fit in there."

By now, I felt dizzy and intoxicated. My head swirled. Red refilled my cup with cold tea to refresh me. A yellowish dog, busy chewing on the bones underneath the table, lit up a distant memory. I bent down to pat him. He sniffed my hand, then growled.

Obviously, he failed to sense familiarity. I suddenly felt like a stranger in my familiar land. Everything seemed to have been turned upside down. Of course, I did not bemoan the reversal of the blowing wind. However, I was afraid that we would be thrown overboard again if we were threatened by another sudden onslaught of changes. We had been ruled by someone who had groped for his way around the stones in the river. When this country was under Mao's reign, our people regarded him as the red sun of the East. A saviour. Today, our people still looked at him with awe, a source of wisdom. *What would happen next?* I wondered, as though I were reading the plot of a Sherlock Holmes novel. There were depressing signs of the future of this land. Without vision, a nation perishes. Without dreams, people slumber. The little boat that carried us in the river is at the mercy of the waves and winds. The rosy and promising future is fatally flawed, as Teacher Blue pointed out. *Am I troubled by our ancient philosopher's worries and Qu Yuan's riddles?* Yes, but I am more worried about how to live a normal life.

I was asked to join my cohorts in singing karaoke or making a foursome at a card game or mah-jongg table, but I declined. It seemed we could freely choose the enjoyable pastime. But I seemed to be a living relic fallen out of time, wrestling with the change of the moon.

"Little Bright, now an engineer of the human soul, let's ask him to give a speech to conclude our dinner today," I heard Bubble saying while I was still lost in thought.

I did not know what to say. After a moment, I stood up, holding up my wine cup. "I have only three words to share with my friends: Life goes on." And then added: "Like the river."

Just then, my mind took a trip back in time: Principal Jia, Master Fu, Landlady Liu, Ear, Moon ... all were coming back to the dining table.

I drained the last drop of wine from my cup.

25

WHEN THE BELL buzzed, classes began.

At 9 a.m. on the sports field, all the students assembled for a public meeting. On the platform, banners bearing slogans with big, bold characters hung high. The students were seated in rows on the ground, surrounded by crowds of adults. They had come to watch the prosecution. A military truck screeched to a halt close to the brick stairs leading to the platform. A dozen men, handcuffed and clad in yellow prisoner uniforms, were pushed off the truck by the stone-faced soldiers carrying rifles.

Just then, a stern male voice began to shout slogans from the loudspeaker. The students repeated the shouts, throwing their right fists high in the air.

"Execute the criminals!"

"Restore social justice!"

Amid the echoing cries, all the handcuffed men began to shake—one tall man looked more terror-stricken than others. Holding a microphone, the Chief of the People's Court in Temple County announced: "Comrades, Teachers, and Students, today we are here to answer the call of our great leader to crack down on the criminals in our county. The People's Court has rendered verdicts for all the criminals standing on the platform. All shall be executed today for the crimes they perpetrated. Those crimes include manslaughter, rape, robbery, assault, vandalism, theft of public goods."

Then, the name of each criminal was read out. As his name was called, the man, shaking like a leaf and flanked by two soldiers, knelt at the front of the platform, his head buried in his chest. The Chief then listed the man's crimes one by one.

I stood amid the multitude watching the show as a theatrical offering. My feet were unsteady too when I saw those men returned to the truck and driven to their execution.

Those who had been standing began to disperse. Some chased the departing truck to the execution ground by the river.

On the ground, the silent students remained seated, anticipating a speech from the school principal. A bespectacled man in his fifties scurried to the platform and shouted into the microphone: "Teachers and students, today the Party has taught us a good lesson. All people must obey our laws and orders. If you dare to violate these laws, you must be punished and executed. Ours is a country ruled by law, and we cannot allow criminals to destroy our social order. Students, never forget today's lesson."

The man was Principal Ren.

I was totally shaken by what I had seen and heard, realizing I could stand it no longer. I began to smell gunpowder in the air, which made me retch. I slipped away amid the shouting. I shut myself in the darkness of the teachers' dormitory, and it took me some time to stop trembling. That night, I was haunted by the same nightmare where I kept falling down a dark shaft into a bottomless pit.

The following morning, mists clouded the surface of the pond surrounded by willow trees, their long thin branches dancing in the morning breeze. Birds were chirping on the trees. Wild ducks swam in the pond in pairs. Under the trees, some students were holding books and I could hear them reading English.

The morning breeze ruffled my hair, cooling me down while I waited outside the classroom. When the bell rang, I faced 50 pairs of probing eyes. I was nervous. My right hand was shaking when I wrote on the blank blackboard:

Lesson One: I Have a Dream

I had studied Dr. King's full speech at college and had memorized it. Now, I was teaching an abridged and edited version. I'd noticed that any reference to "the Lord" or "God" in the speech was deleted from our high school textbook. For instance, the glory of God was neatly replaced, and "God's" children became "our" children.

"Has anyone heard of Martin Luther King or the American Civil Rights Movement in the Beautiful Country?" I asked. As I had been taught, when I said "America," I literally spoke of "a beautiful country" in our native language. Silence fell over the classroom. Then I heard the rustling sound of pages being turned. Finally, some students nodded; others shook their heads.

So, I gave an intro and kept it short.

"Before learning the words and expressions," I said, "let's try an interesting experiment." I then took a jar containing a syrupy substance out of my bag, placed it on the desk together with bundles of disposable spoons, and asked the class to line up to one side.

The procession went past me slowly. Every student's face was filled with curiosity. The first female student licked her spoon gingerly after scooping it into the jar.

All at once, she jumped with joy, shouting: "It's honey!" Then the whole class erupted with delight.

Watching the last student as he sat down, I related my story of the bowl of bitterness at Phoenix Elementary. They all laughed. Then I told them about the Jewish tradition of having students begin their very first class by licking the Hebrew alphabet coated with honey from the blackboard.

"To acquire knowledge is as sweet as licking the honey off the spoon with our tongue," I said. "We can use our knowledge to build a better China."

The class sizzled. Then I asked students to read the passages after me, with banned words being stricken through and replaced:

> With this <u>plan</u> ~~faith~~, we will be able to work together,
> to <u>play</u> ~~pray~~ together, to struggle together, to go to
> <u>work</u> ~~jail~~ together, to stand up for our <u>land</u> ~~freedom~~
> together, knowing that we will be <u>strong</u> ~~free~~ one day.

"What is your dream, then?" I paused to ask the class.

Once again silence descended on the classroom. I glanced at the first name on my list and called out, "Stone?"

A boyish-faced fellow stood up from a row in the middle and said shyly, "My dream is to attend university."

"And what do you want to do after university?" I asked him.

"I ... I ..." Stone shook his head, his voice dwindling to a whisper. He lowered his gaze. "I ... don't know." His face blanched. He looked hurt by my question.

All breathing had stopped; the class was as still as death.

So, I called the last name on the list, "Summer?"

"That's me." My eyes searched for the source of the female voice. A girl with large wide-set eyes stood reluctantly. I repeated my question. "I don't have any, teacher. I just do what my mom tells me."

Amid explosive laughter, Summer retook her seat and dropped her head before casting her gaze back up at me. She looked pleased with herself.

"Without dreams, people perish," I said. "Now it's time to dream a new dream."

The laughter stopped dead. Time to assign some homework, I decided. I asked my students to write a 300-word essay in English that answers the following four questions, which I wrote on the board:

> What is your dream?
> Why is it important to you?
> How will you make your dream come true?
> When will you take these steps to realize your dream?

The bell buzzed again, signalling the start of my next class.

No. 1 High held a weekly teachers' meeting in the conference hall on Saturday nights. As usual, Principal Ren presided, along with the Party Secretary. The room soon filled with cigarette smoke.

Coughing was heard from here and there along with shouting and laughter. Huge swirling fans hanging from the ceiling cast shadows around the conference room. I sat in the corner close to the entrance, sweat dripping from my forehead. The long-haired Moon sat beside me. She bent down to continue reading Jin Yong's *The Heaven Sword and Dragon Sabre*. She had developed a taste for the fantasy martial arts thrillers produced in Hong Kong.

Moon, my childhood friend, had moved away from Phoenix. Now, she had graduated from college and had returned before me to teach English at the school. She had helped me settle in and gave me countless tips on how to conduct myself. A few days ago, Moon had quoted her favourite mantra from Jin Yong for me: "Slay the dragon by using a dragon slayer. If you have this powerful weapon under your command, who dares to disobey your order?"

I had no inkling what she was talking about.

The principal spoke first. After clearing his throat, he said: "Tonight, I'm going to address two important events that occurred during the past week.

"A student named Stone composed an essay that shocked our school community. The essay was written from the perspective of the mother of an executed criminal. He wrote that he shed pitiful tears when she had to pay for the bullets that killed her son before she could collect his body from the riverside. We must take this issue seriously. We need to understand the hearts and minds of such students; what do they stand for? Our school must take immediate action to cleanse these crocodile tears. If we are too lenient, the viper will bite us once it comes to life in our bosom."

Then the Party Secretary called on all the teachers to devise plans to correct the thinking of such students. Being expelled from school remained an option if the student's mind was unteachable. After all, the teachers agreed that our country needed no such successors.

Suddenly, I remembered the boy named Stone who had been the shy student in my class.

"We have another, equally serious issue," Principal Ren said. "There are rumours flying around that a new English teacher called America 'a beautiful country' in class and said the moon in America is brighter than the moon in China. In addition, he asked his students to dream an American dream. What's more ridiculous, this young teacher encouraged his students to lick honey from a spoon in class."

Laughter burst out from the audience.

Moon, who had been listening, poked me gently with her elbow. My face flushed. It took no time for me to realize that I was that new English teacher.

I had been found guilty!

The Party Secretary said: "This is a serious violation of the classroom conduct prescribed in the *Teachers' Guide*. We cannot turn a blind eye to this and will treat this matter seriously."

There was loud buzzing in my head. I do not remember any of the discussions that followed. When the crowd dispersed, I followed Moon mechanically to the teachers' dormitory and then went straight to my room.

I did not sleep well for days because I was so worried about my future at school. *Are they going to kick me out? If so, where will I find a job?*

The following day, word was sent for me to go to the Principal's Office forthwith. I mustered the courage to face Principal Ren, armed with an already prepared self-criticism essay. The principal's face was immobile. But when he opened his mouth, his face turned plump and flabby. It was as though he had two faces. After sitting down at the opposite side of his ping-pong table, I first apologized for making such a mess in class. Then I explained that I had only been applying a pedagogical method I'd learned at college. I paraphrased the famous educator, John Dewey, by saying: "Students will thrive if allowed to experience and interact with the curriculum."

"Excuses, excuses," he said, pursing his lips. His yellowed teeth shone dully under the slanting sunlight entering from the windows.

The weight of his authority bore down on me. My body shook in a cold sweat and I'm sure the terror was visible in my eyes. I could feel the colour draining from my face under his scathing gaze.

"Did you know John Dewey was an opponent of the Montessori child-centred method?" his surly voice asked.

Afraid to meet his eyes, I shook my head, feeling foolish.

"Young man, of course, you don't know. You have lots to learn. You should not follow John Dewey. Let me explain: If you follow the Party, you will have a bright future in China. China has a unique culture with a history that is five thousand years old. We learn from foreigners only to conquer them. We will never forget how the eight allied forces burned down the Summer Palace and how the foreigners humiliated us by enforcing unfair treaties against our will and weakened the sovereignty of our nation."

Finally, he said: "I am speaking the truth."

I was totally confused by his truth and wasn't sure how to respond. His familiar words had taken me back to the era of the Cultural Revolution. Now I understood what Lu Xun, the leading figure of modern Chinese literature, implied in his short story *Kong Yiji* about the four layers of meaning in the Chinese word *hui*, which means to return, repeat, go around, circle.

"You must follow the *Teachers' Guide*," the principal said. "Any deviation will no longer be tolerated."

His voice rang in my ears for a long time.

Before leaving, I bowed to the principal and vowed to accept the Party's criticism and to obey the rules of the school. When I returned to my room, I located the *Teachers' Guide for Senior High English* that had been given to me when I reported to the principal's office on my first day. Under the heading "Important Teaching Tactics," it said: "Provide guidance on how to adapt foreign concepts to serve China; Focus on what to think, instead of on how to think."

Under "Pedagogical Tips," it read:

"Americans are deeply oppressed by the ruling class. Only white people have dreams, and the black and poor people live in deep misery."

Recommended reading: *Uncle Tom's Cabin, The Little Match Girl.*

Quotation from Plato's *Republic:*

"Foolish leaders of democracy, which is a charming form of government, full of vanity and disorder, and dispensing a sort of equality to equals and unequals alike."

I thumbed through the pages. Similar guides were supplied for each lesson for teaching *Gettysburg Address, The Emperor's New Clothes, The Farmer and the Serpent, The Three Musketeers*, and the like.

For a time, I was confused. I asked myself if the English textbooks were true or false. If they were false, then the guidebook was true. If the guidebook was false, then the textbooks were true. *If truth is false, is false true?* Was John Dewey right when he said that we do not learn from experience but from reflecting on experience?

26

AFTER THAT NIGHT, the pages of the *Teachers' Guide* filled my head and there was not much space for anything else. I carried it under my arm whenever I stepped inside a classroom, as if wearing an amulet guarding against bad luck. I had regretted my silly aberration. I felt I'd been duped by my own untamed imagination. Inside the classroom, I noticed eyes watching me as school leaders sitting at the back of the classroom monitored the progress of my remedial efforts. They had slipped into a corner in hopes to catch me off guard.

I'd trained myself not to digress in class, no doubt disappointing the spies. I felt the weight on my soul, feeling like a huge dark wave was hovering, threatening to engulf me. In my mind, I kept seeing a fake, self-lecturing me dancing in the white chalk powder before the blackboard.

However, it did not take long for my mind to be tamed and tethered.

Soon, I grew accustomed to the popular pedagogical method: cramming. "Repetition is the mother of success," I had been told, so I began each class with a daily quiz, followed by a weekly test. I had finally learned that nothing was more important than exam writing. After all, the goal of the students was to pass the university entrance exams.

Our nation and I happened to have the same birthday. So, my personal celebration always felt redundant, drowned out in the fireworks. On the night of my twenty-second birthday, as I was busy marking exam papers—not an exciting task—I heard soft knocking.

"Hi, Teacher, I have questions to ask you." It was Summer, who had previously dropped in a couple of times. She held her English textbook in front of her chest with both hands.

I let her in. An electric fan on the table was swaying its blunt blades rhythmically as it moved the air.

Tonight, Summer wore a tight-fitting white shirt adorned with two embroidered chrysanthemums on the front. I averted my eyes. The room was warm, and droplets of sweat appeared on her forehead above her lovely face. As usual, she sat on the edge of my bed.

"In 'The Emperor's New Clothes,' what do the clothes symbolize?" she asked.

"You're asking an interesting question, Summer. But it's not going to be on the exam," I told her.

Still, her big languid eyes looked at me pleadingly, pressing me for an answer.

"The emperor does not wear any clothes, but everyone says they see the clothes except one truth-telling boy. It's a satire by Andersen about hypocrisy," I said.

"Teacher," she said, lowering her head shyly. "You're still wearing the emperor's *old* clothes."

I felt my face redden. My mind went blank, unable to find words. I heard the drumming of my racing heart.

"You pretend you don't have any desire for girls like me. Yet I can see it in your eyes. Your yearning for intimacy is wide-awake. Girls possess intuition, you know." She spoke as if she were my teacher, giving me an important lecture.

She lifted her hands to loosen her hair, which now looked like a waterfall cascading over her shoulders, the released fragrance filling my nostrils. I tried to break free of her gaze, but I was mesmerized. She proceeded to unbutton her shirt, calmly taking my trembling hand, and placing it on her bra. "Don't panic, Teacher. I'm already eighteen." Her voice was seductive.

By now, the softness of her ivory skin had ensnared me; I couldn't resist the temptation any longer. My desire was let out like a prisoner from a cage. I rose and pushed her down onto the bed, allowing myself to be overcome by my own lust.

"I'm bringing you your birthday reward tonight," she whispered in my ear as if sharing a deeply kept secret. "You're the first man who awakened my slumbering dreams," she said, the memory bringing a shine to her eyes.

By now, my body jerked as if it were on fire. Before I could pull off her underwear, I ejaculated on the bed sheet. I heaved a loud sigh and lay beside her like a deflated balloon. In my mind, I had imagined a scene like this a thousand times, part of a nocturnal ritual when I took the untamed lust into my own hands. Now, when it came to experience the reality of it all, I was useless.

"It's okay." She put her face onto my bare chest, stroking my hair with her free hand. "Don't be scared," she whispered like a mother calming her child after a nightmare. Then, she began to massage my thighs.

"What's this?" Her delicate hand paused.

"Oh, it's a birthmark. It started with a tiny dot, now grew to this palm-like size."

"So is your dream," she said.

She was right: it was this birthmark that nurtured my hard-earned dream.

I suddenly realized I hadn't turned off the lights in the room. My body began to tremble, afraid someone had witnessed what had happened. Mosquitoes buzzed around above my head in the open net.

After that night, I tried to avoid her during the day. But I spent many sleepless nights thinking of her. I now kept my windows shut tightly for the whole summer lest a trace of her nocturnal fragrance permeate the walls of my room again. Many times, however, guilt consumed me. So, I resolved to erase her from my mind, like brushing off the chalk on a blackboard. But I failed, and the nightly imaginary sex scene continued. Each time, I promised to quit the next day, but couldn't control my impulses. At times, I couldn't help but feel how helpless a man was.

Sometimes, I tried to convince myself there was nothing dirty about expressing sexuality, but it never worked. No one around me would even dare talk about sex, and neither did anyone in the books I read or the movies I saw. Clearly, I must be the only man in the world who entertained such dirty, lewd thoughts.

Summer, the season that gripped the hearts and minds of thousands of students everywhere, was finally here. It was June and the university entrance exams were over, the campus almost deserted and the school was half-asleep. One July night, a half-moon appeared in the star-filled sky.

When I roamed the campus, I could not help but ponder my reality. *What will my future be like?* I asked myself. I never liked politics, but it always chased me like a shadow I was unable to shake off. I knew how to speak English, but I was unable to read the language of the school. It wasn't the money I cared about, although teachers earned less than the elderly lady who sat at the school entrance selling tea eggs. It was what made me feel fulfilled inside that counted. My loneliness grew and began to loom large. In just two years, I'd lost my early enthusiasm for teaching.

Just then, I noticed a crowd gathered in front of the bulletin boards by the school's entrance. I remember that the execution posters from the People's Court had been displayed on the board when I first came. All that seemed to have occurred a long time ago.

I stopped behind the crowd and scanned what had been posted: the names of the students who had been successfully selected by the various colleges and universities. It was no surprise that No. 1 High was again listed as the top high school, supplying more students to the three most prestigious universities in the country than any other schools in the province. My eyes kept searching. I found her. Summer's name was on the bottom of the list, and this meant a lot to me.

Suddenly, our crowd was disturbed by yelling behind us. I noticed another crowd in the distance. Not far away, a student tore some textbooks and exam papers into pieces. Others followed. Soon, the books and papers were piled up in a heap in the middle of the quad. A young student poured a bottle of alcohol onto the heap and set fire to it. The books were on fire, sending ashes flying overhead. The crowd began to gather around the black smoke swirling over the flames, shouting and laughing.

The familiar scene was caught in the flame of something still ablaze in the book of my memory. But I could not reconcile the two images split in my mind. *Are there any similarities between these two fires?* I asked myself.

A young girl squeezed in from behind. She wore glasses and seemed to be under a spell. She broke abruptly from the crowd, jumping oddly in circles, screaming and shrieking. Then, she took off her pants and tossed them onto the fire. Removing her blouse, she began to dance naked around the blaze, waving her blouse above her head, as if swirling a red silk shawl. The people in the crowd covered their round eyes briefly with their palms, shouting: "Watch this girl! Come watch!"

"Oh, my heavens!"

"Oh, my sky."

A school security guard ran onto the scene. Two men put a blanket around her and carried the struggling girl off the schoolyard.

"The poor girl. Her name is finally on the list—after three years! But now she's gone crazy," I heard other students whispering.

By now, I'd learned to distinguish between the three aspects of me: body, mind, and soul. When I said "I," I didn't necessarily refer to "me." Often, I was not me. I wanted to step out of my body and let my pure soul flow into this world without being chained as a captive. Only when I brought together these three aspects could I proudly say: "I am the genuine me."

Suddenly, the idea of the "three aspects of goodness" struck me:

the Party required the loyalty of your whole being: body, mind, and soul. *If I am not a master of my own body, can I be a master of my own thoughts? Or dreams?*

Now, there was a good deal of truth in my thoughts. Finally, my guru, Sherlock Holmes, came to reside with me as my roommate. But this time I did not think backwards; rather, I thought forward, contrary to my guru's coaching.

When a new term began in September, I heard the news that Stone, the author of the notorious essay, "A Mother's Tears," had disappeared. Then, sometime later, the office of the Public Security Bureau in the city of Nine Rivers contacted our school to inform the principal they had found a body in the river. In his schoolbag, they found an exam booklet from No. 1 High of Temple County.

Did Stone jump into the river, like the ancient poet, because his dream died? If I hadn't opened the window to his sweet dreams, would he still have swallowed the bitter death? Or did his death have nothing to do with me? Was this because of his disgraced essay?

For a long time, I couldn't wash away his country-faced innocence from my mind. Such a young man with a soft heart, full of promise. But there was no doubt it was Stone's death that helped wake me. I felt a sense of resentment and estrangement that I couldn't explain. Bubble had called me an engineer of the human soul, but I had failed miserably. Sometimes, when I looked at the chalk-smeared fingers of my right hand, I felt I was looking at the hand of a murderer. After every class, like Lady Macbeth, I washed my hands clean again and again in the pond water, listlessly peering at the semi-cheerful wild ducks in a pond partially circled by the indifferent willow trees, still as the earth. My mind seemed filled with secret jealousy. Other times, the chalk I clutched, making it shriek on the face of the blackboard, suddenly loomed like the red brick Master Fu had gripped to crack open the skull. The more I thought, the more crestfallen I became. The black face of the board. The white chalk. The red brick. Everything confused and baffled me.

Everything in me was jumbled together. I had a strong feeling that I would refuse to be an accomplice. I had to preserve whatever was left inside of me. Otherwise, I would have to split my face to become a two-faced man, split my heart to become a double-minded person. Maybe split my body, as well, one body for the day, one for the night. Like First Emperor of China who had cut the head of the mountain in two. Like Teacher Dai, who had cut our brains into two halves.

I had misjudged the short-lived school career I had chosen. No, I didn't choose, I only messed up in the multiple-choice questions, believing "mess" to be "mass." I was chosen. My Sherlock Holmes talent no longer helped me.

In those days, however, trying to shine in another area without approval was like moving a mountain to the sea. But I felt I was choosing not for myself, but for my soul.

Nevertheless, "To be, or not to be?" was *not* a question I considered when I was looking deeper into my inner self. I would not look back, but ahead.

My mind nodded its head in agreement.

This was a historical moment in my book. In my life. And within me.

27

THERE HAD BEEN no rain for a long time. A spell of drought had once again descended on the land.

The scorching sun beat down mercilessly on the red earth, which burned like a fire underfoot. The heat baked the riverbed, and the mud cracked like the skin of a dying tree. The grey air was dusty and arid. Exposed debris on the riverbed teemed with flies. The cloudless sky, the retreating river, the thirsty trees along the embankment, the land moaning under the weight of heat, opening its dry mouth waiting for rain.

The newspaper headlines said the county officials had required the regional army to shoot cannonballs into the windless sky to make an artificial rainfall. The cannons, which sounded like distant thunder, could be heard in the evenings.

But no rain appeared although the newspapers continued to shout arrogant slogans claiming that man would conquer the sky. More cannons were shot madly skyward, but the sky did not cringe or wink. It looked down at the emptiness of the land with condescension.

One weekend evening, Moon and I were strolling on the embankment along the river. A young boy ran past, trying to send his paper kite into the sky. Despite his efforts, the kite dove downward relentlessly, like a bird that had lost its wings. The boy lifted his head toward the sky, apparently in despair. Just then, a flock of sparrows flew overhead.

"You need to wait for the wind, boy, to fly your kite," Moon said to him.

I looked more closely at the boy; his face was so familiar to me. I was thinking I had seen him somewhere. He seemed to be a younger version of me. Suddenly, I remembered my dream about the kite at the mercy of the wind. The scene seemed to remind me that I had to leave this patch of windless sky, or I would be like the dying kite, grounded by hopelessness.

"Are you going to anchor here forever?" Moon said, looking at me.

"I hope not."

"I'm leaving for Shenzhen at the end of this term."

"What are you doing there?"

"Interpreter."

"Did you kneel down before the Party Secretary begging for permission?" I said half-jokingly.

She shook her head.

"I've got to admit." She paused and then asked matter-of-factly: "Do you remember that I have the dragon sword?"

Tears clouded her eyes, as if she had just removed a blindfold and her eyes were trying to adjust to the blazing sun. She averted her gaze from mine and turned her face toward the river. *What is her sword?* I wondered. It still stood as a baffling mystery to me.

I always found Moon to be as mysterious as the moon in the night sky.

"Do you want to go with me?" She looked at me hopefully, but was trying to sound casual, as if tossing a ping-pong ball to me when we were at play.

"Me? I'm scared of your sword," I teased, but she was not amused.

Then, I shook my head to bring me back to earth, adding in a serious tone: "I want to attend graduate school. You know that."

The smile dropped from her face; she said nothing, apparently trying hard to hide her disappointment. And agony.

There was a long pause between us. Whether I had offended or hurt her, I did not know.

The silence remained, but it was punctured by the ringing coming from a bicycle carrying a woman sitting behind a man, leaning her head against his back and clinging to his waist. Both of us looked away, pretending not to see the lovers.

"Now I see we are not of one mind. You're chasing your dream," she murmured. "I will chase mine."

I looked at her beautiful eyes, saying: "Deal."

"Are you still in love with Lily?" she asked.

"Who said that?"

"That's my conclusion."

"Which is false," I said firmly. "I hope you understand in due course."

"I always do. Well, no, most times I don't, actually."

Moon's eyes flooded with tears again. "I'm not worthy of you."

"Don't say that, Moon. You know and I know that we are best friends."

"Best friends ought to share secrets. But we don't."

I did not know what to say to persuade her not to throw away our friendship.

"Remember the 3/8 demarcation you drew?" I asked. "The early war did not prevent us from becoming friends. We should not give up now."

Suddenly, Moon looked tense and shuddered at my mention of the past.

"My past was dead and buried a long time ago. Don't let me exhume my old tomb and hand you my memory box," said she absentmindedly.

"Correct. Correct."

"What's left in me, however, is a new shadow of my past." A strand of long hair obscured her face.

"Yes, of course. It's the same for me. We have walked through the dark valley hand in hand. To be honest, we need a fresh start. With a fresh heart," I said, trying to rein in the unwelcome thoughts that were already galloping like a hundred untamed horses in my mind.

"Only this matters nowadays," she said, pulling the strand of hair off her face. Then she nodded, appearing to have awakened from a deep reverie.

"Moon," I said, "can I beg a favour from you?"

"From me? Anything."

"Can you seek mercy of the school on my behalf?"

"For what?"

"The mercy to let me go. Usually, they don't. They want to control our destiny."

"Why do you think I can do it for you?"

"You have the dragon slayer," I said, teasing.

Once again, Moon did not seem impressed. She frowned at me. And sighed.

"If you need money to gift, you let me know," I said.

"You're being naïve. And honest. But do you promise one thing?"

"What is it?"

"To share with me the news of the fruit of your dream?"

"A done deal!" I said, as if delivering the note of my promise to be enfolded in her earshot.

After that, I tried to lift Moon's mood, but failed. My heart sank. I was sure my feelings of guilt must be obvious on my face.

Surely, Moon must have noticed it.

The following week was foggy. One foggy morning, after class, I received a package stamped with a portrait of Queen Elizabeth II. It was a pleasant surprise from Teacher Blue from Oxford University. Inside was a paperback entitled *The Rape of Hearts*. As I read on, tears slid down my cheeks and the page blurred. In the book, she had written in English: "I gave away my body; they raped my mind, but I have kept pure my soul. Our soul is indestructible, incorrigible, inscrutable. It's unborn. It is free!"

Teacher Blue's story was one of sorrow and grief. Her father was a professor of English, and Blue studied English as a child. Unable to tolerate beatings by the Red Guards, her father jumped off the teachers' building. As a result, Teacher Blue was sent down to the village to do manual work. One day, the village head held a red seal stamp on one hand, and placed his other hand on her bosom, grinning: "Want go to college?" Later, Teacher Blue went to college but soon found out that she was pregnant. She did not strangle the baby to death like the white-haired girl, though.

Tragedies in her life did not come to crush her but helped realize her hidden potential and power. She used her life, which was reflected in her novel, as a glass mirror for the world to see human souls.

By now, I could say to Teacher Blue that I had grown into a different person; I had changed. The face reflected in the mirror was not my portrait or me anymore. Like a beggar on the corner of the street, I used to stuff myself with whatever the world offered, and felt content with a morsel from a leftover meal. Now I wanted the chance to have the emperor dethroned from my inner world, if not from the outside world. This sudden realization delighted me.

I was out of time.

But transformation is happening, I thought.

That night, in my dreams, a new dream was born when I saw in my mind's eye the publication of my own English novel: *Dancing in the River.*

PART THREE

All the rivers run into the sea, yet the sea is not full;
unto the place from whence the rivers come,
there they return again.
—Ecclesiastes 1:7-8

28

~~~

IN SEPTEMBER 1986, I travelled upstream to the capital city of our province to attend RCU, River City University.

A roof of glazed blue tiles covered the 70-year-old, three-storey structure that housed the English Department. Japanese cherry trees dispersed delicate white blossoms along each side of the boulevard, paved in marble, that led to East Lake. In early spring, when the trees were in full bloom, visitors swarmed the campus to catch a glimpse of the magnificent display, to inhale the fragrance, to capture the moment in little black boxes.

That first day, most of my classmates—ten graduate students— were already seated in a circle. I took a spot beside my roommate Sky, a bespectacled young man with thick glasses, which made me associate him with piles of books. I couldn't possibly speculate about his hair. A cluster of curls hung down over his forehead while the rest of it was straight and long, almost to his shoulders.

Old Sun, another roommate, stepped into the small seminar room with a broad smile. The night before, the three of us had dined together at the campus cafeteria.

"Old Sun, you're our big brother, please let me have the honour to pay for you tonight," Sky said, after the three of us seated ourselves, handing him a mug of hot tea.

"No need, no need," Old Sun said, shaking his head.

"Already a department head in a college before you came? Amazing," Sky said.

"You must be very smart. In the future, counsel me more about being smart, I mean people smart," I said.

"Certainly, certainly." Old Sun smiled, mimicking the late Chairman Mao's dialect. "I came from Chairman Mao's home province."

Chairman Mao himself visited RCU in 1958 when his close friend, Chancellor Li, headed the school. Chairman Mao had stayed at a quiet villa in a far corner of the island on East Lake when he swam across the Yangtze in July 1966. During the Cultural Revolution, however, the Red Guards tortured Chancellor Li to death.

Sky stood up and broke my train of thought. He began to recite Su Dongpo's "Gone with the Waves," and added: "Gone with the waves is our beloved Chairman Mao."

Sky and I chuckled, but not Old Sun, whose smile drooped. "You shouldn't joke about Chairman Mao. Seriously."

"Guilty, guilty," Sky replied, still jeering.

"Seriously, watch your mouth and thoughts."

"We do, we do." Our laughter died.

"Do you want to hear a secret message?" Old Sun asked.

"Of course."

"This secret may help change both of your thoughts," Sun said. "Since we are roommates, I need to care about you."

"What secret?" I asked.

"Our English department will select two students by the end of the second year, to study in the U.K.," Old Sun whispered.

"How do you know?" I asked.

"I have my way." Old Sun sipped his hot tea, eyeing both of us. "Do you want to go?"

"I do!" Sky blurted.

"I may not be qualified," I said.

"That's why we need to make our best efforts here to meet the qualification," Old Sun said.

"But how?" I asked.

"You figure out by yourself." Old Sun folded his hands before his chest.

Obviously, Sky and I were interested in this bait.

❧ Dr. Solomon entered the classroom carrying a box of Bibles. He had a long, thick beard. Teaching the Bible was prohibited, we were told, but it was approved when the head of the department changed the subject to "The Bible and English Literature."

Dr. Solomon handed out the syllabus and outlined his course requirements, including the term paper. Then he asked us to open to the Book of Genesis, and read it with his nasal American voice:

> In the beginning, God created the heavens and the earth. The earth was without form and void, and darkness was over the face of the deep. And the Spirit of God was hovering over the face of the waters.

He paused, peering over his reading glasses.

I looked up to the ceiling; it remained silent. I bent my head, unable to look up for fear that Dr. Solomon would read my mind. The origins of the universe and humans were found in Chinese mythology. As is tradition, Pangu is seen as the father of the universe who divided the heavens and the earth out of the void, while Nuwa created the first human from dust. During the Cultural Revolution, however, both Pangu and Nuwa fell out of favour with the Red Guards and Darwin was anointed father of the new myth.

This made me think of one of Qu Yuan's mysterious and opaque poems.

Does the Book of Genesis supply answers to the heavenly mysteries? If our ancient poet Qu Yuan had found answers to his 172 questions in the Old Testament, would he have committed suicide?

Probably not, I guess.

But if that was the case, we would not celebrate the Dragon Boat Festival, I thought.

Just then Dr. Solomon whispered: "Does anyone believe in God, as the Bible says?"

There was silence.

"What's the name of the god in the Bible?"

I raised my hand timidly. I wanted to find out whether the god in the Bible was the same god my grandma used to call upon. "Is Jehovah the same god as the Chinese god of the heavens?" I asked.

"God has many names. The Israelites call Him Jehovah," Dr. Solomon explained. "But there is only one God. I offer this discussion for your term paper if you're interested."

"How can we believe in God if we can't see him?" Old Sun asked.

"We cannot see God in a bodily form, because God is spirit. We see God by faith."

What is faith, then? Is the concept of faith the same as superstition? My head began to spin.

Still, we were not convinced. Seeing is believing, this has been our motto. Or you can call it our faith.

Sky closed his Bible and lifted a hand, saying: "Our Chinese god was stoned to death a long time ago."

This caused some chuckling.

Dr. Solomon resumed his reading. When he came to Chapter Two, he paused to emphasize verses 15 to 17:

"Then the Lord God took the man and put him into the Garden of Eden to cultivate it and keep it. The Lord God commanded the man, saying: 'From any tree of the garden you may eat freely; but from the tree of the knowledge of good and evil you shall not eat, for on the day that you eat from it you will surely die.'"

Dr. Solomon paused to survey the class. "I'm going to leave these passages for you to digest. However, since this is a literature class as well, I want you to reread *Hamlet* and think about Hamlet's statement in the dialogue in Act 2, Scene 2. When Hamlet says, 'for there is nothing either good or bad, but thinking makes it so,' what does he imply? How can you apply the biblical concept of knowledge of good and evil to this oft-quoted statement? I suggest this would be a good topic for a term paper."

Then, Dr. Solomon got up from his chair and wrote "knowledge of good and evil" on the blackboard with his left hand. He printed the word "evil" with such force that the chalk snapped. Suddenly, it dawned on me that Dr. Solomon was not writing on the blackboard, he was writing on my mind; the blackboard was not a simple board, but rather a slate of human brain. Unlike the chalked words, however, erasing words seared on our brain is almost always problematic.

Indeed, the human mind can be a battleground for good and evil.

Even before the class was dismissed, my head was buzzing with new ideas and questions. In Mao's time, knowledge was evil; now in Deng's era, knowledge is good. Shakespeare said there is no such thing as good and evil and both were created by human minds. Now the Bible says knowledge is both good and evil. I was totally confused. I began to doubt that I could do the work. It would be a big loss of face if I failed graduate school.

I seemed to be falling down a dark hole. I had seen education as an endless, light-filled journey to find answers to life's questions: a series of lessons to help me discover my purpose and destiny. In this sense, I viewed education as a part of life itself.

Now, a tempest threatened even those rays of hope.

The house I had so laboriously built began to crumble, its foundation shaken as by a massive earthquake. The things that made me feel good and proud became the very things that now made me doubt myself.

I used to be droplets in the river that the wind blew into waves, smashing me into the rocky cliff, the force breaking me apart into separate pieces until I had become foam that dried in the sun. I had been separated from the river; I was no longer a part of it, not even droplets anymore.

I would never forget this day when I broke myself into pieces.

One evening, leaving the library, I saw a girl walking in front of me. Seen from behind, her figure looked much like that of Summer, whom I had not seen since she left for college. Now, I could not help but think of her, so I wrote her a letter.

A few days later, I came back to our dorm to see a letter lying on my bunk bed. Old Sun collected mail for everyone on the fifth floor. I tore open the envelope. It was from Summer:

Dear Teacher,

I was so glad to receive your letter, which was a big surprise for me. Years flew by like the river, like my days at No. 1 High.

I still remember the size of your birthmark. You said you'd never celebrated your birthday. When I asked why, you quoted Mark Twain: "The two most important days in your life are the day you are born and the day you find out why."

Have you found out the why?

Remember the mother-wife puzzle? Who do you save first?

When I asked, I saw that dilemma in your eyes. The ought-to-be-right or the ought-to-be-wrong has been kicked about at the whims of our minds.

But now I realize that I need to save myself first!

This upcoming Saturday night, Mr. Sword, a rising rock star, comes to perform at River City Stadium. I hope you can come.

May our minds be rocked and awakened by this newfound reality.

Your student,
Summer

I held the letter in my hand for a long time, reading it a second time to look for clues or hidden messages. In my head, I replayed the image of Summer running toward me and my arms extending to embrace her. Then I would hold her and kiss her lips, her face turning as red as a tomato. I tried to keep the image still in my mind.

Suspense hurts.

As I waited for it, time seemed to stop.

Finally, Saturday evening arrived. I rode my Everlasting-brand bike to the stadium. Under the dim light, a girl wearing a black, flat cap with a protective visor stood up and waved to me. It was Summer. My heart jumped with joy, as sweat beaded on my forehead. I did not look into her eyes, as I did not want her to read my thoughts.

"Happy Birthday, Teacher," Summer said, handing me a can of iced Coca-Cola, my favourite drink, as we waited for the concert to begin.

"Thank you, Summer. But I don't even remember my own birthday."

"I could never forget the day that you woke up my dream. But now I realize that living a normal life is my dream." She sighed.

"What happened?" I turned to gaze at her. "What made you so moody now?"

"Nothing—I was born like this. I'm only a weak gal. You know that."

"But you used to be bright, like a summer sun," I said.

"All pretense. I'm tired of putting on a fake face."

I did not know if I could nod or shake my head. "How's college?" I changed the subject.

"I did well in all my classes. I'm working on my graduation project now."

Just then, dazzling spotlights on the stage began to swirl and roam all over the stadium, accompanied by loud clapping and shouting. The audience primarily consisted of young college students, and the "educated youth," who were sent down to the countryside to receive re-education during the Cultural Revolution. These youths were deprived of formal education, prime years and a normal family life. And now people call them the "lost generation."

Meanwhile, the performance was about to start.

"I'm going to get married after graduation, Teacher."

"What?" The noise was overpowering so I leaned close. I could smell the fragrance from her hair and feel her warmth of her breath.

"I'm getting married," she whispered again.

"To whom?"

"An overseas Chinese, living in Vancouver, Canada."

"But how?" I paused, to rephrase. "I mean, how did you know this Canadian?"

"A friend of my mother introduced us."

"Did you meet him?"

Summer shook her head. "No. But I saw his pictures. He looks like a nice fellow. After my graduation, he's coming to our hometown, to hold the wedding."

"Are you going to Canada, then?"

"Yes. I don't want to return to Temple County. Old memories would torture me."

"What memories?"

She turned away. Her eyes were filled with tears.

On the stage, under the spotlight, the singer was clutching a microphone almost to his lips, singing his new song, "Nothing to My Name:"

> *When do you leave with me?*
> *I used to ask endlessly.*
> *But you always laugh,*
> *Saying nothing's left for me.*
> *I wanna offer you my pursuit, my freedom,*
> *But you always laugh, saying it's all nonsense.*
> *Oh, when do you leave with me, oh, when?*

The title of the lyric had multiple meanings, which represented the status of the lost generation, of us, as well. *All is nonsense. All is nothing. Nothing is left for us. We have nothing ...*

Our country had just climbed out of the ashes of the Cultural Revolution and the road of reform is full of obstacles. What will happen if the Eastern winds blow us back to the old days? I wondered.

The music was loud and so was the audience. All I could see was the backs of heads but I felt the hunger burning in their eyes. Although the rock star sang vigorously, his tone was sad and desperate. At the song's climax the audience stood up singing and shouting with him. The overheated stadium seemed on the edge of exploding.

The two of us sat quietly as the stadium emptied.

Summer rode with me on my bike along University Boulevard. She then sat with me on the grass behind the statue on campus. By that time, the moon had begun to hide behind the clouds.

"So, what's happened?" I inquired.

"Don't know. I just want to hide. Anywhere."

She told me her story. Summer's mother had been a young and beautiful actress in a troupe of performers in Temple County. As a child Summer was told that her father had died of cancer. Just before departing for college her mother revealed that her father had been stoned to death onstage. Because of his role as a landowner. Summer was devastated.

I was dumbstruck.

"Was he struck by a brick while performing a play called *The White-Haired Girl*?"

"How did you know?"

Suddenly I had a vision of the player dying in a pool of blood, but I soon shook it off as if dusting a dirty garment. I did not want to revisit that bloody scene.

"How can I continue to live and serve this country where my father was killed, and no one suffered consequences? As if nothing had happened."

"That's why you wear a hat now?"

"To cover the wounds." She nodded.

I brushed away her tears with my palm, then held her in my arms.

At that moment, with her body in my arms, feeling her breath, I did not know what to say to her. I just stroked her hair with my hand. Only moments before, when I had first held her, I could hardly resist the urge to kiss her. Now, I felt I was an evil snake before the face of an angel.

When I rode back alone along University Boulevard, it had begun to drizzle. I could not brush away the sight of Summer crying in my arms. I thought of my mother, of the rainy night when she went away with two men and then turned to gaze back at me.

Just then, I thought of the tree of knowledge, of good and evil in the Book of Genesis. *Does God use the tree as a metaphor for the human mind?* Shakespeare thought so. If you eat from the tree, then you are a human being. Humans are compelled to think about good and evil. That is why Hamlet said that good and evil were created by human thinking. Thus, it was logical to conclude that our thinking creates our own conditions. In other words, our world is a product of our own thinking.

Thinking created China, thinking created America, thinking also created Canada. If we want to change our world, we must first change our thinking. If we think of good, we ingest goodness; if we think of evil, we taste evil. In this sense, our outer world is created by our belief system; the world is merely a mirror of our mind, so it is useless to change mirrors. The human mind is a battleground, and the sound of gunfire is louder than in a real war.

To infer further, our human destiny lies in our own thinking process. Thus, if we want to be the master of our destiny, we must first control our own thinking.

What is the metaphor for "the tree of life" in the Bible? I wondered.

It must be the opposite of the tree of knowledge. There is a difference between life and death, immortality, and life's struggles.

The tree of life must be from God. If you eat of it, you will be immortal, as God is immortal, I reasoned.

When I reached my dorm, the rain had stopped. The Northern Star had pierced through the dark clouds and was now shining brighter than all the other stars. It dawned on me that an interesting term paper was in the making.

29

IT WAS ANOTHER foggy morning on campus.

I scurried to the library building to search for scholarship guides for American and Canadian universities. On the fifth floor, I caught sight of Old Sun bending over a table in a secluded section marked "VIP Zone."

"What are you reading, Old Sun?" I asked.

Looking up, he pressed his right index finger to his lips, then waved me closer.

"Look here," he whispered, pointing to the yellowed pages of an old volume. "The legendary *Golden Lotus*. This is the only volume, which is kept locked up in the curator's office."

"How did you get it?" Curiosity was getting the better of me.

He looked around and whispered mysteriously: "I'll tell you when I get back."

That evening, Old Sun and I sat at our desks. As usual, he combed his hair ten times from back to front, then another ten times from front to back, using a comb made of tiger bones. Next, he poured hot water into his face basin, which had been placed on the cold, naked cement floor. After immersing his feet in the steamy water, he rubbed his left foot against his right one.

As he went about his nocturnal ritual, he began to talk.

He told me he had submitted a 100-word outline of his term paper on the protagonist of *Golden Lotus*, Amorous Lotus Pan, then asked to make an appointment with the curator, who approved his visit to the VIP section.

"You're a genius." I smiled at him.

"But it's a secret just between us," he responded: "Otherwise, I might be in trouble."

"I would not tell my left hand if my right hand had touched the secret book," I said.

He felt satisfied. Then he told me that a grad student from the joint Sino-U.S. MBA program had recently been kicked out of school; the poor guy bought sex from a young prostitute working near the railway tracks. He had been caught in the act by a security guard from the railway station. This had occurred on a Saturday night during the *River Elegy*[6] discussion week, when all the students were required to watch the six-part documentary at an outdoor cinema.

"Poor guy!" he exclaimed.

"How do you find out about this stuff?"

"We, the Party members, have weekly meetings and we make decisions about these types of things," he replied.

I looked at my roommate with awe.

"Have you ever thought of joining the Party?"

"Me? Oh, no."

His inquiry shocked me. Honestly, I had never thought I would be qualified. I did not possess any political sensitivity or skills. Nor was I people-smart, as Dean Yin used to say. In addition, I did not want the Party to probe into my family's sorrows again.

"When you're a Party member, you enjoy lots of benefits and privileges. But loyalty is a top priority. Our five-thousand-year-old history boils down to two words."

"Two words?"

"Yes, allegiance and obedience. The rest is not that important. Think about it. You don't have a future in our country unless you join us, Victor."

---

6. *River Elegy* is an influential six-part documentary shown in China in 1988. The major theme includes the decline of traditional Chinese culture.

"How do I get along with the Party, win her favour?"

Old Sun paused to ponder. "From the bottom of the ladder."

"Bottom? Ladder? You're confusing me, Old Sun."

"Who is the first contact of our Party?"

"Our Party secretary!"

"Yes, you got the key now. Start from there, then climb the ladder to the top."

"But how?"

"How? Is it more opaque than Shakespeare? We have 5000-year wisdom. Read *The Golden Lotus*, Oh, no, no!" He blushed, then corrected himself: "I mean … I mean, read *Dream of Red Chamber*, the dream book. It's the bible of the human mind, the Chinese mind, to be exact. Have you found out the primary theme of the *Dream Book*?"

I shook my head.

"You know it can be summarized in one word?"

"What is it?"

"Revolution!"

"What?"

"Smashing rivals, that is to say."

I shuddered. "But how?"

"Where there's a will, there's a way."

Too complicated for me. I heaved a long sigh.

I thanked him for his consideration and told him I would seriously consider his counsel. But I never again raised the subject of joining the Party. Whenever I thought of the Party, all I could see was my father's agony and my mother's tears.

"I heard that you wrote the English test," he said.

"Yes." I knew he was referring to the Test of English as a Foreign Language.

"How did you know?"

"I know that I know," he said. Then his face turned stern. "Sky's thoughts are very dangerous. Don't stay too close to him."

"He's just a poet, with a poetic imagination," I said.

"To tell you the truth, it's not what you do, but the motive behind what you do that matters. To become a Party member, you must always put the Party's interest above everything else, including your family."

"Everything?" I asked.

"Yes, everything. Your mind, your body, your soul." He nodded. "We are a brick, a red brick, so to speak. Wherever and whenever our country needs a brick, we are here, to be moved to where it's needed."

Suddenly I recognized why I had not been nominated as a triple-good student at college. My *motive* was problematic because I did not put the Party's interest first.

"But how can I know the Party's interest?" I asked.

"That's why in every unit we have a Party Secretary."

"Right, right, Old Sun. Listening to your wise counsel is worthy of ten years of reading or studying. I need to consult you more often."

"It's my mission." He was satisfied.

However, I had already decided not to mould myself into a red brick. I was disqualified, period. *How about studying in the U.K.? The ladder is too high for me to climb. The stakes are too high.*

➤ One sunny day, an old classmate, Sam, paid me a surprise visit. He wore a black Western-style suit with a red tie and white shirt. He was in high spirits. He said he had come to say goodbye before leaving for law school in the U.S. He was being sponsored by a law professor that his father knew. Sam had translated the professor's book into Chinese, which was to be used in universities across the country.

"I'm getting married, Victor," he declared.

"Congrats," I said. "A double happiness fell on the door of your head."

"Guess who I'm marrying?" he said mischievously.

"How could I know?"

"Helen!"

"Peter's girlfriend?" I blurted.

"She's mine now."

"Oh, sorry. I meant that I didn't know you had a crush on Helen at college."

"She proposed to me."

"Really?" I said, truly shocked. But I smiled and changed my tone immediately. "That's great, Sam!"

"Who can resist a beauty?"

"I can!"

"Are you saying you will marry a homely girl?"

"To marry or not to marry, that is the question," I said, teasing. "But, Sam, do you recall our Professor Yang's motto: 'A beauty is never faithful and the faithful are never beautiful?'"

"*Dicto simpliciter.* Every rule has an exception. The professor was wrong."

"What are you talking about?"

"Latin."

"Professor Yang is a moron, then?" I said.

"*Ad hominem.* You attacked our professor personally instead of his argument."

"But Helen … Everyone knows what she did to Peter."

"Hasty generalization! Your sample is too small to draw a safe conclusion."

We laughed until there were tears in our eyes.

"Where did you pick up all this Latin?" I asked.

In response, Sam showed me the book he had translated: *Law and Logic: There Is No Law Without Logic.* "Here is a copy for you, Victor."

"Thank you, Sam. I will study logic carefully from now on, and become a lawyer too," I replied. "By the way, what happened to Peter?"

"Shortly after going to teach in Xinjiang, he quit. I heard he's a rich entrepreneur now."

"Good for him; a smart fellow."

Suddenly, the feeling of jealousy climbed up inside of me and tainted my pleasure at Sam's happiness. This made me uneasy. *Why was Sam so lucky? He had a powerful father (who became a minister of justice in the province after Deng came to power), a beautiful bride and a chance to go to America. Is it because people had different fates?*

As we parted, he said he hoped to meet me again in the U.S.

➤ One Saturday night, music filled the air and I salivated at the wafting smells of food. In the crowded dining hall, which had been converted into a dimly-lit ballroom, merry-eyed dancers gyrated around the room.

There was no disc jockey, or band, or dazzling coloured lights. Instead, huge stereo speakers had been placed in each corner of the hall on chairs, broadcasting dance music and pop songs. It was a perfect place to flirt, poke fun, seek out friends, and ultimately, maybe, find love.

It was on one such evening that Sky met Linda when he asked her to dance. In her late twenties, Linda had come from America to teach English. Sky offered to teach Linda Chinese, and in return, Linda helped edit and polish Sky's written English. The operator began to play "The Moon Represents My Heart," ensuring the first dance would be a waltz with tender lyrics:

> *You ask me how much I loved you*
> *And how deep?*
> *My feelings are genuine*
> *My love is real*
> *As the moon represents my heart.*

Seeing the various dancing couples intoxicated by the waltz, I felt lonely but could not muster the courage to ask someone to dance. I stood in the corner, enjoying the swirling melody.

If you wanted to discover joy in the dancing hall, I told myself, you had to reinvent yourself. So, I imagined I was someone else. Sometimes, it is an escape and a great relief to imagine you are not yourself so that you don't shoulder the responsibility of your own thinking and its consequences.

Then I thought of Summer. Since that night, I had frequently desired her company but I hesitated and, ultimately, resisted. Now, I imagined that I held her by the waist, waltzing to the melody, as she smiled. Suddenly, I saw her tears. My body was trembling; I couldn't take it anymore. I left.

Early March saw the cherry blossom trees in full bloom, their pink petals adorning the trees and dusting the marbled pavement below. Once separated from the trees, they gradually faded, withered, curled, and died under the feet of the smiling, camera-carrying crowds. I hoped the fallen petals couldn't feel anguish, like humans.

Do petals have fates, like people?

They are blown away by the whimsical wind, crushed underfoot, gradually decomposing and returning to dust.

Creative Writing was my favourite class. It was taught by Professor Adam, who had written many books, including *The Flying Pigs*. He circulated his books in class on the first day.

"Many authors write from their intuitive mind rather than their rational mind," he told us. "Coleridge's *Kubla Khan*, for example, is such creation. While asleep, the poet had a vision of reading beautiful sentences in a book. When he woke, he recalled all the sentences that would become the famed *Kubla Khan*. William Blake was another poet who treasured the sacred gift of imagination.

"What materials do we select to create our stories? It's through the mind's eye that we discover truths, both about ourselves and about the world around us. Reality is not single-dimensional; it is multi-faceted. When we look at reality with a single lens, it creates an illusion. Our subconscious is like a stream or river constantly running through us, day in and day out, serving as a mysterious source for material and an inspiration for many geniuses like William Blake and Henry James. This realm is accessible to everyone, including you and me."

And then the professor said to the class: "Tonight, before you go to bed, I want you to invite Shakespeare to have a cup of tea."

"Who?" Our surprise was unanimous.

"I said to invite Shakespeare—or Hemingway, or another author of your choice."

"But how?"

"Use your imagination," Professor Adam said. "Tonight, quiet your mind, close your eyes, and imagine Shakespeare's sitting with you, then engage him in conversation. Ask him about *Hamlet*, ask him about your writing. Then write down the answers that come to your mind. This is your first writing assignment."

I decided I would invite Qu Yuan and Job, the biblical figure in the Book of Job, to engage in dialogue on the heavenly questions.

Then we read excerpts from Sigmund Freud and Carl Jung about the unconscious or subconscious. After class, when I opened the pages from *The Interpretation of Dreams* and *Modern Man in Search of a Soul*, I tried to figure out which one could explain my frequent childhood nightmare of falling into a dark, endless pit.

30

ONE EVENING BY chance, I met Justin, a Canadian studying Chinese history at RCU. We met at the English Corner, a place on campus where students came to practice their spoken English. After that, we met frequently to discuss the Needham question. (Joseph Needham was a British sinologist who had written a series of volumes called *Science and Civilization in China*.) His question was this: Why had modern science developed in Europe, but not in China?

"Have you discovered the answer yet?" I asked him one day.

"I think so," he replied, his tone serious. "In Western eyes, China is a victim of its own success because the virtues of the past may become the vices of today, and the essence of human civilization does not lie in history, but in future advancement."

When winter vacation arrived, Justin asked me whether I was interested in taking a literary trip to Qu Yuan's burial place. I'd long wanted to pay a visit to Qu Yuan Temple.

So, one morning we boarded a train.

"Justin, I have a question for you," I said. "What's the difference, if any, between Chinese and Canadian students?"

He had a habit of knitting his brows when thinking hard. "Almost all Chinese students fear and obey authority. They go in the same direction the wind is blowing and seek social approval. In contrast, most Western students are free to make their own choices and then take responsibility. In general, Chinese students almost always try to be the same as others, while the Western students try to be different from one another."

I looked at him, puzzled.

"Look," he said. "In Chinese, ji (己) is self. Yi (己) denotes other. Is there a difference between those two words?"

"In terms of strokes, both are almost the same, save for the latter where a line extends up in the left side," I replied.

"Exactly. Most people in China see themselves in others and that's why they need to follow the crowd. In a Westerner's mind, you must become an individual first and then become part of society which, in turn, is made up of a group of distinct individuals."

I did not want to believe him, but I didn't try to argue with him either.

If self becomes other, then "I" becomes "you"—your thoughts are my thoughts. My life is lived in the lives of the multitude. My purpose and goals aren't my own.

At that moment, the train's public intercom system called out the next stop. It stopped for a few minutes, then resumed its journey.

My train of thought resumed as well.

My people lived like this for thousands of years! My grandma lived it, my parents lived it and now I live it. If Grandma is a circle, then Mother is a small circle within a big circle, forming a big black hole sucking in all outside circles. I eat one piece from a mooncake, thinking all the cakes in the world are the same. That is the essence of Chinese education: one for all, and all for one.

In this sense, I was a circle too, but I refused to be sucked into the circle of circles. Now I understood that I could live a different life with a different me. *I am not you; you are not me.*

I read somewhere that conformity is a disease of the mind; when you think the thoughts of others, you no longer have a mind of your own. That's why we have the expression "losing one's mind."

The Cultural Revolution was an example of collective insanity. The lesson was both painful and stunning: most of the people could be wrong. Holding a popular opinion does not mean you are standing on the right side.

The same can be said of tradition.

My people had fallen into the trap of tradition, charmed by the longevity of practices filled with sets of old rules. Most of these precedents had been put forth by a two-thousand-year-old saint, Confucius, whose voice still echoed in the land. "Things have always been done this way" is always on the lips of my people. Such presumption is fallacious; obviously, old things are not necessarily good. We must re-evaluate the merits with new eyes. Otherwise, we and our children will be drinking from the river of everlasting myths.

Will the same winds sweep the land again?

Likely, unless we change our consciousness!

Old ways of thinking won't create a new social order. Justin was right. For a long time, I did not know or even dare to think about what I wanted. I was like a leaf that had once been on the branch of a tree. Now, it had dropped to the ground and was blown away by the wind, ceasing to be part of the tree.

Just then, I could hear the intercom broadcasting Bob Dylan's songs.

Early in the afternoon we arrived in Prosperity City in a bone-chilling wind. We saw big red slogans on street banners and heard speakers talking about the massive migration that would take place; a gigantic hydroelectric dam was to be built nearby on the Yangtze. It was to be a hydraulic powerhouse, a feat of human engineering that would boost China's intellectual pride. The Great Wall of China is the only human structure on earth that could be seen from space when man landed on the moon, we had been told. I later learned this was a myth.

We checked into the Patriotic Poet Hotel, which had been newly renovated.

"Foreigners can't stay at this hotel," the receptionist said to Justin.

"Why?"

"No why. It's our policy. Look, this is a small town, we are not open to foreign tourists yet," the woman said apologetically.

"This must be a mistake. Qu Yuan is famous all over the world. Look, my friend came all the way from Canada. Canada, does it ring a bell? From Dr. Bethune's hometown! Dr. Bethune, still remember? Is China going to close the door on Dr. Bethune's countryman?"

"Every rule has an exception," Justin said in Chinese.

"Justin, this is China. We must handle it in Chinese way," I whispered in English.

"Wait here." The lady rose and went inside.

Moments later, a middle-aged man came in, and studied Justin's Canadian passport. "You came from Canada?"

"Yes, studying at CRU now," Justin said calmly in Chinese, cooling the heat stoked by my half-true overstatement.

"You speak fluent Chinese." The man looked Justin up and down.

"Yes, I also studied Qu Quan. That's why we're here today."

"Look," the man turned to the receptionist, "our friend came from Dr. Bethune's hometown. Do we have reasons to reject friends coming from far?"

Thanks to Chairman Mao's essay called "Dr. Bethune," the Canadian physician is a household name in China. Finally, Justin got the best room in the hotel, plus a free bottle of Qu Yuan Liquor. And free breakfast coupons. I had become much smarter now, I reckoned, but still needed to work on my people skills.

Exhausted from our strenuous journey, we soon fell into the realm of dreams.

The following morning was cloudy and windy. The whole town was quiet but looked festive. Red posters of blessings hung on every door. It was a "small feast" day, the first day of the celebration of the Spring Festival.

Surrounded by bushes and trees, Qu Yuan Temple lay at the

foot of Mount Phoenix, overlooking the river. A wooden plank with carved calligraphy hung over the entrance. A gatekeeper was cracking sunflower seeds, skillfully spitting out the husks. That day, there were few visitors.

A collection of poems written by Qu Yuan hung on the walls of the calligraphy section. We walked to the Asking Heaven Pavilion on the top of the hill, where we could see the river in the distance, flowing like a yellow serpent under the grey sky. Feeling as though I was on holy ground, I sat on one of the wooden benches. My thoughts flew out like birds from a cage, soaring to the sky.

I imagined that a long, long time ago, the young poet had followed an ancient circular path, just like the routes of our people's history—long and zigzagged, like human life. There, he had looked up to the star-filled heavens, where he could decipher the routes of the sky, the destinies of humans and the fate of the land. Then, he waited for the shimmering of the awakening light, born from the eastern sky, to shine upon a land still in slumber. In the far distance, as far as the naked eye could see, he saw our human dreams floating between a cloudy sky and a misty earth.

When you stood under the boundless sky, everything would become possible, he would think. The hill's pinnacle afforded him the freedom he desired; the open expanse afforded him untethered imagination. His cries were answered by the echoes in the heart of the open sky and repeated in the river of history flowing through the civilized land. He searched for answers to his big questions, so big that none of his descendants could answer them. Did he know the answers himself? Maybe he did. He listened to the stones but they were silent as death. How had death come upon one of the greatest poets who ever existed under the sky?

Legend had it that he had asked his heavenly questions after his discovery of mysterious paintings (or graffiti) on the walls of an ancestral temple.

On our way out, a crowd began to gather before an altar where

a statue of Qu Yuan stood. The smoke from burning incense floated in the air, ashes dancing in the wind. For the worshippers, Qu
Yuan was their hero, their saviour, their god.

We walked along the riverside to our hotel. Lying on the bed, I
turned on the TV and watched an interview with scientists on the
upcoming construction of the Great Dam of China.

Soon, I fell asleep.

I awoke before dawn as Justin continued snoring in the bed
next to mine. I felt light as a shadow. I tiptoed out of the room as if
walking on eggshells.

It was freezing outside. A dense fog had settled over the countryside. Not a soul could be seen in the deserted streets and almost all
the houses were dark.

I found myself walking toward the bend of the river visible at
the mouth of the lonely lane, but I did not know why.

In the distance, I noticed a human figure. Walking closer, I
found myself stepping into another time and space. An old man was
sitting on a stool holding a long, thin bamboo pole that extended
into the middle of the river. He wore an ancient gown like those I
had seen in the movies. His hair was white, and he sported a long
beard. Thick fog draped itself like a shawl around him.

Before I recovered from the startling sight, the old man spoke
without turning his head. "What are you searching for, young man?"

"I want to find answers to my life."

"Have you found them?" I heard him say.

"Not yet."

"When you ask, you already have the answer. When you seek,
you have already found."

"What? I don't understand, sir."

The old man turned his head toward me. His eyes shone as if a
fire burned there. They reminded me of the story of the Monkey
King, who had burned in an alchemist's furnace for 49 days.

His eyes seemed to penetrate my inner being, my soul. Without speaking aloud, he said: "He posed every statement of fact as a question in his poem and the answers are within the questions."

"But how?" My bewildered eyes blinked.

"By seeing it in spirit, not in person."

Perplexity rippled through my brain.

"If you are in spirit, you see the future, not the present, because future is in the present, just like answers are in the questions."

This remined me of Mr. Yi's riddle when he said I need to think *from* (not of) the future.

Are they talking about the same vision?

"Are you saying," I stammered, "perspective … vision … changes reality?"

"Yes, as if already fulfilled," he said nodding, his hand twirling with the tails of his long, white beard. "The greatest mystery in the universe!"

"So metaphysical!" I said. "But why did Qu Yuan commit suicide?"

"He killed his body and freed his soul. People discovered his body but lost his soul, and the answers to those questions are now lost to destiny."

The silence grew between us. I took time to absorb the conversation, like savouring a rice dumpling after opening the fragrant lotus leaves.

"Did he ever say, '*the road ahead is long and endless / yet I will be searching far and wide, or up and down?*'" I asked again.

The silence held.

Eventually, the old man sighed. "He was wrong, pointing people in the wrong direction. A big mistake in his life too. When you look outside, you search for things, kings, men. In fact, truth lies within; you can never find it from without. Answers can only be found in the human soul, not in the human mind. Today, people almost forget the divine questions and turn them into rice dumplings."

Had we been searching in the wrong direction for generations?
I was puzzled.

"Let me show you an example. What do you see before your
eyes?"

"Isn't it a river?"

"You see a river; I see human consciousness. You see water; I
see minds. You see fish; I see souls."

Heaving a sigh, the old man then became a long shadow, disappearing in the air like wind blowing over the river, leaving me
standing in the cold, shivering. In another strong gust of wind,
everything merged before my eyes: the old man, the ageless river,
and the shadow were all one.

I raced back to the hotel and entered like a shadow.

When I opened my eyes, I found I was already sitting up in bed.
I touched my right hand with my left, checking to see if they were
real. It was as if they had been separated for a long time. Yes, they
were real flesh, but I felt cold. I rubbed my eyes and wondered if I
had seen a ghost while sleepwalking or had been dreaming and
having a wordless conversation with a ghost. It seemed that, for me,
the answers to the heavenly questions would remain hidden in my
subconscious.

31

THE DECEMBER MORNING was upon us when we arrived in Guangzhou. The cold north wind did not blow in the southern city; instead, it was mild. The ocean breeze blew in our faces, filling our nostrils with the warmth of spring.

Our ears soon buzzed with the sounds of Cantonese dialects mixed with the hustle and bustle of the cobbled streets beneath arching sycamore trees. The sun was already high and dazzling in the early morning.

When we looked up at the skyscrapers in the skyline, the sun hurt our eyes and we had to squint.

The Grand China Hotel was listed in Justin's travel guide, *Lonely Planet: Travel Inside China.* A nearby plaza housed the famous Friendship Department Store. Our Cantonese-speaking taxi driver stopped and a young doorman in hotel uniform took our luggage, leading us into the lobby through a revolving door.

At dusk, we walked along the crowded sidewalk to Friendship Plaza. Two stone lions crouched on either side of the entrance, their round, cold eyes looking down on us. A girl by the entrance stopped us, saying in English: "Show your passport, please."

"What passport?" I asked in surprise.

"This is a foreigner-only zone, sir," the young woman replied coldly.

Justin produced his Canadian passport. I was shocked and irritated by another *only*. My face flushed to my ears. I felt sweat running down my spine.

"This is China, and you are telling me that a Chinese is not allowed to enter and shop in this plaza?" I raised my voice and, of course, the girl could hear the anger in my tone.

"You're right, sir. We accept only foreign currency here," the girl said dismissively. She then turned her face away, ignoring my presence altogether.

"That's unheard of," I grumbled.

Other than that, I could hardly speak. I did not know how to explain this peculiarly Chinese logic to my Canadian friend, who remained as silent as the marble floor. He said nothing; he did not want to embarrass me. I felt ashamed and walked away angrily with Justin following.

"It's okay, Victor," Justin said when he caught up with me.

"Of course, it's okay for you, because you're a foreigner and you enjoy preferential treatment in China."

Jealousy, which is more frightening than rage, surged inside me.

"It's you who think yourself inferior—no one else. Because you identify yourself with your emotions," Justin said.

"It's a fact—not an emotion."

"If you mix your emotions with facts, that's an emotional response."

"You think so? I don't. What would you do if you were in my shoes?"

"We only have two options: either face the facts before us and accept them or challenge them and change them. I would challenge them until there are changes."

"But this is China."

He sighed. "I have heard the 'this is China' excuse ten thousand times and my ears have grown calluses, to borrow a Chinese expression. Everyone in China is waiting for a saviour but you may wait another hundred years. As Chairman Mao said, a thousand years is too long; you must seize the moment now."

"Easier said than done," I replied.

"Of course. But if you don't do it, or I don't do it, it's going to be the same for another hundred years. You could be a Martin Luther King, a Dr. Sun Yat-sen,[7] or a nobody. The choice is yours."

When we returned to the hotel, our heated argument continued.

"Who do you think you are? You are only a 'foreign devil,' a Caucasian ghost," I yelled, slamming the door shut behind me.

"That's what you say but that is not who I am," Justin said calmly.

Then he talked about his theory, learned as a psychology major. "Your mind can play tricks on you."

How different we were, and how he had just shown me a concrete example of the differences between us, I heard myself thinking.

I stood unmoving, straining to calm my emotions.

"I'm sorry, buddy," I said. "I should not have vented at you."

"No worries. That's what friends are for. Friend*ship*—you and I are in the same ship," he joked. "I warned you that I would never give up an opportunity to debate with you."

We laughed. That so-called Friendship Store had almost ruined our friendship. I regretted my emotional outburst. Although our argument was over, this incident left a lasting psychological impression on me.

That night, I pondered Justin's theory. Thinking affected our emotions, and that led to the release of words based on our thoughts. We are controlled by our emotions but that is not who we are.

The next morning, Justin and I decided to try some Cantonese dim sum at the Delight Restaurant. Although my ears seemed to reject the Cantonese dialect, my stomach was hungry for Cantonese cuisine. A busboy led us to a secluded area because Justin was a foreigner, I thought. The waitress handed me a Chinese menu, asking us whether we were interested in a special order.

"What special order?" I was curious.

---

7. A Chinese politician, physician, and philosopher known as the father of modern China.

"Monkey brains," she said in Cantonese.

"What?" I could not understand her.

Justin looked at her, also perplexed.

"Come. I'll show you." She motioned us to follow her.

She led us to another partitioned room where several men were speaking Japanese. An animal-like head stood in the middle of the table. A hammer stained with fresh blood lay beside the head. In a wired cage, there was a live monkey with its head opened, red blood dripping along its body. Its skull was as large as a human head.

"Delicious!" One of the men scooped up some blood from inside of the head, and sipped it, shooting a thumbs-up at us; the others lifted their wine cups, saying "drink up" in Japanese.

Justin ran out of the restaurant and vomited in the gutter.

I did not know what to say. I'd never heard that people could suck up a monkey's brains in a restaurant. That evening, it took me a while to recover from that awful encounter. I thought of the monkey's head and the blood spilling over its fur.

Were we very much like that monkey?

On Sunday, it was raining. We went to a ticket booth, handing over some of the people's currency. The old man moistened his fingers by spitting on them before counting the paper notes. The raindrops drummed on the roof of the bus as it sat at the station. Soon, the bus drove away, eventually leaving the busy city streets and, turning southward, heading to the border city.

Shenzhen used to be a small fishing village. Today it's a special economic zone.

About an hour later, our bus was stopped at a checkpoint and diverted to Gate 4 where passengers stepped off and lined up in two queues. I turned over my ID and bus ticket to the uniformed guard.

"Where's your pass?" he demanded.

"What pass?" I asked, confused.

"Special pass for Shenzhen."

"I didn't know I needed a pass."

"Can't enter without a pass."

"Where can I get a pass?"

"Not my business." He pushed me away.

I said goodbye to Justin and turned back to Guangzhou.

The next morning, the hotel telephone rang. I was told to come down to the lobby.

"Hi, Victor," Moon said, extending both of her hands and smiling.

The previous night, I'd managed to get hold of Moon on the phone and now she was here.

"Welcome! You should've told me you were coming."

"Sorry. I didn't know I needed a pass to see you."

Moon was wearing a black skirt and stockings. Her high heels clicked on the tiled floor of the lobby. Her black hair cascaded down to her shoulders, wavy in the middle and curled at the bottom. She ushered me into a black Mercedes Benz parked outside the hotel. We drove off.

"Do you still read Jin Rong?" I asked.

"Not anymore. I used to numb myself by reading fantasy and romance. Now I read Lee Iacocca's autobiography and the *Wall Street Journal*."

She handed me her business card.

"Vice-President of Marketing, GE Medical Equipment Group," I read. "Well! I have eyes, but I didn't notice Mount Tai," I said, referring to one of the most sacred mountains in China. "I never knew that your ambition was as high as the moon."

"That's why I'm called Moon. I've always hung high in the sky," she said, then compressed her lips. "Do you want to join our English interpretation team after graduation?"

"Me? To be or not to be, that is the question," I joked.

Then I told her that I'd applied for a scholarship to study abroad and that, if I was accepted, I would be leaving in July.

"Interesting. How has Shakespeare treated you so far?"

"I've learned a lot from the master," I said. "There's no good and evil unless you think it so."

"I had forgotten all about Shakespeare. But I'm more like Shylock, whom Shakespeare hated," she said.

"If you have money, you can do anything."

"That's what you've always said. Not me."

"I think and therefore I am. We identify ourselves with our mind."

"What do you mean?" she asked.

"People think we are our minds."

"Of course, we are."

"But we are more than our minds. Remember the 'to be or not to be' dilemma? We are who we are."

"I can't argue with a philosopher. But in Shenzhen we only argue about money—nothing else," she said, waving a hand.

"You've turned into a capitalist."

"You will too, one day."

By now, the sun had risen high in the soft sky. Moon turned her black Mercedes off the highway and then, flanked by skyscrapers, into the financial district in the heart of the city. I imagined the view from the top of one of the tall buildings; crowds walking in the streets would look like ants crawling on the ground.

Looking up, I could not see the sun, only shadows.

After settling in at the Hilton, Moon and I met Justin at the Golden Dragon Café next to Stock Exchange Plaza. A huge dragon curled on the wall at the entrance, flames of gold spitting from its mouth as it lay watching the people.

Inside, a massive chandelier hung from the domed roof, its golden light flickering on the glass windows and on the smooth, white-tiled floor. Beethoven's Fifth Symphony filled the room.

The candles on our table wavered, seemingly to the music's beat. Diners, most in professional attire, talked in voices that rarely rose above a whisper. A server handed us two elaborately bound menus, written in English and Chinese and offering western dishes.

Moon had reserved a table beside a window so that we could watch the flow of the bright, busy streets. The table was set for four with the best china and silver cutlery atop a pristine white table-cloth. A white linen napkin folded into the shape of a flower stood on each plate.

Covertly watching Justin spread his napkin over his knees, I followed suit.

The server brought us some ornate cups filled with aromatic coffee. It tasted bitter but was seductive on the tongue. Moon smiled and added honey to the brew. Then she joked about my honey-licking experiment at No. 1 High.

I burst into surprised laughter, almost spitting out my half-chewed chicken breast. A man from an adjacent table swivelled to look at me, giving me a common parenting signal meant to hush me. Our giggling stopped. I was used to shouting, not whispering. Shouting was seen as a sound of power and strength, I thought. That is why our people are addicted to shouting.

Moon and her husband had just returned from their honeymoon in Hawaii.

"I'm curious, Moon," I said. "Do you have a Party Secretary in your joint venture?"[8]

"No," she replied. "No mandatory political studies, either. Shenzhen is an experiment based on the free market model."

"Let freedom reign all over China," Justin commented, sipping his coffee with visible pleasure.

I'd felt poverty and tasted frugality. Amid a sudden shift in the political winds, I felt uncertain and frightened; I seemed to have lost the ground I'd walked on solidly for so long.

---

8. China's government mandates that foreign investors in certain industries, such as medical equipment, form joint ventures with a domestic Chinese partner.

32

IT WAS RAINING the next morning. I rose early to see Justin off at Luohu Customs on his way to Hong Kong, or Fragrant Harbour.

Today's Luohu must be different from when Fool-the-Second had been there seeking an opportunity to escape Phoenix many years ago, I thought. I passed the gigantic statue of Deng Xiaoping facing south. A few sparrows perched on Deng's motionless shoulders stained with bird droppings. Over the years, Deng had waved his magic wand and cast his spell for change. Over about ten years, a small fishing village was now transformed into a metropolitan city. Here, the old world had disappeared before our eyes. I wandered the streets for a while, not knowing where I was going, then hailed a taxi

"Where to?"

"Anywhere. Just give me a taste of the ocean."

"Seafood Restaurant?" the young driver was bewildered.

"No. Just give me a glimpse of the blue ocean."

The driver seemed relieved and we drove off.

"In the far distance, on the opposite side, that's Victoria Harbour," the driver said. "When night falls, you can glimpse the lights."

We chatted and I asked him if he liked the special economic zone.

"It depends. Many people prefer an iron bowl of rice, or guaranteed job security. If that's what you want, this is not a place to be. It took me a while to get used to it."

As we arrived, the driver said: "Pay me Hong Kong dollars?"

"Sorry, sir. Only have the people's currency."

On the beach, I basked in the winter sunshine, gazing up at the patches of blue sky and assessing the shapes of clouds. The air was thick with the ocean breeze and seagulls floated freely in the wind. I felt reassured by a shred of hope. Hope was in the air and at the zenith of the blue sky. I grasped a brief solitude that I had never hoped to feel. In the space of a few days, while spending time at the border city, I began to grow fond of the ocean breeze. My heart felt like a bird and I wanted to fly high in the sky. While I indulged myself in reveries, a man, with a young boy beside him, was holding a kite string, about to launch their kite into the air. The boy's face lit up and he yelled: "C'mon Dad, let me try now!"

The kite floated higher and higher. The boy burst into loud sobs when the wind snapped the tether line and the kite gusted higher and higher until it was a dot in the sky.

Time is like the tether of the kite, which is at the mercy of the wind. When the tether snaps free, the kite flies to the clouds. What does the other side of the sky look like? I wondered.

That evening, I lay on the bed and channel-surfed. I could get CNN live and some Hong Kong movie channels. Amazing! I chose a hypnosis demonstration filmed on a stage in Las Vegas. I watched the hypnotist instruct his selected volunteers on stage: "One, two, three, sleep!" At the sound of his snapping fingers, all the volunteers immediately fell fast asleep, their chins on their chests. The hypnotist gave suggestions and verbal cues to them; he asked them to perform various tasks and they obeyed, like children would. The hypnotist asked a senior gentleman to dance a bit of Swan Lake. He did so, to the audience's warm applause.

After all sorts of comic performances, the hypnotist said: "Now, when I count to three, all of you will open your eyes and be fully awake. One, two, three. Open!" He snapped his fingers and, astonishingly, they opened their eyes and looked around, seeming to have forgotten where they were and why.

This was the first time I had ever heard of hypnosis. Many

years later, I would read Émile Coué's *Autosuggestion* and Dr. Joseph Murphy's *The Power of Your Subconscious Mind*. Those two books helped me better understand the inner working of our subconscious. Like a master hypnotist, our culture had fed us suggestions and cues from off-stage for thousands of years. With a finger-snap, we all fell into a hypnotic trance.

Just as I began to doze off, I heard a soft knock at the door.

"Hello, sir." A woman in a red coat stood across the hall, facing my door. She seemed nervous but older, somehow, than her face and shoulder-length hair indicated.

"Hello, who're you looking for?"

"I'm Anna. I'm your service girl tonight."

"Excuse me? I never ..."

"Is this 1808?" She pointed to the room number, adding quickly: "A lady booked me."

It could only be Moon, I thought. I let her in.

"What type of service do you offer?"

She smiled unconvincingly. "A relaxing massage." While she shed and folded her overcoat, I took a good look at her. In a round face her eyes were almost hidden behind the painted eyelashes and brows.

"Do you want to take a shower while I'm getting ready?" she said, her voice almost granting my body unspeakable power and freedom to act.

"No, no need," I said, fighting down the urge to say yes. "As a matter of fact, I don't much care for massage but, since you're here, we can chat for a bit."

"Okay, what do you want to talk about?" She kicked off her black high-heeled leather shoes. Peeling off her silver stockings, she climbed on the bed and leaned against the soft headboard, one hand fiddling with her hair. Under the bright light of the room, her complexion was the colour of ivory piano keys. Her body was curved like those of the female stars in movies.

I couldn't take my eyes off her.

"I don't know." I feigned a smile, averting my eyes. Covertly, I moistened my dry lips with my tongue.

Staring, she made me feel uneasy.

"How old are you?" I finally got out.

"Twenty two. My final year at college."

"What are you studying?"

"International trade."

Questions were all I could think of to say. "Why do you want to be a massage girl?"

"I need money. Can I get a Coca-Cola from the minibar?"

In Chinese, we call Coca-Cola *Delicious-and-Delight*. I heard the pop as she opened the can. I liked that sound, one associated with the release of energy. I thought of Pavlov's salivating dogs again.

"You sure you don't want service tonight?" She dimmed the lights and began undressing, pulling off her underwear. Then she was lying naked, her thighs stretched out on the bed, like open scissors.

"Come lie down." Her soft voice was seductive. I could not resist the temptation, so I dropped my pants to my ankles, stepped out of them, lay down. I rolled over to steal a kiss.

"You don't touch," she said, both sternly and apologetically at the same time. "You can enter my body, but you cannot kiss my breathing soul. Workers sell their muscles, professionals sell their brains. Me, I sell my body, but not my soul."

Then she turned me over and began to massage my back gently. My whole body was trembling; while one part of me had surrendered another part resisted.

"Are you cold?" she asked.

"Yes, a little bit."

"I'll give you warm." She put her warm body on top of mine after turning me over to face her. Her hands touched mine. I closed my eyes; I desired penetration but could not feel my erection. My body seemed to be frozen when it touched hers. I do not know why.

At that moment, I did not feel like I was living in the same body anymore; my old sense of self seemed to have been separated from my body.

"Are you made of wood or stone?" she scolded, her breath beside my ear. It was sweet.

"Neither. Flesh and blood, like you," I said, turning away from her enticing breasts.

"Then why are you not aroused?" she asked. "Am I not sensual enough?"

I didn't know what to say. I didn't mean to reject her but something inside me pulled me away from any desire.

A heavy silence descended, my reverie finally broken by a soft touch on my right thigh near my noticeable brown birthmark.

Immediately, I remembered this was the sign of my soul. "When it returns, you will be recognized by the birthmark on your body," my grandma had told me once. "When you die, you will return to Heaven as a spirit."

"A mark of karma?" she asked.

"Don't know."

Then she brushed aside a strand of hair from her face. I could hear my soul silently crying inside me, a sound I had not heard for a long time.

33

WHETHER IT WAS by chance or by providence, I did not know.

On the train, I had happened to sit beside Stephen. He was reading the Bible and that prompted my curiosity. So, I began to fire questions at him like a high schooler.

As our conversation deepened, Stephen told me he'd studied physics at Princeton. Now, he worked at the River City Steel Plant. When he told me he was a Christian, I thought he must be a man from the bottom of the Atlantic Ocean.

"Now offer me your right cheek, after I slap your left," I said, teasing.

Stephen pretended to "turn the other cheek," looking pleased. We laughed. He told me his grandma was Christian. "If you believe in God, ask him to save you now," the Red Guards sneered as they flogged his grandma with a leather belt until she died.

"I often asked God why He did not stop the evil in the world," Stephen said.

"And ...?"

"Because God gave humans free will. We can choose good or evil, but every choice contains a seed of consequence. That's what makes us human. Right now, the world is not threatened by the loss of human lives, but by the loss of humanity."

"How can we believe in an unseen god?"

"I know it's hard to get our head around it. However, Einstein came very close to proving God's existence in a scientific way. What does E stand for in $E = mc^2$?"

"Energy," I replied.

"Energy is also called *qi*, or breathing, which is called *pneuma* in Greek. It means spirit. When we say *qi gong*, it literally means the power of breathing. In Einstein's equation, energy is one and the same as mass or material moving in another dimension, travelling at the speed of light. Einstein had essentially proven the existence of God. Energy is a scientific term for spirit. Spirit is matter in its highest form; matter is spirit at its essence. They are one and the same.

"Our ancestors also believed there was one Almighty God who created the heavens and the earth out of chaos. *Tao* gives birth to one, one begets two, two begets three, and three begets everything in the universe. *Tao* literally means the spoken Word of God. The Gospel of John begins like this: 'In the beginning was the Word, and the Word was with God, and the Word was God.'

"There are lot of references of a supreme creator in our ancient literature, including *Tao Te Ching*, and many embedded in our language as well.

"Humans are three-dimensional beings with body, mind, and soul. Our bodies are corrupt, but our souls will be united with God's spirit in eternity. Do you believe in Heaven and hell?"

"My grandma said that all evil men will go to hell and be burned with brimstone eternally," I replied. "I would say eternity is a very long time."

Like other people in Phoenix Town, I'd proudly bragged about the universal truth of atheism. I had to admit, however, that I'd been a superstitious atheist; I believed in fate or karma because I knew that my life had been driven by an invisible force beyond my control, despite my efforts. But for me to believe in God would require a great—perhaps impossible—leap of faith, which seemed to be an impossible mission to accomplish.

When I listened to Stephen, I did not say that I understood him. While my mind wandered off I kept nodding out of politeness. As the train came to a stop, Stephen asked me what my plans were after graduation. I told him about my plan to study abroad.

"Pray to God," Stephen said. "The Bible says whatever you ask for in prayer, if you believe, you shall receive."

I looked at him dubiously.

"Why don't you come to our Sunday service?" Stephen asked, as we parted at the railway station.

One sunny Sunday in March, I rose early and decided to ride my Everlasting bike to Stephen's church. Designed in the Roman style of architecture, the building was near the old colonial district, a gigantic cross atop the façade. The front steps had been tiled with marble stones. Beside the two wooden doors a poster read: The Kingdom of God is Within.

Stephen was delighted to see me and sat beside me, handing over a Chinese Union Bible. "It was translated by a group of missionaries in 1919," he said. "Today, we celebrate Easter Sunday, the day of resurrection after Jesus died on a cross."

"Is Jesus a god, too?" I asked.

"There's only one God, who is a trinity of three personas: Father, Son, and Holy Spirit."

"You are talking riddles, Stephen."

Soon, the congregation fell into silent prayer and a choir started to sing. I was dumbfounded by the lyrics of "Amazing Grace," which affected me deeply.

The preacher was a soft-spoken old man with thick grey hair. He prayed over bread and tiny cups placed neatly on a white tablecloth.

"The bread represents the broken body of Jesus; the wine in the chalice represents the blood He shed for our sins," Stephen whispered.

The minister began his sermon with a parable.

Once upon a time, there was a young beggar living in a small town. Every day, he wandered around, begging for food. His face was dirty, his clothes gave off a terrible stench and his shoes were worn out. One day, he wandered by a beautiful palace, where two stone lions guarded the entrance. The door was wide open. When the beggar saw well-dressed guests going into and out, talking and smiling, he was filled with jealousy.

They must be holding a banquet, the young beggar thought. So he decided to beg on the corner nearby. Every day, he stood there and was fed with the leftovers, and he was well satisfied.

This continued for some time. Then, one day, the master of the palace, dressed in a purple robe, came out and saw the young beggar.

"Why are you begging here, young man?" the kind-hearted master asked.

"I'm starving, Master. I have no food to eat."

"My poor son, why don't you come in to feast with me?"

"Can I, Master?" The beggar sank to his knees.

"Yes, of course. Everyone is my guest." Thus, the master invited the beggar into the palace.

As I wondered about the moral of this parable, I heard the preacher asking his congregation: "Why are we begging outside the palace while the door to the palace is wide open?"

Then the preacher continued: "And my brothers and sisters, are you spiritually hungry? Are you begging for food for your souls? Are you standing outside of the palace, starving like that beggar?

"Our master, Jesus, is King of the palace. He has invited all of us, including you and me, to enter His palace as His guest. His palace is called the Kingdom of God.

"Where can we find the Kingdom of God, you may wonder? Above, in the heavens, or under the sky? The Scripture says in Matthew 6:33, 'Seek first the Kingdom of God and His righteousness, and all these things shall be added to you.' A prominent psychologist, Carl Jung, once said, 'Who looks outside, dreams, who looks inside, awakens.'

"Today is such a day, a day to resurrect our sleeping souls, because Jesus is risen today."

The preacher led the congregation in a hymn before resuming.

"What does the Kingdom of God represent? The Kingdom of God represents a spiritual realm where God is in total control as King, a consciousness wherein human will is in total surrender to the will of God. In other words, it's a state of the God-consciousness in man. I tell you, this has been God's greatest secret, told only to His followers. The Scripture says in Matthew 7:7, '*Ask and it will be given to you; seek and you will find; knock and the door will be opened to you.*'

"Brothers and sisters, we gather here today to celebrate the resurrection of Jesus. All the powers, God's qualities, are within you. Within your mind, Heaven is in your mind, in peace with God. This is the true meaning of resurrection."

A long silence ensued, the whole congregation deep in silent prayer.

The sermon seemed to open a door to an unknown dimension where I began to grasp the very essence of life and humanity.

If God is the only truth, what about every other truth I had understood so far?

My guru, Sherlock Holmes said: "When you have eliminated the impossible, whatever remains, however improbable, *must* be the truth."

Was that still true?

Holmes claimed that his method of reasoning was the only way to discover truth. Could he be wrong? A Sherlock Holmes fallacy? Perhaps. All humans are prone to mistakes and we learn from our mistakes.

How about my hero, Dr. Pavlov, and his theory of conditioned reflexes?

Pavlov observed the behaviour of dogs in his laboratory, then presupposed the universality of such behaviour and applied it indiscriminately to humans. His theory inevitably implies that no difference exists between animals and humans. Is this problematic? Of course! This could be a psychological fallacy.

In physics, Newton's laws had been remedied by Einstein's theory of relativity.

The Earth used to be flat, then became round. The sun used to orbit around the Earth—the examples run on and on. Humans had claimed to have found the truth when we found only a fragment of the truth. A truth, rather than *the* truth! Truth, with a capital T, is not learned; it is revealed from above and enlightened from within.

This revelation coursed through me like a current of electricity.

For the first time in my life, I prayed to God for forgiveness. But I was unsure if God could hear me or would answer my prayer. For most of my life, I had done everything I could to save my face but nothing to save my soul. I looked around. My old world had disappeared; I had a new pair of eyes. Suddenly, I felt the deepest peace in my heart, a sort of peace that I had never felt before, inside where the soul resides. The divide between my body and soul was being bridged beyond space and time. Now my life was presented with a new face with new meaning. It seems that everything I had gone through served one purpose: it happened for me to understand what a life is about.

So far, everything I had learned prepared me for this fateful day. Now, I became a new version.

By now, the chapel was flooded with sunlight. The sun shone down, filtered through the domed skylight, the smiling rays of light revealing dust motes dancing in the chapel.

The light of truth penetrated me.

34

THE YEAR 1989 was the Year of the Snake, which people say is almost always a presentiment of disaster.

One day in May as dawn broke, the morning dew evaporated quickly in the heat. By now, the petals of the cherry blossoms had fallen and died, decomposing into the earth. Bereft of their blooms, the branches swayed in the wind. On campus, students prepared to commemorate the May Fourth Movement, named after student protests of seventy years before in Beijing. That demonstration had sparked a new cultural movement and new way of thinking in China.

Two months earlier, in April 1989, former General Secretary Hu, who had been forced out two years before due mainly to his reform efforts, passed away unexpectantly, marking the end of an era, and sparking the demonstrations.

What we didn't yet know was that, once again, history would repeat itself, and our leader Deng would become a victim of his own success. Unlike Pygmalion, who fell in love with what he had created, Deng would smash his own creation to pieces.[9]

For us, once we had tasted the sweetness of relative freedom, the thought of going back to the old and bitter ways of the past was agonizing. As a symbol of our fight for freedom, a huge Chinese Statue of Liberty had been erected at the heart of Tiananmen Square, where rock star Sword shouted out the lyrics to his song,

---

9. Although Deng had previously supported reforms to open China's economy, he agreed to the use of force to suppress the 1989 student protests in Tiananmen Square.

"Nothing's Left." Thousands of students were protesting in the streets to send a message asking for a more open society. CRU's Student Union urged students across the city to boycott classes and walk out on May 4.

The day before, Sky worked through the night to compose a new poem, "Mama, Don't Abandon Me." He then asked if I could compose and deliver a keynote speech to observe the May Fourth Day.

"Why me?" I asked.

Sky was a member of the Student Union Council.

"I see the sparkle in your eyes, Victor."

"When?"

"From the way you presented your term papers. You possess intimate knowledge of good and evil."

"Intimate? I'm flattered, Sky, but let me think about your proposal."

"After hearing you, I now realize that it's not science we need most. Science can turn us to a Frankenstein monster."

"What about democracy, then?" I asked.

"Maybe. What do you think?"

"Not even democracy that we need most. Democracy can be a yo-yo game, depending on who controls the diabolo. Remember, democracy enthroned Hitler."

"Are you saying the May Fourth Movement was futile now?" he asked.

"You said that, not me."

We chuckled.

"Not necessarily," I said. "It's a step up in the ladder of consciousness."

"What consciousness?"

"Conscious of being human, being beyond good and evil, being checked by reins of reasoning, most importantly, having faith in life."

"Victor, those insights are so deep, so transcendent."

"Thanks, Sky. Remember *Alice in Wonderland*? What does the Cheshire Cat say to Alice?

"We're all mad here," Sky replied. "Similarly, to err is human, to forgive, divine. Do you forgive me?"

"Forgive you what?" I gave him a puzzled look.

"For misreading you. Me thought you're another Old Sun."

"I beg to differ, since we have tons of Old Suns. Tons of King Lears as well."

"So, what're you scared of?" Sky asked.

"Not scared of anything, I've never spoken like this in public. You know, stage fright."

"Everyone has a first time. If you don't do it, your fright will remain with you forever. You know what, Victor, I had the same fear too, but I killed it. No longer afraid."

"You're absolutely right, Sky."

Eventually, something inside me spurred me to take on the task. That night, I tossed in bed for a long time.

On May 4, a stream of university students went to the streets in support of a student hunger strike at Tiananmen Square. Ironically, Tiananmen literally means the Gate of Heavenly Peace. When I stood on the platform that morning, I spotted Old Sun at the back of the crowd, aiming his piercing gaze at me. He must have seen that I was a changed man. Anyway, I took a big step, jumped to the platform, then began to address the crowd, my head raised high, my right hand waving:

> My fellow students and citizens of the land:
> On October 10, 1911,[10] on the very ground on which we now stand, our forefathers lit a fire. They shed their blood, and many lost limbs or even lives. Unfortunately, this newly kindled fire was extinguished by the heavy downpour of an evil rain. But the seeds of hope they sowed in this soil never died.

---

10. The Wuchang Uprising was part of the 1911 revolution that led to the overthrow of China's last imperial dynasty.

Today, we stand before Dr. Sun Yat-sen's statue to continue with the unfulfilled dreams of our forefathers who lost their lives for the great cause of seeking civil liberties, freedom, democracy for this great nation.

Our nation has come to an important turning point: continue with our current course of reform and liberalization, or reverse its course by returning to the old road. The choice lies before each one of us.

The Statue of Liberty was a gift to the people of the United States. If no one gives that gift to China, we must erect that statue with our own hands, our own hearts, even our lives. History tells us that freedom is not freely given by the mercy of the rulers. I am not asking you to take up arms but I urge all of you to muster your courage, to raise your voice, to bring your hands together in solidarity, to show that we will not back down unless the wheels of our country move forward, not backward.

About two centuries years ago, Napoleon Bonaparte said: "China is a sleeping lion. Let her sleep, for when she wakes, she will shake the world."

We have been sleeping for too long now and today is the day to wake up and roar like a free lion …

Rounds of applause exploded from time to time from the excited crowds and interrupted my speech. The remainder of my words were drowned in the uproar of the human sea. I stood on the platform, trying to fight back tears. But they fell like raindrops. I did not know why.

For a long time, I stood on the holy ground, unwilling to leave. Still, the air was filled with roars rushing toward the sky.

After the demonstration, Old Sun sought me out, warning me that I would probably end up in jail.

"Is this ... that ... serious?" I squeezed out the broken words out of my distraught thoughts.

"Nothing is more serious than opposing the Party," Old Sun replied. "Have you heard of butchering a chicken to scare monkeys?"[11]

"But I ... I ... never opposed the Party."

I lost words and tried to stretch the silence. A shadow fell from the naked lightbulb hanging on the white concrete dormitory ceiling. I placed my hand on my kicking heart to prevent it from jumping out.

Thanks to the reference letters from Dr. Solomon and Professor Adam, I'd been awarded a scholarship and was anxiously awaiting a visa from the Canadian Embassy. I was glad that I had kept this a secret by redirecting the visa letter to my father's house, as it was Old Sun who collected all incoming mails.

Then I remembered Stephen.

More than anything, I wanted to share my scholarship news with him—I would meet him in church on Sunday.

On the way, I stopped in the middle of a long bridge across the river. Gusts of wind blew through my hair; a tugboat churned its way upstream, like an old man hiccupping and climbing slowly up a hill.

In the east, the Yellow Crane Tower stood on the age-old back of Snake Mountain, 50 metres high, silently overlooking the noisy, yellow-mud river. The tower became famous because a twelfth-century poet had written about a very old yellow crane—a symbol of spirit, I guess. The poem evokes an image of the land's perpetual emptiness and the loneliness of the sky when the sad bird eventually disappears.

I thought of the sad, nine-headed bird in a similar legend in a

11. An old Chinese expression that refers to making an example out of someone in order to deter others.

land that has birthed a great many of them. But the past seemed long gone, like the bird.

When I approached the church, a small crowd was cooing over a swaddled baby in a basket at the church's entrance. The infant's eyes were closed, and droplets of tears inched down her cheeks. An elderly woman wiped away the tears with her wrinkled hand, bending over the infant.

"Where's the mother?" people in the crowd called out.

No reply.

"What happened?" I asked.

"An abandoned baby girl," the lady said.

I had heard that more and more baby girls were being abandoned due to the one-child policy. *Her mother's heart must be as hard as stone,* I thought. The scene reminded me of the Bible story about the pharaoh who wanted to kill all the firstborn babies. Drawing the connection between the two events troubled me.

Then, I heard someone say the church had been closed permanently. I looked up to see that two long pieces of white paper had been affixed to the doors in the shape of an X. The cross atop the entrance was gone.

I ran to a telephone booth. I wanted to talk to Stephen. At the other end of the line, an indifferent male voice said that Stephen had been arrested.

"Arrested? Why?" I asked.

"For an illegal gathering at his residence," the voice said coldly. Click.

I was dumbstruck and felt dizzy: What's going on in this world? I wondered. It began to rain. Soon I was soaking wet.

A three-word telegram lay on the table when I finally reached my dorm: *Return Forthwith Father.*

Having a telephone in our household was still Mama's unfulfilled dream.

35

"WHY DIDN'T YOU tell me, Mama?"

Bedside, I was looking at my mother's withered body, sobbing. Mother had been diagnosed with late-stage liver cancer and had only a few days to live. In the front room, a coffin smelling of fresh paint, leaned patiently against the wall.

"Heaven wills it, my fated time. No one can challenge fate. I heard the calls from the god of death," Mother said.

Mother struggled to move her weakened body, and removed the jade bracelet from her wrist. "This was from your grandma, who received it from her grandma. According to our tradition, this jade will pass on and on. But I want you to bury it with me. An amulet, turned a curse."

I nodded and choked back tears.

Father brought in some of Grandma's soup. His eyes were red and his face looked haggard. His breath was a mixture of alcohol and tobacco; he hadn't shaved for days. He sat on the edge of the bed, pulling Mother up to spoon-feed her with the soup.

"I want to tell you something, before I leave," Mother mumbled. "Son, I want you listen too, you're not child anymore."

"Old Song," Mother murmured. "It's not what you thought, I'm clean. I did not steal money. They … forced me, to confess … the rest, I don't remember." Mom faltered; no tears dribbled down.

A new madness seemed to seize my convulsing father.

"Bastards!" Father yelled, jumping up, the veins of his temples bulging. "Worse than beasts." In a fit of rage, Father hurled a china bowl against the wall, smashing it to pieces.

"Please, calm down. Does not matter anymore. I now burying all misery and pain in my grave. I only hope, it not happen again, to my children. Sorry, Old Song, cannot care for you anymore. Bye, my son." Mother closed her eyes, tears slowly rolling down to her tear-filled pillow.

Father's sobs became wails and he stormed from the room. Grandma told me later that the china bowl he'd destroyed was the same one that had held the water that sealed my fate.

My fate in the china bowl was finally broken. The spell of me was finally broken! The curse was finally broken!

I sat beside Mama through the night. Opening her eyes in the dead of night, she screamed: "Run, son, run quick!" When I calmed her down, she told me two giant men with spears were sitting on the roof, waiting for her.

When Mother gave her last breath at midnight, the wall clock stopped ticking. She never opened her eyes again. She did not need to tend to her morning chores anymore. She sleeps in a realm where there is no time and no space.

Many years later, I deeply regretted that I had missed the opportunity to introduce Jesus to Mother on her deathbed. The guilt tormented me for years. At that time, my mind had not been transformed; my faith had not matured. But later, I was relieved to learn that the departed will be given a last opportunity when Jesus comes again.

Grandma was heartbroken at the death of my mother. For her, it was a final, crushing blow.

"Oh, Heavens, why didn't you take my life and give it to my daughter?" Grandma wailed. "Don't let me live under such a curse."

Grandma was totally beaten down. "I am an accomplice of the god of fate," she said.

That night, Grandma grabbed a butcher's knife from the kitchen and, raising it high over her head, chopped at the old wooden bench late into the night. Eventually, her cursing turned into a stream of reproachful mumblings. The old bench was smashed into halves under the furious chopping.

My family and I buried Mama with the old bracelet. At the funeral, my three-year-old nephew came home in the company of my elder sister. "Uncle, I want Grandma's bracelet back," he cried.

"No, Sunny, it's not yours to have; it belonged to Grandma." I stooped to pat his head, saying, "How about I buy you a wrist-watch?"

When my dejected sister overheard my mention of a watch, her face turned pale suddenly. "No, no, not a good idea," she said, dragging her protesting son away.

Perplexed by her abrupt reaction, I could not help but wonder: *Did I say something wrong?* Then the image of my father's Soviet-made watch came to me, its chains swirling and spiralling before my very eyes. The terror of the past still lingered in our subconscious. I sighed.

The following night, my younger sister sobbed when we seated ourselves for dinner. "I dreamed last night," she said, " Mama crying and telling me she's starving to death." My sister refused to be comforted until I agreed to burn hell money at Mama's tomb site after the meal. For Mama to buy food in the other world, my sister said. In my mind, Mother had concluded the physical part of the journey we call life ... or rather, bodily life. My townspeople still believe they are protected by our departed ancestors living from an underworld. Now, I realize this thousand-year-old conviction had chained the souls of our ancestors to the mountains.

(Born out of the crevice of a gigantic boulder, the legendary Monkey King had been chained beneath the Five-Finger Mount by the Emperor of the Heavenly Palace due to his rebellious act, according to *The Journey to the West*.)

On June 4, Father's eyes were glued on the television. The night before, we watched Sword, quavering with rage, singing his "All is

Nothinged" (a better version of translation) in front of the anguished students at Tiananmen Square. Martial law was declared and curfews were enforced in Beijing. The People's Liberation Army was commanded to clear the protesting students from Tiananmen Square. On the TV screen, a battalion of tanks rolled onto Everlasting Peace Boulevard. The streets in Beijing were plastered with wanted posters bearing photos of students on the run.

"You threw eggs onto stones," Father yelled at the black-and-white TV screen. "You think those students can remove the mountains?"

"That's a callous thing to say, Father," I grumbled.

My father trembled with anger and his high-pitched yelling shook the house.

"Have you heard of the fable where the old man removed the mountains, Dad?" I said.

"Lie! That's lie." Father looked at me, his eyes bulging, "My son is out of his mind, he believe such lies."

Suddenly, my eyes reddened, tears at the ready. I knew those were the shameful tears for my great cowardice. But I fought them back by swallowing them in my belly.

A few days later, I received a letter from Hong Kong.

June 6, 1989

Dear Victor,

When you open this letter, I'm in Hong Kong. Tears streamed down my cheeks when I bid farewell to Deng's statue at the Louhu border.

The students in Beijing sacrificed their lives for our dreams. It saddened me when I woke up to the fact that freedom is not free; it comes only at great costs.

Now, I'm on the run and in exile.

Very ironic, isn't it?

Remember how you ranted about the beautiful Esmeralda in the hunchback movie? Linda is that gypsy girl, and the fate of the young poet has now befallen me. Linda offered to marry me so that she could help exile me from my own land.

When my spirits are low, I think about what you said to me about human destiny. Maybe you're right; we can be our own masters. I could not bear it one minute longer if I believed our destiny is controlled by an unknown hand. But to solve the greatest Sphinx riddle, I must seek my own answers. I don't want to be devoured by the beast when it's my turn to answer the riddle.

I will write again after I hear back from you. In the meantime, I have a lot of thinking to do. I wish you a smooth transition to your new life at the University of Calgary.

Your friend forever,
Sky

P.S. Justin flew back to Toronto from Hong Kong on June 4.

P.S.S. I heard Old Sun was the only student on the list who would be sent to study in the U.K. Well, happily ever after.

One day, Grandma set the table for the evening meal and I sat beside my sullen father.

"Get out of the seat!" he yelled at me. "This is your mother's place."

Before we ate our evening rice, Father had set an extra pair of chopsticks and a bowl of rice reserved for Mama. It is our tradition that the family invites the departed to dine for 49 days before the departed finally bids farewell. (I had totally forgotten about this tradition.) Father always drank at meals. His brain was filled with cigarette smoke and alcohol. When he wasn't smoking or drinking, his mind seemed empty.

I felt pity for Father.

As usual, he sat on his wooden armchair with two arms adorned with sweat smears. This ragged chair was special to him, and he would prohibit anyone from sitting on it. Once I jumped on it before meal. Father seized my collar dragging me off, throwing me to the ground. Amid my tears, he barked: "This is ALL I have now. Don't you take it from me!"

Father always chose to speak rough language that was hard to swallow. Revolution had robbed him of parenting words and conscious volition, which made me sad.

After our meal we sat facing each other. I told him of my departure to study in Canada. Father poured himself another tumbler of alcohol as if drinking up his mishaps, fears, shames and shadows of the past, all stitched together, while dragging on his cigarette. The rift between us seemed too wide to close. Suddenly his face reddened and he pounded the table, sending a china bowl trembling off the edge to the cement floor.

"Why you abandon your homeland?" He stopped to hunt for words. "Last night, our ... our ... local police, police ... came see me, your what speech ... and the like."

Father's gaze was stabbing the air filled with his cigarette smoke and odor of alcohol. His eyes were red and bloodshot.

"What speech?" I was surprised.

"They say ... they ... say ... anti...er...anti.revo...lu...tion." His tongue was rolling in his smoke-filled mouth, "I'm an old head now."

"What?" I was speechless and scared.

I know that I had brought no honour, only shame, on him.

I failed to find words from my muddied thoughts to fill the silence. My heart thudded with despair.

"You better ... go confess ... if you leave ... my ... door, you do not ever come back again!" Father's rage bubbled.

Suddenly, he stumbled to the other room and slammed the door behind him. No doubt the power of alcohol had affected him, but his drunken words hit me harder than his fists. Although I was used to father's eruptions, that night's outburst toppled my crumpled father-son equation. A father cannot be a father forever, and a son cannot be a son forever. Of course, I was not talking about our blood relationship. Staring at the empty chair, sniffing at the smell of my father's fury, I fancied Wordsworth's whispering while watching the rainbow in the sky: the Child is father of the man.

While I was struggling to find a go-between to facilitate a reconciliation, I thought of Red. She was the best person to pacify my father. She'd attended Mother's funeral; I had already told her of my study plan.

One evening, I left my father's house and paid Red a visit. Uncle Wang was sitting by the doorway. Since Brother Steel was in prison, the front door of his house had been kept open and would not close until the homecoming of the son of the house. When he saw me, Uncle Wang jumped with joy. "My son, my son! You finally back." He opened his arms and held me tightly, as if I would slip away.

Red came to my rescue. "Dad, it's Little Bright," she said softly. "Don't recognize him anymore?"

"No, he is my *son*!" Uncle Wang cried. "My only son."

Red quieted her dad down and sent him to his bed.

Before I arrived, she had been knitting a red wool sweater, which sat on the couch in her room. Red fetched a china plate and a fat ripened peach; she tried to slice it, but her hand trembled when the blade hit the pit inside the peach.

Giving up, she used her hands to tear open the ripe fruit and offered half to me. I bit into it with relish, my lips stained with the red freshness of the fruit.

Juicy, pleasant, and seductive.

On the table was a small tank containing a pair of goldfish, one larger than the other, swimming and wagging their coloured tails. As they swam closer, I tapped on the glass. They hurried to the bottom in terror and hid behind fake plastic mountains.

"The fully-fledged bird is flying far and high this time and will never return to its nest. No one can bind your wings," Red said calmly, returning to her knitting.

"How do you know I won't come back?"

"Remember what you said, female reasoning?"

"Yes, the right hemisphere brain, instinctive, you learned fast, applied, and solved a decade old mystery!"

Both of us burst into laughter.

"Can I ask you a personal question, Red?"

"What?"

"Why are you still single? I heard you rejected all your suitors."

Red looked at me but didn't say anything. Then she rose, entering her bedroom. I followed her as she opened the door of her wardrobe and pulled out a red silk bag, which she unfolded before me. "Because of a solemn promise, you remember it? " She eyed me calmly.

I hung my head; my mind slowly flew back to Turtle Beach ...

The effect of her words set my face ablaze. The sly innuendo I took as mockery.

The yellowed piece of the *People's Daily* was tied with two red ribbons. "This newspaper is as old as you. It has been with me for 27 summers when your grandmother handed it to my father after your birth. The bloodstains on the paper remind me of the traces of a sacred betrothal."

My eyes filled with tears. I looked away, enveloped by a new wave of guilt and shame. I could find no words to describe my feelings. The crumpled paper, which had once held a part of my placenta, also smelled of my birth. It warmed me to the memory of the moment when I heard my own first human cry.

From the reverie, I pulled back my galloping thoughts.

"Do you hate me?" I lowered my voice and head.

"Hatred's birthed in the mind but love is born in the heart. No ambivalence existed in hearts. Never regretted my decision."

"So Shakespeare was right," I said.

"Who's Shakespeare?"

"Never mind. He is one of my teachers."

"Love and hate cannot coexist at the bottom of your heart." Her voice was gentle and soothing like a young mother murmuring to her baby.

She then asked me to stand closer and tried on the newly knitted sweater. Her hair touched my cheek. I felt out of breath. My heart drummed. A current passed through me. I heard the pounding of her heart, felt the heat of her cheek. Her body was instantly writhing against mine.

When I unbuttoned her clothes, she closed her eyes, breathing hard. She yielded totally to my desire, which, like a tethered tiger, once unleashed, darted toward its prey. Finally, she felt my erection. I felt something warm, and damp ejected from inside of me, like a flood rushing out after the gate is lifted.

Red clutched a pillow, then put it over her mouth and muffled her screaming and groaning. I felt fresh perspiration oozing from her soft flesh. I felt as though I were riding in a rocket shooting to the sky, excitement running through me. Then the rocket plunged from the sky and into the ocean.

When I came to myself the innocent evening had ripened into a young, warm night. I looked at Red who was breathing rhythmically beside me on the bedsheet, which was dotted with fresh stains of wine-red blood. Strands of her hair covered one eye. I brushed back her hair and gently kissed her forehead, still flushed with pleasure. Two dimples showed on her cheeks when she smiled. Looking at her face, I forgot to tell her how beautiful she was.

For a moment, I imagined I'd been living a delicious dream. She was not the girl I had known as a child. Our childhood intimacy had been only skin deep. Now, I had the true sense of her; she was the spirit of Mount Phoenix that Grandma had hunted to heal my soul.

For the first time, we were lying on her mat with our heads close together. Her skin seemed luminous in the dark. There was smile on her face.

When I left, stars flickered in the northern sky. The Chinese moon hung in its fathomless firmament and winked flirtatiously at the earth. For the first time in my life, I felt the very moon was shining for me, on my face. A shadow had been born from its gleam; it walked with me, like a phantom haunting the lonely beach. But I was not afraid of phantoms anymore. My old fear had died. I had buried it in my mother's grave.

Night had silently spread its dark bedsheets for the tired earth to sleep on. The empty streets wound in silence along the belly of the yellow earth. Sleep hugged the jagged peak of Mount Phoenix closely and drifted silently over the land, enveloping it gently. The dim lampposts glowed on the lonely streets, sending down rays of hope in the darkness and illuminating swarms of harmless flying insects dancing in the yellow light.

The houses did not talk; they were dark, their windows open. The winds of sleep were flowing in and out freely, as if they owned the obedient houses, the aged town, the growing dark against the sky.

Just then, I heard my mother's groans and a new life cooing in the dark silence. I saw the joy on my father's face when he held his newborn son in his arms. From this native earth had sprung my young life.

How many roads must a man walk down?
Before you call him a man?

267

I found myself humming as I walked and felt my young face glowing in the moonlight.

How far does this road go? a young voice asked in my mind.

Endless, another voice said.

I fell silent, walking on the familiar, deserted streets with my head held high. I felt a swell of pride, a feeling of rebirth filling me with elation. My mind travelled with me on the narrow road that we still call the "horse-way."

The mystery of life must have been solved by love, I thought, feeling as though I were a whole man, heading toward my destiny.

36

ON THE DAY of my departure, Grandma's tiny feet tottered on the heaving gangway as she saw me off at the wharf.

"When coming home?"

"Do you remember the tale you told me, Grandma?"

"What tale?"

"About the celestial bird with nine heads."

Grandma paused to recall. She seemed to remember something, then thrusted her wrinkled hand into her breast pocket from which I'd stolen money.

"Here for you. Don't want to bury with me." She drew forth a small, wrapped parcel.

"What is it?"

"Imagination." She tried to straighten her stooped back, while unfolding the yellowed deck cards. "My old feet are rooted to this earth. Time is like a butcher's knife; it cut off my wings a long time ago." She sighed. "Go fly toward the sky, where the river flows, where you can find home. Actually, the whole world is your home now."

Her voice was cracking and tears filled her eyes.

I held the imagination firmly onto my breast.

I had read in a science magazine about how a mother bird teaches a baby bird to fly. The mother first drops the food just outside the nest to motivate her baby to flap its wings, then drops it farther and farther from the nest to motivate the baby to fly. Once a fully-fledged bird is ready to leave the nest and take flight on its own wings, its mother would never expect it to fly back home.

To me, Grandma was an angelic bird appointed by fate to show me the true meaning of life. When the night was dark, she had not seen the blackness but the radiance of the stars. She accepted the whole of her life, a realm beyond joy and sorrow, pleasure and pain, a place where she beheld truth and found freedom.

My vision blurring, I gazed at this beautiful soul, who endured sorrows as though dining at a banquet, who faced torment as though enjoying a companion on a lonely night, who never complained that the night was too dark or too deep, who always held the present in her hands with her thousand-year-old patience. She knows that, as one who experiences life, you create the world inside you, a place where you do not necessarily suffer in the face of pain. She stood in life like the mountains, unmoved by the winds of pain.

This is the secret to life that Grandma imparted to me.

With tears clouding my eyes, I craned my neck to see if I could find Father in the crowd: no sign of him. This saddened me greatly. But there were no police in sight, either. When I had travelled upstream to college Father had come to see me off and it was here that we said goodbye.

The *New Red East* sounded its horns impatiently, once, twice. I heard the crackling chains clutching the rusty anchor that had dropped into the riverbed. The rising wind was muttering around me, tide was slapping at the foot of the sluggish pier.

My destiny was calling me. I boarded the vessel.

On the deck, I bid farewell to my late mother who slept in the mountains like a baby in a new world. Now, she needed no sun or moon. The earth was her bed, the mountain her pillow, the clouds her blanket. Now she could freely stretch her feet as far as the tail of the river.

As the gigantic vessel travelled downstream, passing the half-sided mountain, I looked up, sensing the shadowed wings of the mythic bird. In the back of my mind, I will always call this place my home, my roots. However, when the roots of a tree grow deep in the ground, they are not jealous of the new branches and leaves stretching heavenward. If they do not have the heart to allow the growth of new branches, it means they are rotten at bottom. Yes, the leaves chase the ground, but that is because they are dead; a young leaf always leans for the sky. Let the dead bury the dead, my heart echoed.

In my mind's eye, I could see the faces of our old ancestors, those saints and poets, floating above in the shadow of the mountains and on the rolling waves of the river. I met their tired gazes, looking at me with censure and indignation. But those gazes could not quiet me anymore. Now the winds wrapped me with warm peace. My heart would no longer shiver like a child. As I examined my own being and beheld my inner self, I saw a new river, a new world where I could swim, smile, dream ...

Because I am a new man now!

I thought about the sword of King Solomon and the two women claiming to be the true mother of the crying child. *How about a true motherland?* My thoughts moved as fast as the flowing river. *If the land were cut into two halves, could a child still find his mother?*

The destiny of a river is to flow into an ocean. By the same token, the fate of humans is to seek out and walk toward their destiny.

My thoughts flowed on. Memories coursed through my mind as if they had just happened yesterday. I had journeyed on the old river on sands of sorrow and the waves of dreams, a river that flows from the oldest memory to the new day.

I looked up at the sky, thinking everything that had happened in my life had spurred me to dive deeper than the surface of life into an uncharted dimension. Now, I had stepped out of the bondage of mind and emotion and awakened to the truth within me.

After all, our life journey is a soul's journey, onward and upward and, ultimately, inward.

Out of the blue, I wanted to shout at the top of my lungs:

Wake up, mountains; you are swallowed by your own
shadows.
Stop crying, River, your cries are drowned in your own
tears.
Yesterday is no more!

For me, life has been like a journey on the river. You cannot control the torrents, the rushing tidal waves flowing eastward, but you can enjoy the journey by triumphantly dancing in the river. The purpose of this journey is not to find a place to house our body or mind, but to find a home to anchor our soul.

When the next morning broke and the young sun rose on the horizon, I was awakened by the whistles of a passing ship bobbing upstream. The *New Red East* heaved three long answering blasts of its horn.

Screeching seagulls flew above the ship, as if welcoming the rising of a new sun. The air was filled with the smells of the green sea under the reddened sky. I could feel the breath of the ocean and the beauty of the morning light penetrate my body and fill my soul.

The end is in the beginning, I thought.

On the horizon, the cries of the yellow-mud river were at once silenced by and absorbed into the vast bosom of the blue sea, becoming one with the expanse of water. The sea stretched wide its arms, embracing the river. It is true the river does not have the same qualities as the sea, but when they become one, they are in intimate union, as though arriving together after a long journey home.

The sky and water seem to merge, the sunlight dancing over the water. Amid the morning mist, I saw my future, but it did not lie ahead of me, it lay within me.

In the mist, I imagined I saw a snake-like figure with a human face emerging from the water. He looked like the white-haired ancient I encountered the morning I visited Qu Yuan's birthplace.

The sun was now suspended in the sky, casting a thousand glittering suns onto the surface of the sea. I was in the sea; the sea was in me.

Between the sky and the sea, the mythical bird flew toward Heaven.

As you think, so you are. As you sow, so you reap. Thinking *is* sowing. Hence, our destiny lies within, not without.

Is this the mystery of fate?

The eye of my heart opened. A man was walking toward me on the water. He opened the door of his heart, asking me wordlessly:

"Have you found your answers yet?"

"I have, sir," my heart answered.

"Are you aware of who you are now?"

"I am."

My vision brightened at last. As my inward eye opened and dove into the sparkling blue water, I saw my own mind dancing in the river.

Acknowledgements

FOR THIS MOMENT, there are not sufficient words in my mind to express the depth of my heartfelt gratitude to those who have made this book possible.

First, this book would not come into existence without the love and support of two important women in my life: my grandmother and my wife, Rachel.

My grandmother was a good storyteller. The weird, uncanny tales I heard at her bedside lit the fire of my imagination, which became my only toy to play with in my childhood.

My wife, Rachel, is the most beautiful woman in the world. Over the long years, she never stopped whispering to my heart endless words of faith and of love when I agonized over my past and the writer's block.

Also importantly, I am deeply indebted to the following people, all of whom have contributed to the making of this book:

To Michael Mirolla, thank you for inviting me to submit my manuscript for the chance to win the Guernica Prize. Your kindheartedness worked miracles for this book.

To the jurors of the 2021 Guernica Prize for Literary Fiction, thank you all for your audacious verdict that changed the fate of this book.

To Bänoo Zan, thank you for your beautiful words said of this book at the prize ceremony; you moved me to tears.

To Roxane Christ, thank you for your encouragement and support when I was struggling with my first draft.

To Brenda Adams, thank you for your painstaking effort to read and improve my manuscript.

To Guo Liang, thank you for the delightful discussions on writing and on Orhan Pamuk over the years, and for your insightful critique of my manuscript.

Last but not least:

To Du Qiong, thank you for the kind permission to use the photo of Guanyin Pavilion for my book cover.

About the Author

GEORGE LEE was born and raised in China. He earned an M.A. in English literature, a Juris Doctor degree, and a Coaching Certificate in Canada. Now he is an attorney, family mediator, and life coach. He lives with his wife and children in Vancouver, Canada. *Dancing in the River* is his debut novel.

Printed in August 2022
by Gauvin Press,
Gatineau, Québec